The President frowned

"Why would Shen-wa want Snyder alive... Ah. So that he'll know what we know about the Red Star, and can make preparations against our responses in advance."

"And Snyder might know if Shen-wa is the person behind these attacks, and possibly his location," Brognola stated.

"Striker certainly has courage, breaking into a Red Chinese maximum-security prison just to ask a man a question."

"Whatever gets the job done, sir," the big Fed said as a dark shadow swept past the window.

As a second shadow appeared, Brognola dived forward and tackled the President to the floor just as something exploded outside, the titanic force of the blast rocking the White House.

Other titles available in this series:

Storm Front
War Season
Evil Alliance
Scorched Earth
Deception
Destiny's Hour
Power of the Lance
A Dying Evil
Deep Treachery
War Load
Sworn Enemies
Dark Truth
Breakaway
Blood and Sand
Caged
Sleepers
Strike and Retrieve
Age of War
Line of Control
Breached
Retaliation
Pressure Point
Silent Running
Stolen Arrows
Zero Option
Predator Paradise
Circle of Deception
Devil's Bargain
False Front
Lethal Tribute
Season of Slaughter
Point of Betrayal
Ballistic Force
Renegade
Survival Reflex
Path to War
Blood Dynasty
Ultimate Stakes
State of Evil
Force Lines
Contagion Option
Hellfire Code
War Drums
Ripple Effect
Devil's Playground
The Killing Rule
Patriot Play
Appointment in Baghdad
Havana Five
The Judas Project
Plains of Fire
Colony of Evil
Hard Passage
Interception
Cold War Reprise
Mission: Apocalypse
Altered State
Killing Game
Diplomacy Directive
Betrayed
Sabotage
Conflict Zone
Blood Play
Desert Fallout
Extraordinary Rendition
Devil's Mark
Savage Rule
Infiltration
Resurgence
Kill Shot

Stealth Sweep

A GOLD EAGLE BOOK FROM
WORLDWIDE®

TORONTO • NEW YORK • LONDON
AMSTERDAM • PARIS • SYDNEY • HAMBURG
STOCKHOLM • ATHENS • TOKYO • MILAN
MADRID • WARSAW • BUDAPEST • AUCKLAND

Recycling programs
for this product may
not exist in your area.

First edition July 2011

ISBN-13: 978-0-373-61546-9

Special thanks and acknowledgment to
Nick Pollotta for his contribution to this work.

STEALTH SWEEP

Printed in U.S.A.

The soldier above all others prays for peace, for it is the soldier who must suffer and bear the deepest wounds and scars of war.

—General Douglas MacArthur,
1880–1964

No matter the obstacles, I'm determined to carry on the fight, my solemn tribute to the men and women, soldier and civilian, who give their all to protect the innocent, and strive for the ultimate goal of peace.

—Mack Bolan

PROLOGUE

Oskemen Valley, Kazakhstan

Impatiently, death waited to be released.

The rumbling sky was the color of oiled steel, and a cold rain fell in a heavy mist upon the rocky landscape. Jagged granite peaks soared high enough to rip through the dark storm clouds, a thick forest of pine trees glistened with moisture, and muddy creeks gurgled along twisting ravines until leaping off cliffs to unexpectedly become waterfalls.

With a low mechanical growl, a massive diesel locomotive slowly arched over a rocky foothill, the huge engine briefly eclipsing the crescent moon as it rested on the horizon. As the long freight train began the serpentine descent into the darkness below, a dull thump sounded from one of the sealed cargo carriages, then the corrugated roof blew off to sail away into the dripping trees. A moment later, a dozen spheres abruptly rose from inside the carriage on an exhalation of compressed air. Shooting high into the misty rain, the spheres snapped out curved wings and glided away from the chuffing locomotive just as it disappeared into a brick-lined tunnel.

As they skimmed low over the treetops, the outer covering of the strange devices crumbled away like dry ash to reveal sleek falcon-shaped machines, the wings and angular bodies painted a flat, nonreflective black. There were no running lights, no exhaust, no sound of an engine, and the machines sailed through the stormy night as silent as ghosts.

Spreading out in a search pattern, they circled the rolling foothills several times until visually confirming their location, then sharply banked away from one another and streaked away in different directions at nearly subsonic speeds.

SET ON TOP of a huge pile of broken slag was the curved white dome of a Kazakhstan military radar station, the outer protective surface oddly resembling a giant golf ball. Inside, the freshly painted walls were covered with amazingly lewd centerfolds from hardcore Spanish and Ukrainian sex magazines, along with posters of the white sandy beaches of the Caspian Sea to the far west. The coast was naturally rocky; the sand had been flown in by the Soviet Union government to create a private beach for its upper echelon. But now everybody had access to the little resorts. It was one of the more benign legacies of the brutal political regime.

Wrapping a dry cloth around the worn wooden handle, Sergeant Aday Meirjan lifted the softly bubbling pot. “Tea?” he asked over a shoulder.

“Thanks!”

“Sugar?”

Hitching up his new gun belt, Private Dastan Alisher frowned. “What am I, a barbarian?”

“I’ll take that as a yes.” Meirjan chuckled, topping off the pair of cracked ceramic mugs.

Hanging from the domed ceiling, clusters of humming fluorescent lights brightly illuminated a curved bank of controls, glowing radar screens and squat, utilitarian radio transmitters—the softly beeping heart of the radar station.

Near the exit was a bubbling samovar, the delicious aroma of freshly brewed tea mixing with the stink of ozone wafting off the high-voltage transformers powering the antiquated electrical equipment. Positioned alongside the door to a cramped washroom was a hand-carved wooden gun rack filled with an assortment of weapons: old WW II German-made 9 mm "grease guns," a pair of American Browning Automatic rifles, crude AK-47 assault rifles and glistening new AK-105 assault rifles equipped with grenade launchers and telescopic sights. On the floor below were crates of ammunition for each weapon. It was a miniature United Nations of death-dealing man stoppers.

Listening to the gentle beeping of the radar screens, the weary soldiers leaned back in their heavily patched chairs and took appreciative sips of the strong tea, the sweet brew bringing much needed freshness and clarity to their tired minds and limbs. This had been a long shift for both of them, and their time in Fort Purgatory was not over yet.

Located in the barren western region of the nation, Oskemen Valley was a good fifty miles from the gleaming skyscrapers and raucous discotheques of Oskemen City, and an equal distance from the horribly radioactive wastelands of the old Soviet Union nuclear test sites. While the radar station carried the official title of Listening Post 47, unofficially it was better known as Purgatory, a dead zone caught between heaven and hell.

Only a decade or so earlier, the valley had been the military foundry of the Soviet Union, with dozens of busy factories and manufacturing plants turning out an endless supply of missiles, torpedoes and artillery shells. But with the collapse of the USSR, the Russian soldiers fleeing back to their homes had taken everything they could sell for quick cash on the black market. Almost overnight, Kazakhstan had become an independent nation, and a major world power, equipped with hundreds of abandoned underground silos full of thermonuclear ICBMs.

The Kazakhstan government neatly removed itself from the deadly nuclear crosshairs of the rest of the world by simply giving the United Nations all fourteen thousand of their remaining Soviet nuclear weapons. It was a political tactic nobody had ever thought of using before.

Concentrating what limited resources the country possessed on constructing schools and repairing roads, Kazakhstan still maintained a strong conventional army, with hundreds of radar stations positioned along important passes through the steep mountains to keep a careful watch on the despised Russians to the north, and the equally distrusted Chinese to the east. Every other country along its borders could be safely ignored, as they lacked the technological ability to seriously threaten Kazakhstan.

Once they'd finished their tea, Alisher refilled the mugs this time, while Meirjan checked the steadily beeping radar screens. The noise would most likely drive most civilians mad, but to a soldier it was the beautiful music of peace. The rainy skies above the valley were empty of any aircraft, rockets or incoming missiles. Although why in the name of God anybody would want to invade the isolated valley, the sergeant had no idea whatsoever. But it was his job to guard the place, not ponder the intricacies of international politics.

"Anything coming our way?" Alisher asked, passing his sergeant a steaming mug and reclaiming his seat.

"Not in the sky," Meirjan stated confidently.

"So, tell me about your pet project," Alisher asked. They needed to talk about *something* to pass the time.

"Are you really interested?" Meirjan asked, arching an eyebrow.

Alisher gave a polite smile. "No, just bored."

Sgt. Meirjan shrugged. "Fair enough. I found the parts stuffed in a truck, ready to be hauled back to Moscow." He rose from his chair and walked to the main console. Set among the array of standard circular screens was a hexagonal one tinted a dark blue. Luminous arms swept around the circular screens as the dish mounted on the roof steadily rotated, but on the hexagonal screen a luminous bar moved up and down in counterpoint.

"Can't be very important if they left it behind," Alisher stated with a sniff. "Strange looking thing."

"The Soviets also left behind several thousand working nuclear weapons," Meirjan reminded him brusquely.

The private snorted. "True enough. How does it work?"

"By combing an active radar beam with a passive sonic receiver, sort of like sonar."

"What is that for, flying submarines?"

Glancing sideways, Meirjan frowned. "My guess is that the Soviets wanted something to detect American stealth bombers by the noise of their engines."

"Oh. Kind of useless in the rain, isn't it?"

Reluctantly, Meirjan began to agree, when suddenly the blue screen started to blare a warning tone. Stepping closer, he frowned as a pair of small objects appeared on the blue screen. They were coming in low, arching around the huge Soviet factories just like birds, but moving way too fast.

"What are those, Sarge?" Alisher asked curiously, taking a sip from the mug.

"Don't know yet," Meirjan growled, dropping into a chair and adjusting the controls. The Doppler radar screens were clear of any airborne traffic. But the stealth radar clearly showed incoming craft. Wiping a hand across the blue screen to dislodge anything on the glass, he blinked as more objects appeared out of nowhere. Two were diving straight for the SAM—surface-to-air missile—bunkers, whereas another pair was going to the fuel depot, and the rest were heading for the radar dishes hidden on the mountainside…and the disguised listening station.

"Those look like ARMs," Alisher said slowly, setting down his mug. It missed the table and noisily crashed to the floor. Neither soldier noticed.

"Yes, they do," Meirjan muttered, trying to fine-tune the controls.

"Is…is this another intelligence test for the new guy?" Alisher asked, a surge of hope in his voice. "Like that bucket of steam the colonel asked me to get last week, or that hoop snake you wanted me to kill?"

"Maybe…" Meirjan said hesitantly, a hand poised above the alarm button. The Doppler radar was still clear. The logical explanation was that these weird blips were merely a glitch in the software, or better yet, just a practical joke from one of the other watch officers stationed at the post during the day. He relaxed a little at that thought. Yes, of course. What else could they be? That made a lot more sense than a salvo of antiradar missiles appearing out of thin air!

Just then, the first pair of blips reached a radar dish on the nearby mountainside. Immediately, that screen went blank, the foggy window facing that direction brightened with a flash, and there came the sound of a distant explosion.

"Those are missiles!" Meirjan snarled, flipping the red toggle switch.

Instantly, a howling siren cut loose outside, and whole sections of the control board came alive as the SAM bunkers, and electric miniguns hidden in the forest, cycled into action. But Meirjan bitterly cursed as their targeting systems swung harmlessly past the salvo of incoming missiles. Sweet Jesus, they couldn't find them! Every radar screen was clean and green; only the experimental stuff registered the enemy ARMs.

His heart pounding wildly, Meirjan briefly glanced at the exit door. Then he spit a virulent oath and tore the cover off the control board to try and jury-rig a connection between the Soviet X-radar and the defensive-fire control system. With luck, it would take only a few moments....

"Red flag! Red flag! HQ, this is forty-seven, we have hostiles," Alisher crisply said into a microphone, his hands quickly adjusting the controls on the old radio. "Repeat, we have—"

Just then, the entire universe became filled with white-hot pain for the two soldiers, but it lasted for only a second.

SPREADING RAPIDLY across the misty sky, the missiles slammed into the open concrete bunkers, detonating all of the surface-to-air missiles in the honeycomb launcher. The roiling explosion ripped the fortification apart, setting off the rest of the missiles, supposedly safe behind a fireproof wall. The combination blast ripped the night apart, the halo of shrapnel spreading out for ten thousand yards.

As sleepy soldiers stumbled about the barracks, grabbing boots and Kalashnikov assault rifles, another machine crashed to the ground directly before the front door, the explosion blocking the entrance. Then two more crashed in through the glass windows and detonated in midair. The fiery blast blew a hurricane of body parts out the windows only an instant before the massive stores of ammunition in the basement levels were triggered.

The roof was designed to withstand a direct hit from World War II artillery shells, but the new bricks walls weren't and they actually bulged out slightly before shattering into total annihilation. Chunks of men, masonry and machines sprayed across the landscape, the civilian cars in the nearby parking lot peppered by steaming pieces of their former owners.

Only moments later, the remaining four SAM bunkers were obliterated, closely followed by the fuel depot, the rooftop Gatling guns, the main armory, and then a parking garage draped in heavy canvas. Briefly, the array of T-80 tanks, and a hundred other assorted military vehicles were exposed to the elements before the winged machines streaked in through the open sides of the structure to slam directly into the armored door protecting the massive stores of shells for the military behemoths.

Accelerating constantly, the first flying machine slammed full-force into the resilient barrier, merely denting it slightly and setting off a howling alarm. Then a second one hit, widening the dent into a breech, and the third punched through the seriously weakened door. As it fell aside, three more of the black machines swooped inside, moving almost too fast to see. A startled corporal wildly fired his AK-101 at the bizarre invader flying by his post, but missed it completely.

"Hello, headquarters?" a lieutenant sputtered into a telephone. "This is Oskemen Valley, and we are under attack by—"

Reaching the main storeroom, the machines found their targets, held a brief electronic conference and then promptly exploded. A deadly halo of burning thermite and stainless-steel buckshot filled the interior, killing a dozen more soldiers and rupturing thousands of rounds of assorted ammunition stored for the mothballed Soviet tanks. The first series of explosions ripped away the fireproof curtains and set off the sprinklers. Then the hammering concussion and tidal wave of white-hot shrapnel reached the main stockpile of military ordnance.

In a stentorian thunderclap, the entire five-story garage was torn from its foundation and lifted into the misty rain on a staggering column of writhing flame and black smoke.

Fifty miles away, in Oskemen City, an amateur astronomer stationed on the roof of the Amanzholov University caught a glimpse of the rising mushroom cloud in her telescope, and fell to her knees, begging for deliverance from the coming apocalypse.

After only a few minutes, a dozen raging bonfires dotted the rugged mountain valley. Everything of any military value was gone, completely eradicated with pinpoint accuracy. However, the roads and bridges were unharmed, along with the huge abandoned Soviet Union weapons factories. Only the windows were gone, the dirty glass shattered by the powerful shock waves.

As the military fires raged unchecked, a warm air rushed through the dark buildings, blowing away the years of accumulated dust from the forges, cranes and conveyor belts sitting patiently in the darkness....

CHAPTER ONE

Baltimore, Maryland

A rosy dawn was just beginning to crest above the horizon in the east, but the shoreline highway was still dark, the heavy traffic an incandescent river, an endless stream of headlights and brake lights. The expensive cars streamed by, the yawning drivers hidden behind tinted windows.

Keeping one hand on the wheel, Mack Bolan, aka the Executioner, changed lanes as he downshifted gears. "Are we talking about a 'stolen arrow' scenario?" he asked, glancing at the cell phone clipped onto the polished mahogany dashboard. A newspaper lay on the passenger seat, the checkered grip of a big pistol just barely visible beneath it.

"I can't say more on an open line," the voice of Hal Brognola replied over the stereo speakers positioned around the luxury car.

"Understood," Bolan growled. "See you in fifteen."

"Make it ten," Brognola countered, and disconnected.

Taking the next off ramp, Bolan merged into the city traffic.

A few minutes later, the soldier turned a corner and saw the flashing neon sign for the Blue Moon Café. It spite of its proximity to the luxurious Crystal City Mall, this was a genuine, old-fashioned, greasy spoon diner that never closed. The coffee was perfect for degreasing tractors, and the pot roast could be used to patch tank armor, but the chili was spectacular. Best of all, the customers were a wide assortment of humanity, so the occasional predator went unnoticed. Bolan had met Brognola there on a few occasions.

A handful of cars stood in the parking lot, most of them positioned directly on the white lines of a space to make sure nobody dinged the smooth finish of the doors. Parking the sleek McLaren away from the other vehicles, Bolan turned off the softly purring engine and got out, deliberately leaving the keys in the ignition and the door unlocked. Crystal City wasn't the best neighborhood, and he knew that by morning the expensive car would be gone, stolen and stripped into parts, completely erasing his tracks, and the vehicle's connection to the Colombian drug lord he had permanently borrowed it from the previous day. If there was one thing the Executioner had come to rely upon, it was the insatiable avarice of humanity.

Pausing for a moment, Bolan patted his windbreaker to memorize the exact position of every weapon he carried: a switchblade knife in his pants pocket, a Beretta 93-R slung in shoulder leather under his left arm, a .357 Magnum Desert Eagle under the right, spare ammo clips in the pockets. Satisfied, he moved across the parking lot, his shoes crunching on the loose gravel.

A swatch of bright light streamed from the entrance of the diner, and as Bolan approached, the shadows near a rusty garbage bin shifted.

"Hey, mister, is this yours?" a raggedy old man asked, proffering a shiny alligator skin wallet. "I found it near the curb, and—"

Instantly stepping aside, Bolan felt something move through the darkness exactly where his head had just been. Brushing back his windbreaker, he drew the 93-R.

"Move along," he whispered in a voice from beyond the grave.

Hesitantly, the two men paused, lead pipes clenched in their scarred hands. Then they looked into his cold eyes, and quickly eased away until the shadows swallowed them whole.

Holstering his weapon again, Bolan then walked around the Blue Moon diner twice, purely as appreciation, to make sure no professionals had it under surveillance. Those two fools were of no real concern, just a couple of muggers.

Going inside, Bolan found the diner packed with people hunched over tables and industriously eating. There was a constant clatter of silverware, a dishwasher chugged somewhere unseen, and a radio thumped out a stream of golden disco music from yesterday. The smoky air was rich with an enticing mixture of smells, including coffee.

Bolan took a table in the corner with his back to the red-and-white tile wall, getting a direct view of both the front and rear doors.

After a few minutes, a waitress walked to his table with an order pad. She was an aging beauty with titian hair that came from a bottle, and magnificent cleavage that seemed natural. Her name tag said Lucinda. The plastic had been cracked and repaired with tape.

"What'll you have?" she asked, making the sentence one word.

"Chili and coffee, both hot," Bolan said.

Lucinda tried to push the Midnight Special, but Bolan pushed back, and they didn't quite come to blows before she relented. Tucking a well-chewed pencil behind an ear, she walked away in defeat, dodging tables and the fumbling hands of drunks.

The diner was busy, the customers a mixture of truck drivers, college students, pimps, clerks, tourists and a couple of slick willies who might as well be wearing a placard to announce their profession as the independent salesmen of recreational pharmaceuticals. Several of the pimps had some of their female employees along as company, so there was a lot of dyed hair and bare skin on display, but everybody was cool. The Blue Moon was neutral territory, the Switzerland of the Maryland underworld.

A scrawny Latino boy, who seemed far too young to be working at that hour, came over with a steaming mug of coffee, and got Bolan started just as a couple of state troopers entered by the front door. They sauntered past the soldier, joking with the fat guy behind the counter, and ordered some meat loaf sandwiches to go.

The cops departed just as Lucinda returned with his chili, along with a basket of sourdough rolls that Bolan hadn't ordered, but deeply appreciated. He thanked her, and she accidentally-on-purpose bumped him with her bare thigh a few times before realizing that Bolan was simply being nice and not making a pass. Lucinda grudgingly accepted the rejection and walked away.

Not his type, Bolan noted, using a napkin to clean the spoon. However, even if he had been interested, he still would have done nothing. There were certain people in the world that a wise man only treated with respect: the very old, the very young, and anybody who would be left alone with your food for a significant length of time.

As expected, the chili was delicious, rich and meaty. Taking his time, Bolan ate slowly, keeping a close watch on the clock hanging slightly askew on the badly painted wall. The ten-minute mark had come and gone, and he was getting ready to go hunt for his friend when Hal Brognola strolled in through the front door.

Instead of his usual three-piece suit, the stocky Fed was wearing a loose vest, a red flannel shirt, denims and work boots to try to blend into the neighborhood. More important, his hair was mussed, and there were scratches on his cheek.

To Bolan, the man looked haggard, as if he was chronically short on sleep. But that was an occupational hazard in D.C.

Slung over Brognola's shoulder was a laptop that probably cost more than what most people in the diner made in a month. As he went past the other customers, some of the pimps viewed the device with marked interest. Then they saw the Justice man glance back, and quickly returned to their meals.

"Sorry I'm late," Brognola said, taking the opposite chair at the table. "I ran into an old friend."

"And he had just found your lost wallet." Bolan didn't phrase it as a question.

"Something like that," Brognola admitted with a shrug. As his jacket swayed open, he briefly exposed a shoulder holster and an old-fashioned snub-nose .38 revolver.

"Leave them alive?"

"Unfortunately. Getting this to you intact was a lot more important," Brognola said, placing the laptop on the table. He pushed it over. "I'm eager to hear your opinion on this matter."

Flipping open the lid, Bolan saw the monitor flicker into a scene of a rainy mountain valley. He concentrated on the brief recording. It was obviously taken from a series of security cameras, grainy and unfocused, shifting abruptly from one angle to another. Then the explosions started, and the recording ended soon after that.

Scowling, Bolan watched it again, then sat back and took a sip of the coffee. It was cold, so he waved at Lucinda for a refill.

"Anything else ya want, sweetie?" she asked hopefully.

Her upper thigh pressed warmly against his hand on the table, and she shifted slightly to let him feel the play of the tight nylon against his skin.

"Just the coffee, doll," Bolan said, leaving his hand in place, but quickly lowering the lid on the laptop. "We're talking some business, ya know?"

"Yeah, sure," Lucinda said softly, topping off the mugs.

As she turned, Bolan smacked her on the rear. She gave a little jump, then looked backward with the kind of primordial smile of the sort that once had toppled the city of Troy, and walked away with a pronounced bounce in her step, just to let the man see what he had missed having for desert.

"So, when's the wedding?" Brognola chuckled, watching as the smiling woman disappeared behind the counter.

"Next week, in Vegas. Come as Elvis," Bolan replied with a straight face, then returned to business. "All right, from the Cyrillic writing on some of the street signs, and the poor condition of the buildings, I would guess this was taken in the Ukraine."

"Close. Kazakhstan."

"Somebody blew up a radar outpost in some remote mountain valley. What does this have to do with me?"

Reaching inside the pocket of his flannel shirt, Brognola produced a small envelope. "On my orders, the NSA did a scan of all cell phones in the area during the time of the attack, and they recovered this."

It was a blurry shot of a burning building with a bird flying by, silhouetted against the flames. Bolan started to ask a question, then paused. Barely visible in the firelight, he could see that the bird was armed with missiles. Obviously, it was some kind of an unmanned attack vehicle—UAV—a drone. Then the implications hit him. One drone couldn't have done that much damage in a week. There had to have been several of them, eight, maybe ten. And if their first target was the radar station…

"It looks like somebody cracked the heat-signature problem on the engines," Bolan muttered, returning the picture.

Tucking the photo away, Brognola nodded. "Unfortunately, yes. In my opinion there is no question of the matter. These shots are of a new type of stealth drone, fast, silent, radar-proof and incredibly lethal."

"Fair enough. Then why are we meeting here and not in your office?"

"Because nobody else in the Justice Department agrees with me on this. Not even the President thinks that there is any real danger to America."

"And what makes you think there is?" Bolan asked.

"Just a gut feeling."

Bolan accepted that. Over their long years working together, he had learned to trust the man's instincts. They had saved the soldier's life more than once. "Haven't the British been secretly working on a new stealth UAV?"

"You know your weapons. Yes, it would have worldwide strike capability, and carry a complement of thermonuclear weapons."

With that kind of range and firepower, the British drone would be enormous. "How close are they to finishing it?" Bolan asked, leaning back in the chair. It creaked slightly under his weight.

"Decades, at the very least."

"Then there is no way that this was a field test by the British."

"Not a chance in hell. And even if the Brits had a working version, why bomb Kazakhstan? There's nothing there of any importance." Turning the laptop around, Brognola tapped a few keys and shoved it back. "Or at least, that was what I thought until these pictures were relayed back from a WatchDog satellite doing a pass over the area the next day. Pay close attention to what wasn't damaged in the strike."

Arching an eyebrow in frank surprise at the statement, Bolan carefully looked over the wreckage from the attack. The photos were black-and-white, but crystal clear, and he soon spotted the pattern in the destruction.

"Somebody is getting ready to do a Hitler," Bolan said in a low, hard voice.

"Yes." Brognola sighed, as if releasing a heavy burden.

Once more, Bolan looked at the pictures of the smashed defensives of the Oskemen Valley, and the completely unharmed bridges, tunnels, electrical power plant and, of course, the old Soviet factories. It would seem that somebody knew their history.

For a long time after World War II, military strategists had analyzed the attack pattern of Hitler's army, trying to figure out why he would pass by one town to attack another. The strikes almost seemed random, even chaotic, until some clever paper-pusher in the Pentagon compared the invasions to Hitler's supply list.

None of the blitzkriegs were random—they were all precise hits on factories that he wanted to take intact, scientists he wanted captured alive, or mines that he desperately needed undamaged and fully operational, so that his engineers could regularly upgrade the backbone of his army, the panzer tank.

"Anything else been hit?"

"Unknown. Too many of the smaller countries surrounding China are third world nations. Their capital cities are relatively modern, but the outlying farms are still operated by sheer muscle power."

True enough, Bolan supposed. "The people operating the drones probably hit the valley during a storm to try to disguise the destruction as lightning strikes," he stated.

Brognola nodded. "Now, given the location of the valley..."

"Along with its complete lack of nuclear weapons."

"...I think that we can easily make an educated guess who is behind all this," Brognola growled, closing the lid on the laptop. "Our old pal, Red China."

"You mean the Red Star," Bolan corrected. He had tangled with the Communist spy agency before and found them a lot trickier, and much deadlier, than the KGB had ever been, even in its glory days.

Across the diner, a couple of pimps started shouting at each other over who owned what street corner, and suddenly switchblade knives snapped into view. Instantly, Lucinda hurried over with a pot of boiling coffee. As the pimps rose, she spilled it on the table and everybody quickly retreated to avoid getting scalded. Wheeling out a bucket and mop, the scrawny Latino youth started cleaning up the mess and the frustrated pimps took their fight outside and away from the other customers.

"This could just be an internal coup," Bolan suggested. "The Red Star has wanted to seize absolute control over China for a long time."

"Maybe," Brognola admitted, folding his hands on the table. "But the worst-case scenario is that they're planning to expand the borders of their nation, and seize everything they can—Russia, Laos, Vietnam, Japan, India—giving them an unbreakable stranglehold on the east, paving the way for a Communist expansion such as the world has never seen before. And after that..."

"World domination?" Bolan said, pulling out some loose bills from his pocket.

"Nobody has seriously tried that in a long time," Brognola added. "I've been wondering when it would happen again."

"Where's the Farm on this?" Bolan asked, paying for the food and leaving a generous tip.

"Both teams are in the deep bush of South America handling another matter," Brognola replied, typing on the laptop's keyboard. A second later, the screen turned blank, the hard drive gave a loud buzz, then went silent and a puff of smoke rose from inside the machine.

"Barbara says it would take at least a week to extract Able Team and Phoenix Force. That is, without full military intervention," Brognola continued, pushing aside the hot laptop. There were scorch marks on the tabletop where it had sat.

"So I'm alone on this."

"I'll try to rustle you up some tactical support some friends overseas. There's an Israeli hacker who owes me a favor, Soshanna Fisher. But yeah. Basically, you're alone on this." Brognola gave a wan smile. "You've been there before."

"Only out of necessity," Bolan said, then rubbed the back of his neck. "This is a pretty wild-ass theory, Hal."

"Yes, it is, Striker."

"And you're probably dead wrong."

"Sure as hell hope so."

"But if you're right…"

"Yeah, I know." Brognola sighed.

"I'll call if I find anything," Bolan said, offering his hand.

The men shook.

"Any idea where to start your search?" the big Fed asked. "China is mighty big. But—"

Bolan interrupted, standing. "I'm headed for Hong Kong first."

Pushing back his chair, Brognola frowned. "What for?"

"To ask somebody about the drones," Bolan replied, heading for the door.

Before the big Fed could respond, his cell phone vibrated.

Checking the screen, Brognola saw the call was from one of his contacts in the NSA. Only minutes ago, the *Lady Durga*, the flagship of the Indian navy, a brand-new, state-of-the-art, nuclear-powered aircraft carrier, had been reported sunk off the Sea of Bengal after entering a fog bank. All hands lost. It was a major blow to India.

Plus, at the exact same time, a research lab in South Korea got hit by lightning during a rain storm and mysteriously burned to the ground. They had been working on a new type of radar. The entire staff of technicians and scientists were dead, and all of their records destroyed, along with the only working prototype.

"Move fast, Striker," Brognola muttered, snapping the phone shut with a savage jerk of his wrist, "because it looks like its has already hit the fan."

CHAPTER TWO

Northern Laos

Five trucks jostled along the old dirt road meandering through the steaming jungle. Razor-sharp machetes welded to the grilles and bumpers helped trim away the hanging vines and thorny creepers that regularly overgrew the winding road. By this time the next day, there would be no trace that anybody had driven through the jungle at this point, which was the precise reason this particular road was used so often.

High overhead, tiny monkeys ran and chattered in the treetops, while at the noise of the engines colorful birds took wing. They erupted from the bushes and flew into the air like living fireworks, briefly filling the sky with wondrous colors. Somewhere in the distance, a tiger roared, announcing a fresh kill, a crimson snake slithered through the flowering wines and hordes of unseen insects endlessly sang their secret song.

In the rear of each truck was a single large trunk, securely strapped to the metal floor and surrounded by armed guards, their scarred faces grim and unsmiling. This was their second run of the month, and everybody was eagerly thinking of the exotic pleasures their bonus would purchase once the five trunks were delivered across the border. Heroin was very big business in China, and no country in the world grew it better than Laos. The much vaunted black-tar heroin from Turkey was laughable in comparison.

"Sometimes I wish that I was Chinese and the government would subsidize my opium," a young private said with a laugh, nudging the trunk with the steel toe of his army boot. "Think of it! They buy at fifty a kilo, then sell it on the streets at ten. Ten!"

"Perhaps there is something good to be said about communism, after all," another private replied.

"The drug is just another way to keep their slaves from rebelling," a large corporal growled without looking up from his French comic book. "We use whips and chains, the Chinese use heroin. What is the difference?"

"Shut up, all of you," a grizzled lieutenant muttered, dropping the ammunition drum from a massive Atchisson autoshotgun, only to slam it back into the receiver. "Never talk about business in the open."

"Way out here?" a private asked. "Who is going to overhear us, a lizard working for Interpol?"

"I said be quiet," the lieutenant repeated, clicking off the safety. "That's a direct order."

Grudgingly, the troops obeyed, and went back to polishing the dampness from their AK-101 assault rifles, and daydreaming about the fleshpots of Vientiane. The capital city offered many tender delights for a real man with hard cash.

Sitting in the second truck of the convoy, Tul-Vuk Yang pulled a slim Monte Cristo cigar from the breast pocket of his military fatigues and bit off one end. Spitting it away, he then thumbed a gold lighter alive and applied the hissing flame to the tip of the expensive cigar. Once the tip was cherry-red, Yang removed the flame and drew the pungent smoke deep into his lungs. Ah, wonderful! The foolish Americans used all sorts of bizarre chemicals to cure their broadleaf tobacco in only a few hours—arsenic, lead, formaldehyde—while, the Cubans allowed their tobacco to naturally cure in direct sunlight. The process took a month instead of six hours, and aside from the obvious health benefits of not breathing in vaporized arsenic, the difference in taste was beyond belief.

"Magnificent!" Yang sighed, exhaling a long stream of dark smoke.

"Sir?" the driver asked, glancing sideways.

"Nothing, my friend. Pay attention to the road! The rebels have been planting more and more of those homemade bombs these days, and—"

A thunderous explosion ripped about the jungle as the road just behind the convoy violently exploded, smoking pieces of men and machinery spraying outward in every direction.

"Incoming!" Yang shouted, the cigar dropping from his mouth. Clawing at the radio in the dashboard, he pulled up a hand mike. "Alert! Red alert! We are under attack!"

Instantly, the five trucks increased their speed, and soon were racing along the rough dirt road at a breakneck pace. Following close behind, the barrage of incoming missiles chewed a path of destruction after them, coming ever closer.

Just then, a fiery dart streaked between the first and second truck, the exhaust blowing in through the open windows.

"Close!" the pale driver yelled.

"Too close," Yang growled, scanning the sky for any sign of the enemy helicopter. The bastard had to be tracking his trucks by the heat of the engines. There was only one solution for that. He thumbed the mike alive.

"Everybody use your grenades. Throw them randomly, as far away as you can!"

Moments later, the jungle shook from multiple explosions all around the convoy. Bushes erupted from the soil, and trees toppled over. For an intolerable length of time, it seemed to the drug runners as if the entire world was exploding all around them.

Then the vines parted before the first truck and there was the Dee-wa Bridge, a modern box trestle that spanned a white-water gorge to reach the other side. Yang grinned at the sight of China. Nobody sane would dare to attack them there! The Chinese Red Army was bad enough, but the Red Star agents were psychopaths, genuine sadists who loved torture and bloodshed. No one dared to offend the dreaded Red Star!

"We're safe!" the driver yelled, as the first truck bumped onto the bridge and rapidly accelerated across the smooth, perforated flooring.

"Not yet," Yang replied, drawing a Very pistol, and firing a round straight upward.

The flare arched high into the sky and exploded into scarlet brilliance. Almost instantly a missile slammed into the sizzling flare and detonated in a controlled thunderclap.

Laughing in victory, Yang fired more flares as fast as he could, every one targeted by a missile and then swiftly destroyed.

"Last truck is on the bridge!" a voice announced over the radio.

"Now we're safe." Yang chuckled, lowering the flare gun.

That was when he saw a flock of big black birds hovering over the Dee-wa Gorge, as if they were nailed to the empty air. He blinked in surprise, then screamed as the winged machines cut loose with all of their remaining missiles at point-blank range.

The entire length of the Dee-wa Bridge was engulfed in a fireball from eighteen antitank missiles. The steel mooring ripped from the concrete beds, and the trestle writhed like a dying thing, twisting and convulsing, rivets flying and welds cracking until the bridge was smashed into a million pieces. Smashed and on fire, the armored trucks tumbled down into the gorge, the men already dead from the bone-pulverizing concussions.

It took the burning vehicles almost a full minute to reach the bottom of the gorge, and trees were flattened for a hundred yards from their meteoric impact. Then a pair of drones arrived to crash among the smoldering wreckage and ignite their self-destruct charges of thermite. Soon, a raging chemical bonfire filled the area, melting the metal trucks into slag, vaporizing the cargo and forever completing the total annihilation of the infamous Yang Moon Convoy.

Patiently, the rest of the Sky Tiger swarm waited until their miniature computers were assured everybody was dead, and the cargo of opium was beyond recovery. Now the machines automatically switched to their secondary targets, and swooped away to find the next bridge of any kind that crossed the Dee-wa River. The wild waters had a different name in each new territory, but the drones were concerned only with bridges and dams. At each one, a drone would smash into the structure and set off its payload of deadly thermite. Burning at the surface temperature of the sun, the lambent fire destroyed everything it reached. Concrete, iron, granite or steel—nothing could withstand the hellish infernos.

Less than an hour later, there were no functioning bridges between Laos and China, and the drug trade between the two nations was terminated for the time being.

Hong Kong International Airport, Hong Kong

THE AIRPORT WAS bustling with crowds of people arriving and departing, and nobody seemed to be paying any attention to the Chinese soldiers standing on the overhead catwalks carrying QBZ assault rifles.

Maintaining a neutral expression, Bolan gave them only a cursory glance, then ignored the guards completely, just like everybody else. The Customs line moved swiftly, faster than he had expected, and soon he was standing before a small Asian man who scrutinized his passport as if knowing it was a fake. Except that it wasn't, aside from the name imprinted on the federal paper.

"And what is the purpose of your visit, Mr. Dupree?" the customs inspector asked, looking at the passport. "Business or pleasure?"

"A little of both, hopefully." Bolan chuckled, looking past the two men going through his luggage. "Seems like quite a party out there. Is today something special, like your Independence Day?"

"Liberation Day," the Communist corrected, studying the fictitious travels of Adam Dupree, a sewage pump salesman from Detroit, Michigan. "But that is not today. You are just in time for the Hungry Ghost festival. A colorful celebration from our more primitive past."

"Got some mighty pretty girls on those floats going by," Bolan replied, giving a wink.

The Customs official almost smiled. "I cannot speak on such matters. You understand?" The passport was returned, and the suitcase snapped shut. "Enjoy your stay. Break no laws. Next, please!"

Bolan tucked the passport inside his plaid sport coat.

Taking the suitcase, he merged into the next line and passed through a glistening arch that looked like something straight out of a science-fiction movie. It even gave a low, ominous beep when he passed through. A moment later, the woman sitting behind a glowing screen waved her hand and a guard stepped aside with a nod.

The inspectors had found nothing illicit, or illegal, in his belongings because there was nothing to be found. He didn't have so much as a penknife or a sharp pencil in his pockets. Smuggling weapons through airports was getting tougher every year, and while Bolan hadn't expected the airport to have the new-style body scanners yet, he was very glad he had decided to play it safe. The modified X-ray machine had given the woman at the console a clear view of his naked body. Everything was revealed without the traveler being bothered by the inconvenience and embarrassment of disrobing or receiving a pat-down. These days, the dreaded cavity search was reserved only for people who acted unduly nervous, or broke the rules.

Exiting the airport, Bolan took a moment to look around at the bustling crowd of tourists, hustlers and armed police. Outside the terminal, the air was much warmer and a lot more noisy, with people talking in a dozen different languages. Most were Asian, and Bolan could detect the subtle difference between the Chinese, Japanese, Cambodians and Macauns, the other recent acquisition of Red China. But there were also a lot of European blondes and British redheads mixing with the Asian ravens.

The Hungry Ghost festival didn't start until the next day, but there were dozens of floats being prepared, along with an army of pretty woman practicing dance steps. Bolan was impressed. Their elaborate costumes covered every inch of their bodies, yet, somehow, the dancers still managed to exude an aura of sultry eroticism. What the Brazilians did with partial nudity, the locals in Hong Kong did with simple body movement and grace.

Before he'd left the States, Bolan had Barbara Price, mission controller at Stony Man Farm, arrange for a gun drop with the CIA.

Turning his attention to the line of cabs parked along the curb, Bolan easily spotted one bearing the faded logo of a half-moon, the symbol he was told to look for. As he walked that way, the other cab drivers shouted out their prices, and special offers, but the soldier ignored them. He had just traveled halfway around the world, and his contact was driving a specific cab.

"Taxi, mister?" a tall Asian driver asked, lowering his MP3 player. Instantly, the screen went dark. "Clean and cheap! Best rates in town!"

"Now, I heard that the Star Ferry is the fastest way to reach the Kowloon District," Bolan said, tightening his grip on the suitcase.

"True, but very smelly!" the man countered, swinging open the door. "Hong Kong means fragrant harbor, only nowadays it refers to the reek from the industrial plants and pollution!"

"Well, my business is handling sewage…." Bolan said with a shrug, and stepped into the cab.

The cabbie closed the door, then got behind the wheel.

Quickly, Bolan checked the work permit on public display. The faded card was sealed inside a sleeve of foggy plastic, but the picture matched the driver. The name listed was Samuel C. Wong.

"Where to first?" Wong asked, starting the engine.

"Madame Tsai Shoe Repair," he replied.

Shifting into gear, Wong gave no outward sign that the name meant anything special as he started the engine and pulled away from the terminal.

Merging into the stream of traffic, the cab was soon

ensconced in a wild mixture of old and new vehicles—sleek hybrid cars and old ramshackle trucks that seemed to be held together with bailing wire. Huge BMW flatbed trucks hauling machinery muscled past flocks of people pedaling furiously on bicycles. Neatly dressed businessmen and women zipped along on scooters, while burly men covered with tattoos roared by on motorcycles, mostly Hondas and Suzukis.

As the cab stopped for a red light, Wong glanced into the rearview mirror. “Check under your seat.”

Warily, Bolan did so and found a flat plastic box sealed with duct tape. Thumbing off the tape, he popped the top and pulled aside an oily rag to reveal a slim 9 mm pistol, a sound suppressor, a belt holster and a box of standard ammunition.

“You took a big chance carrying these so close to the airport,” Bolan said, disassembling the pistol to check the internal workings before reassembling it even faster.

“Not really. I also deliver small packages for the local Customs inspectors,” Wong said with a laugh. “The local cops understand how the world works. As long as I only break the little laws, nobody asks about the big ones.”

“Fair enough.” Bolan screwed on a sound suppressor. Then he opened the box of ammunition, but as he started to thumb some rounds into an empty clip, he happened to look at the bottom of one brass casing.

“Damn it, those bastards have found me already,” Bolan growled, peering out the window. “Quick, pull over! We’re a sitting duck in this thing!”

“What’s wrong?” Wong asked in confusion, quickly shifting gears as he arched through the busy traffic. Horns blared at the maneuver, but the other vehicles melted out of the way.

“I’ve been made,” Bolan replied, brandishing the empty

handgun. "When I hit the sidewalk, you run. Get clear fast!" He tried to put as much concern into his voice as possible.

"No, let me help!" Wong countered, savagely braking to a hard stop alongside a bright yellow fire hydrant. "Just tell me who—"

Flipping the useless pistol over, Bolan grabbed it by the sound suppressor and clubbed Wong directly behind the ear. The man crumpled with a sigh onto the wheel.

Dropping the weapon, Bolan reached around the moaning driver and grabbed a sleek .22 pistol. The safety was off the assassin's weapon, and there was a round already in the breech for immediate use.

"What...don't..." Wong mumbled, flapping his hands.

Ruthlessly, Bolan smacked the man in the temple with the HK and heard the deadly crunch of bone. Shuddering all over, Wong went still forever.

Rifling through the pockets of the dead man, Bolan unearthed two spare clips, a switchblade knife and some cash. But there was no cell phone or wallet. Hastily tucking everything into his jacket, Bolan exited the cab and walked casually through the array of vendors and pushcarts. Turning a corner, he snapped the switchblade into life and took refuge in a dirty alley that reeked of garbage.

Nobody seemed to be looking his way, so Bolan went deeper into the alley until reaching a small slice of sunlight coming in between two buildings. Quickly, he checked over the pistol and then the ammunition. Thankfully, both were clean, unlike what was in the box under the seat.

Every bullet had a manufacturer's stamp on the bottom of the shell to show the lot number, location made and date. The police often tracked criminals by the brass ejected from a weapon. On the other hand, every major intelligence agency in the world made their own ammunition, which always lacked the stamp on the bottom. That was standard operational procedure. The cops knew something big was happening in their town when they found a corpse and empty "ghost" brass nearby. However, the ammunition in that box had carried a stamp, which meant it wasn't CIA issue, and that meant Bolan's cover had somehow been blown. He just didn't know how, or by whom, but staying in that cab would have been his last act on Earth. Out of curiosity, he used the switchblade to pry open a cartridge for the HK, and out poured sand instead of gunpowder.

Just then, a tall figure blocked out the sliver of rosy sunlight.

Instantly, Bolan ducked, and something hot hummed by his head as a hard cough came from the darkness ahead. As the round ricocheted off the brickwork behind, Bolan dived to the side and fired twice, then twice more. The dark figure grunted from the impact of the tiny .22 rounds, but didn't fall. Bolan bit back a curse. The other man had to be wearing body armor! The .22 rounds were doing less damage than a well-aimed snowball.

The silenced weapon coughing steadily, the other man slowly walked into the alley, blasting every pool of shadow.

Tracking the muted muzzle-flash of the weapon, Bolan guessed where his adversary's head should be, then stood and triggered a fast six rounds in a tight group. There came the sound of multiple .22 ricochets off the brick wall, then a hard smack of lead into flesh.

Snarling curses in what sounded like Chinese, the other man fanned the darkness with his weapon until the clip cycled empty. The soft click of a clip being released could be heard, and Bolan surged forward, batting aside the bigger weapon with the HK, and ramming the switchblade upward with all his strength.

He felt the warm breath explode from the other man as the steel found flesh. Gurgling, the man stumbled, his weapon clattering to the ground. Grabbing a fistful of hair, Bolan slashed across his adversary's throat and pushed him away. With blood raining to the ground, the man smacked into a wall and collapsed alongside a pile of garbage cans. A few seconds later the gurgling stopped.

As Bolan searched for the dropped weapon, he listened for any sounds of backup, sirens or running shoes. But nobody in the market had seemed to notice the brief tussle in the dark alleyway, or else the merchants simply knew better than to become involved in such matters. In this part of the world, the first rule of survival had always been stay low and don't get noticed.

When finally satisfied that nobody was coming, Bolan checked over the new weapon. It was a sleek 9 mm Norinco pistol, the official sidearm of the Chinese Red Army. The grip was rough, and Bolan scowled at the realization that it had been cut with notches. No professional soldier would have done that, so this man had simply been a very talented amateur. Just some street muscle, nothing more. Fire-and-forget.

Locating the corpse, Bolan went through the pockets. As expected, there was no cell phone, car keys or wallet. But he discovered four more ammunition clips, a butterfly knife, an enormous wad of cash held together with a rubber band, half a pack of chewing gum, plus something small, rectangular and hard.

Lifting the object into the sliver of daylight, Bolan snorted at the sight of the Hong Kong "octopus" card, a prepaid pass for every form of mass transit in the city. Excellent.

Depositing everything he didn't want into a garbage can, Bolan quickly left the area, zigzagging through the maze of back alleys until coming out a full block from where he had abandoned the cab. Strolling over to a street vendor, he purchased a cup of surprisingly good coffee, and sipped from the cardboard container while walking through the busy crowds.

There was a bad apple in the local CIA station. Maybe the cab driver was the only bad guy, maybe he was just a henchman. Whatever, the Executioner would hand over the information for Brognola to deal with.

It was a wake-up call, though. I can't trust any of the established contacts, rendezvous, or safehouses, Bolan realized. He would have to find his own source of additional weapons, and some way to sneak into Communist China.

Looking over the noisy throng to make sure nobody was paying him undue attention, Bolan turned away from the Asian teenager sitting on a park bench. The young woman was smoking a cigarette, and smiled as their gazes meet, then hitched her denim skirt high on her thighs to show she wasn't wearing anything underneath.

Arching an eyebrow in pretend shock, Bolan then patted his pockets to mime that he was broke. She managed to look sad, then shrugged and turned away to find another big American tourist.

At the corner, Bolan dropped the coffee container into a waste can under the watchful gaze of an armed police officer, then boarded a tram headed for the waterfront. His choices were rather limited at the moment, so he was going to have to do this old school and infiltrate China through the criminal underworld. That would mean risking encounters with a lot of people who would be delighted to bury him alive, but there was no other recourse at the moment. Once the news of the drones became public knowledge, China would slam its borders closed, so time was short. That would mean getting his shoes shined.

Surreptitiously checking the pistol tucked into his belt, he smiled at the memory of the sultry redhead. A mixture of Irish and Chinese, she possessed the best traits of both races, intelligence, grace and a figure that made most internet sex bombs look like cartoon stick figures. Tsai "Pat" Adina was the tenth wonder of the world.

However, it had been a long time since Bolan had last seen the woman. Hopefully, she was still working freelance, and he wasn't walking directly into another trap.

CHAPTER THREE

Engels Air Force Base, Russia

The abandoned freight yard, high on a hill overlooking the air base, was overgrown with weeds and brambles. The small brick building that had once served as an office was almost buried from sight under multiple layers of ivy.

The steel railroad tracks were long gone, and the wooden ties crumbled back into the earth. Only random pieces of rusting machinery lay about on the cracked asphalt, along with unrecognizable piles of trash and windblown leaves. Once, there had been thousands of cargo containers waiting patiently to be shipped across Russia. Stacked on top of one another, the containers had formed cubist mountains that rose defiantly to challenge the Ural Mountains on the horizon. But now there was only a handful of the big steel boxes, most of them rusted through in places to become homes for rats and other small vermin.

Artistically surrounded by a dozen other corroded containers, one steel box was heavily streaked with rust and bird droppings, but still in good shape, and unbreeched. Lying in the nearby weeds were the gleaming white bones of an itinerant worker, what the Americans would have called a hobo. Still clenched in her right hand was an iron crowbar whose sharp tip perfectly matched a set of gouges in the surface of the unopened box. Four years ago, the woman had climbed the wire fence and attempted to break open the container, hoping it was full of stereos, or cell phones, or anything that could be sold on the black market for a fast ruble.

She'd labored for hours to pry open the access panel, and her reward had been a searing burst of pain as 20,000 volts of electricity surged through her body, making her blood boil, her kidneys shrivel, her teeth shatter, then her cooked brain quite literally explode.

The rats and black beetles had feasted well that autumn, but soon the bounty of flesh was gone and only the bones remained, along with a few scraps of cloth, and the relatively undamaged crowbar.

Suddenly, the steel box began to softly vibrate, the dried bird nests and loose scales of rust dancing along the top until tumbling over the ends. With a hard clang an internal lock disengaged, and the lid swung aside just as a dozen spheres blasted upward on a column of compressed air.

Spreading their wings, the drones swooped from the sky, skimming low across the weedy fields of rubbish to fly straight off the end of a limestone cliff. Diving sharply to build speed, the war machines streaked straight down toward the sprawling air base that filled the valley below.

The leaves on the trees shook from the wake of the Sky Tiger drones as they flashed past a radar station and a SAM battery. Spreading out in a curve, the drones separated and began pumping out their deadly cargo of sarin nerve gas.

Coming out of the control tower, a pair of airmen were the first to die, their faces barely able to register the fact before their bodies dropped, twitching, to the tarmac, and then went still forever. A guard in a kiosk set alongside the main hangar saw the drone and reached for the red security phone on the wall, but his hand never finished the short journey before he was sprawled across his desk, red blood pouring from every orifice.

Getting ready for the morning reconnaissance patrol along the Chinese border, the two pilots strapped into the cockpit of their MiG-35 jet fighters actually saw the drones flash by, and managed to get out a warning over their throat mikes before the sarin gas penetrated the seals of their planes. As their vision began to fade, the pilots frantically turned up the flow of oxygen to their masks. That bought them a few precious seconds of nearly unbearable agony, then they slumped over in their seats, convulsing and gushing red life.

Accidentally, one of the spasming men shoved the control yoke forward, and the idling jet engines instantly surged, revving to full power. With nobody at the controls, the MiG-35 started to drift and narrowly missed crashing into an Mi-26 cargo helicopter full of dying paratroopers. Then the MiG ran over a bleeding flight controller sprawled on the ground, and swerved wildly around to clip an attack helicopter and crash directly into a Tu-160 strategic bomber.

Since the MiG wasn't in the air, the air-to-air missiles lining both wings weren't armed, nor were the thermonuclear bombs loaded into the Tu-160. But that made little difference to the maintenance truck carrying a full load of high-octane jet fuel.

The fiery blast engulfed a dozen other war planes, quickly setting their own stores of fuel ablaze, then cooking off the warheads in their assorted rockets and missiles. With nobody alive to stop it, this quickly became a chain reaction of explosions that rapidly escalated into a rampaging cacophony of destruction, shattering windows for a thousand yards, buckling the control tower and even flipping over the cars in the distant parking lot. The heavily armored thermonuclear bombs inside the belly of the Tu-160 were completely undamaged in the maelstrom, as were the underground SAM batteries. But a split second later, the thermobaric bomb inside the Tu-160 ignited.

Designed as it was to explode in the sky above an enemy target and utterly obliterate it, the device's titanic detonation shook the entire base, shattering the pavement back into gravel and burning every trace of the deadly sarin nerve gas from existence. Unstoppable, the hellish shock wave of the Russian superbomb careened along the ground, brushing aside planes, trucks, men and machines as if they were dried leaves. Then the heat flash expanded in a staggering halo effect that set fire to everything organic: corpses, tires, trees, boots, roofing tiles and the drones.

Slowly, a rumbling mushroom cloud of smoke and flame formed above the annihilated air base, and charred pieces of corpses and partially melted chunks of billion-ruble jet fighters rained down across the countryside for miles....

Southern Hong Kong

LEAVING THE PUBLIC TRAM at the downtown station, Bolan walked outside the terminus into organized chaos.

The Kowloon District of Hong Kong was unlike anyplace else in the world. A wild mixture of old and new gleaming skyscrapers rose above wooden shacks, rickshaws racing alongside hybrid limousines. Diesel buses fumed alongside electric streetcars, and trucks of every description rumbled past, carrying the goods of the world. Bicycles didn't flow in streams, but moved in flocks like birds on the wing, and the constant chiming of their little bells was only a background murmur to the orchestra of voices talking, laughing, singing, crying, arguing, pondering, lying, cutting deals or just chattering away.

A hundred vendors were selling everything imaginable from small stalls lining the sidewalks. If the Chinese government deemed something legal to sell, then it was available in Kowloon, usually at a discount price if you bought six of them.

A hand fleetingly touched his hip, and Bolan savagely slapped it away. With a startled cry, the pickpocket moved off fast, cradling his broken wrist.

If there were any traffic laws, nobody was paying attention to them, and Bolan simply crossed through the busy traffic like everybody else, wherever he pleased, the traffic lights seeming to be merely decorations.

Since Hong Kong had once been a British colony, the street signs were also in English, and Bolan easily located the waterfront, although he heard the warning blasts from the tugboats long before he actually saw water.

The crowds were thinner here, and scurried to keep out of the way of the rattling forklifts that wheeled about in conga lines ferrying about an endless array of cargo pallets. The voices were far more impatient, and the use of vulgarity infinitely more prevalent.

Leaning on an iron railing that had been recently painted, Bolan looked across the choppy bay. Since Kowloon faced south, and Mainland China was on the other side of the island to the north, there was only open water to the horizon. In the murky distance was another landmass, oddly named Hong Kong Island. How the inhabitants kept the two islands separate was a puzzle to most outsiders, and a constant source of amusement to the locals.

Though the harbor was choppy, with low swells cresting on the rocky shoreline, the waterway was full of sleek pleasure craft, old fishing trawlers, junks, wooden rafts, futuristic hovercraft and colossal cruise liners that resembled floating islands of light.

There were also a scattering of Chinese navy gunboats, their radar constantly in motion, the deck guns and depth-charge launchers covered with tarpaulins as protection against the salty spray, and the idle curiosity of the much-prized tourists. But the armed sailors on deck were openly carrying 5.56 mm QBZ assault rifles, and stared suspiciously at everybody and everything. Even the tourists. Most of them laughed and took pictures with their cell phones, but the wiser heads turned away and went about their business. China valued tourism, but only to a point.

Keeping to the shadows, Bolan watched the gunboats move along on patrol, blazingly bright halogen searchlights sweeping across every small craft that approached. He grunted at that. These were the new Wall of China, Communist hard-liners more resolute than stone, grim men who couldn't be bribed, or dealt with.

Turning away from the water, Bolan headed back into the maelstrom of chatting people. It had been a while since he had last been here, but the memories came flooding back, and he soon located the Tsai Shoe Repair Shop. The brass sign above the front door was small, almost unreadable, and the windows were in desperate need of a good washing. Yet Bolan knew that the place was one of the most profitable enterprises on the entire island.

The public side of Tsai Shoe Repair was strictly legitimate, with eager cobblers fixing worn-out soles, replacing broken heels and polishing leather to a mirror sheen. New shoes were available for purchase, as well as a foot massage. However, unlike most shoe repair shops, the business occupied the entire five-story building, including the garage next door.

The set-up was simple. A customer walked in for a repair, or maybe just a shine, and had a few minutes to kill with nothing to do except watch television in the waiting room or read magazines. But if he wished a beautiful young hostess would happily escort him upstairs to a wonderland of fleshly delights. The Tsia Shoe Repair was the premiere brothel of Hong Kong, and unlike so many other brothels, the customers here always left with whatever possessions they had originally arrived with.

Walking into the garage, Bolan used the employee entrance to bypass the shoe shop and go directly into the waiting room. As expected, it was empty. The brothel made no money from a full sofa, only full beds.

At the back of the room was an unmarked door that opened onto a short flight of stairs that led straight to the second floor. Halfway there, Bolan passed a burned-out light fixture, and smiled for the hidden video camera. The soldier reached the top step, and as he pushed open the door, a tiny woman rushed forward to grab him around the waist.

"Colonel!" Madame Tsai said into his stomach, tightening her grasp. "My God, I never thought I'd see you again!"

"Nice to see you, Pat," Bolan replied, prying her loose to kiss the woman on the forehead.

The owner, manager and madam of the brothel, Tsai Adina, was extremely small. She barely reached five feet, and cultivated an explosion of red curls to give her an extra few inches. Add spike high heels and she just managed to reach about five feet five. Bolan guessed that she weighed somewhere around ninety-nine pounds, but every ounce was in exactly the right place and proudly on display in a skintight bodysuit that revealed every curve. The front was cut low to show off her cleavage, along with some sort of tattoo on her right breast.

Although surrounded by a cloud of jasmine perfume, Tsai used very little makeup. She wore a slim holster at her side. The madam liked to run a peaceful business, but if there was trouble with an unruly guest, she served as the bouncer and easily convinced most people to leave with the swift application of a French police baton. The handle was only seven inches long, barely visible in a closed fist. But with a snap, it extended to twenty-seven inches of coiled steel, and proved more than sufficient to convince even a meth freak that it was time to go home. As small as she was, nobody sane ever tangled with Tsai Adina twice and lived to tell the tale.

"How are things?" Bolan asked.

"Never better." Tsai smiled, going on tiptoes to kiss him on the cheek.

Although Bolan had been acquainted with the woman for years, she knew him only by his various alias's. His name changed from time to time, but she was smart enough to never ask embarrassing questions. Keeping secrets was part of her stock-in-trade.

"Got someplace where we can talk in private?" he asked.

"Trouble, John?" Tsai asked in real concern. Her face was only inches away, her eyes a deep blue, almost turquoise.

"Not for you," he replied honestly, "and you can call me Matt Cooper."

She looked at him hard for a few moments, then nodded. "Follow me." She escorted him into a second waiting room.

This one was much more impressive than the one downstairs, and a lot more populated. There were several red leather couches full of men, and a few women, with everybody politely trying to not look at one another. The carpeting was thick to help mask any noise from the polishing machines downstairs.

Instrumental music played softly over disguised speakers, and the oak panel walls were heavily decorated with pictures of the female staff members in various stages of undress, along with numerous shots of celebutantes in bikinis, or less, removed from magazines.

Pushing her way through a beaded curtain, Tsai walked along a dimly lit hallway, her high heels clicking with every step. The passageway was lined with closed doors from behind which came the expected cries, moans and groans of adults indulging in the most basic of recreational activities.

Turning left, the woman proceeded through a small room filled with the night shift. Most of the prostitutes were eating dinner or working on laptops. The rest of the women were touching up their lipstick or brushing their hair.

Bolan followed Tsai into an elevator and she pressed a button for the fifth floor.

With a ping the elevator opened, revealing a big sign in the hallway that stated there was a hundred dollar fine for loud talking. More doors lined this corridor, but these were different from the working rooms downstairs. These doors had locks and peepholes.

"How many on staff these days?" Bolan asked, looking down the long corridor.

"Thirty," Tsai replied, pulling a key out of her cleavage and unlocking a door. "Well, twenty-nine, actually. My roommate, Lu-Ann, is out with the flu."

"The nine-month flu?"

"No, just the plain flu." Tsai laughed and she opened the door. "Sneezing and sniffling and such."

"Send her my best." Stepping inside, Bolan relaxed his stance slightly when he saw the room was empty. Bookcases full of paperbacks and CD jewel cases lined the walls, and off to the side, a big-screen TV was set before a curved sofa. The screen was dark, but the DVR underneath steadily counted down as if recording something unseen. There were two beds, at opposite ends of the room, and an open door showed a small bathroom decorated with light blue tiles.

"Welcome to the inner sanctum," Tsai said, closing the door and locking it. "No customers allowed."

"Just friends?"

"Just friends, and damn few of those."

"I'm honored."

Although quite small, the room was very clean, and clearly not designed to entertain clients. There was an easy chair by the window, and a laptop was humming. In the corner was a dresser piled high with folded laundry.

"Okay, who's trying to kill you?" Tsai asked, going to the liquor cabinet and starting to make drinks.

"Best not to ask," Bolan stated, sliding of his jacket. "None for me, thanks."

"No?"

"Working."

Glancing in a mirror, Tsai arched an eyebrow at the weapons on display, but said nothing.

"I need some guns."

"More than those?" the madam asked.

"Better ones, if possible."

"Well, I have a fairly decent armory in the office," she said, thoughtfully biting a lip. "But I know where you can get more. Military stuff, right?"

"Right."

"Yeah, thought so. Well, the Tong hasn't given me any problems for years, but I like to stay prepared."

"Very wise."

"I'll send a girl to bring a map."

"Thanks."

"Anything else?"

"A boat, small, fast, disposable."

Turning to the left, Tsai saw the electric glow of China in the far distance and opened her mouth to speak, then changed her mind.

"When do you want it?" she asked softly.

"As soon as possible."

"Then I had better get moving."

CHAPTER FOUR

Yangtze River Valley, Red China

"No! Please!" Colonel Weng Pei pleaded. "I had to act. Choi Lei at the CIA station said that a specialist was coming from America to deal with something big. He had to be eliminated."

"Shut up," Major Shen-wa Fen muttered, slashing his knife along the man's throat.

As a torrent of hot blood gushed forth, the major pushed his gurgling commander out of the hovering Z-8 transport helicopter.

"You contemptible fool," Shen-wa said in annoyance, cleaning the blade on a rag as he watched the hurtling body vanish into the thick forest below. "Who told him to move on the intel provided by our insider and lay a trap for the CIA agent? I want the Americans stonewalled, learning nothing as they rush about Hong Kong from one false lead to another until they meet the *Lucky Lady!*"

"Mice in a maze," Sergeant Ming Bohai rumbled from the cockpit, angling the military helicopter away from the rolling forest and back toward home base.

Sheathing the blade, Shen-wa nodded. "Exactly! But now…"

Annoyed, he looked out the window, lost in his private thoughts. Was the plan compromised? He didn't think so, which was lucky, because at this point it would be nearly impossible to stop. After five long years of planning, everything was dovetailing into place, and he wouldn't allow anything to get in his way. Certainly not some hot-snot nephew of a politician, a fat fool who had never fired a weapon in combat, and earned his rank by throwing elaborate parties and kissing ass.

No wonder the world hates China, Shen-wa noted, leaning back in the jump seat. We're a joke. As corrupt as the Americans and as decadent as the Russians.

Pulling a small ironwood pipe from the breast pocket of his uniform, Shen-wa tucked it contentedly into his mouth. Sadly, he couldn't light the pipe, as smoking was strictly forbidden on board the helicopter. Something about the smoke bothering the advanced electronics. Still, having the stem between his teeth gave him no small measure of comfort, and it was an aid to clear thinking. How had a CIA agent been dispatched to Hong Kong so fast? What did the spy agency know?

Unlike most of the executive operatives in Red Star, the major was a tall, handsome man with perfectly combed hair, and the smile of a Beijing movie star. He always spoke softly, rarely above a whisper, yet combat veterans jumped as if he were cracking a whip. Nobody in the Central Military Command really understood how the major achieved the effect, not even the president, and every attempt to duplicate it had failed miserably. The aura of command radiating from Shen-wa was a natural talent, and had caused quite a lot of resentment in the regular army. His transfer from counterintelligence into the covert division of the Red Star had been as expected as rain in the spring—normal, natural and to everyone's benefit.

"Sir, can the damage be repaired?" Ming asked, swinging away from the new high-tension powerline towers jutting up from the forest like the skeleton hands of dead robots.

"Most certainly, old friend," Shen-wa replied, smiling around the pipe. "We're fine. For the moment, at least. Your prompt action in telling me about this saved us all. It has helped save China itself."

"Just doing my job, sir," Ming demurred, leveling the helicopter so as not to draw unwanted attention from the workers below.

Childhood hadn't been kind to the sergeant in many ways. It gave him a face from hell, and had started him on the twisted path to his present employment. Unusual for a race known for its rather compact stature, Ming was a hulking giant, well over seven feet tall and with shoulders as broad as a Tibetan ox. His fingers were so large he had to remove the trigger guard from his service pistol to operate the weapon, yet he flew helicopters with smooth precision.

"We're all just doing our jobs," Shen-wa said, lost in thought. The CIA...the CIA...why did that keep echoing in his mind?

Lost in contemplation, he made no further comments as the sergeant expertly piloted the helicopter over the small town of Sandooping, and then proceed up the river toward the gigantic Three Gorges Dam.

Finished only a few years earlier, the Three Gorges facility was the largest dam in the world, with twenty-seven hydroelectric generators fully capable of supplying power to half of China. Once, he had read the exact figures of how much voltage it generated, but then promptly forgot the number. He wasn't overly interested in statistics, only results. The dam had cost thirteen billion euros to build, and so it had been relatively easy for him to siphon off a decent chunk of the funds for Project Keyhome.

The Three Gorges Dam was so huge that it had a series of locks alongside, elevators for cargo ships, and could lift entire oceangoing vessels from the lower runoff located at the bottom, to the vast lake on top. No other dam in the world could do that, and the fact was a constant source of pride for the major. The Chinese had always been creators, inventing black powder, rockets, the compass, and a host of other items that made modern life possible.

And soon they would bring freedom to every civilized nation on the planet, Shen-wa added mentally. Whether they wanted it or not. But first China had to clean its own house.

Receiving clearance from the air traffic controller inside the control tower atop the massive dam, the sergeant landed the helicopter directly on one of three circles set aside for emergency transport.

Even before the sergeant had shut down the complex machine, Major Shen-wa had exited the helicopter and walked far enough away that he could light his pipe.

"Orders, sir?" Ming asked, bending low as he walked under the slowing blades.

"You better go and report the terrible accident to your political officer, Sergeant," Shen-wa directed. "Now remind me again, the colonel was drunk, as usual, and fell off the helicopter...." He paused expectantly.

"A hundred miles to the north, near the abandoned missile base?"

"No, better make it the south, near the rock quarry. That will be much harder to search."

"Yes, sir. A hundred miles to the south, near the old rock quarry," Ming replied, managing to look contrite. "We tried to land to see if there was anything we could do, but the terrain in the area made it impossible."

"And we didn't radio in immediately for help because..."

"We couldn't! The colonel had ordered a halo of full radio silence around the dam."

Removing the pipe, Shen-wa smiled. "Exactly. Such a shame."

"Sir, what if they don't believe me?"

"Then kill them all and throw the bodies into the gorge. In fact—" he gave a hard smile "—do it anyway. It's time that we took over this facility. I'm tired of listening to these cowardly paper-jugglers."

"Yes, sir!" Ming replied eagerly, giving a fast salute.

Shen-wa almost smiled at that, then it hit him. Less than thirty-six hours had passed since the attack on Kazakhstan. There was no way the CIA could have dispatched an agent to China in so short a time period. The colonel knew the bureaucracy of the Agency was horrendous. Whomever Colonel Weng had tried to capture was merely somebody pretending to be a CIA agent. That was the only logical answer.

Exhaling a long stream of smoke, Shen-wa grunted. The old bastard may have done the project a good deed, accidentally uncovering an unknown enemy before he could get close.

"Something wrong, sir?" Ming asked in concern.

"Yes and no," Shen-wa replied, removing the pipe. "After you terminate everybody in the political office, go to Hong Kong and find out who it was that entered the island. He isn't a CIA agent, and we need to know who this man actually works for."

"Perhaps the American...ah...NAS?"

"NSA," Shen-wa corrected. "But no, they are code breakers. More paper-pushers. This was the act of somebody with blood in their veins. A professional. A killer."

"Perhaps the Mossad."

"Yes, that could very well be," Shen-wa answered slowly. "The Israelis are very good at what they do, almost as good as us!" He chuckled, and the sergeant joined in for the sake of solidarity.

"Find this man," Shen-wa said. "Question him thoroughly. Then poorly hide the body, and blame it on the Russians."

"What if he is Russian, sir?"

"Blame it on them anyway. Who can keep track of their internal politics, eh?"

"Sir, yes, sir!" Ming replied with a crisp salute.

Puffing on his pipe, Major Shen-wa watched as the sergeant strode away, loosening the massive .50-caliber Norinco pistol holstered at his side. Just for a fleeting moment, Shen-wa almost felt sorry for the poor bastard, but then it was gone, a random thought lost on the breeze.

Leaving the small heliport, Shen-wa walked to an iron door and waved his identification card before the scanner. There came a subtle hum, and the door unlocked, then cycled open to the sound of working hydraulics.

Stepping inside, the major walked past a huge soundproof room full of technicians busily operating the complex controls of the gargantuan power station. A pretty woman at one of the consoles smiled at him in passing, and Shen-wa politely touched his cap in reply. Lieutenant Lee Jade was a distant cousin, and he had gotten her the job in case he needed some insider information about the daily operations of the dam. So far, he hadn't, but it was nice having family nearby, anyway. After all, family was why he was trying to help China conquer the world.

Reaching a private elevator, Shen-wa showed his identification card to the wall scanner once more, then pressed his hand on a glowing sensor plate. There came a slight tingle as the plate sent a few volts of electricity through his fingers to make sure the hand was still alive, and not detached by an enemy spy in order to facilitate entry. This was another Chinese invention, although he had heard rumors that the West had also created a similar device, for the exact same reasons.

It was a very long ride down to the bottom level, and Shen-wa emerged from the elevator in a cloud of tobacco smoke. Tapping out the glowing ashes into a trash container, he then slowly walked toward a sandbag nest with two soldiers stationed behind the waist-high barrier. They looked strong and fit, even though one was clearly much older than the other. Both men were in full dress uniform, heavily armed and wearing class four body armor. Field soldiers got class two armor, and special forces wore class three. Class four was much too heavy to wear in combat, but the bulky armor was perfect for soldiers who could sit down and rest for most of the day.

"Major!" a young private called out crisply, snapping a strange weapon to his chest in lieu of saluting. The barrel of the weapon was ridiculously large, the ammunition clip even bigger, and there was a bandoleer of 35 mm shells draped across his chest, with two more tucked into loops at his side where he normally would have had a sidearm.

"So, it finally arrived," Shen-wa said softly, looking over the QLB 35 mm grenade launcher.

"Yes, Major!"

"And you passed the mandatory testing?"

"Of course, Major!" the young private stated proudly. "I can fire the QLB in my sleep, and repair it in the dark!"

Hefting his own QBZ assault rifle, the older private grunted in acknowledgment. "He actually can, Major. I've seen him at the gun range. Fast. Faster even than Sergeant Ming."

"Show me," Shen-wa commanded, pointing down the corridor. "Destroy that light, third from the end."

In a blur of motion, the young private crouched as he swung up the oversize weapon and fired. Hot smoke and flame belched from the muzzle, and a hundred feet away a light fixture exploded into debris, leaving a fist-size dent in the steel wall.

"Why nonexplosive rounds?" Shen-wa asked sternly.

"Only the first two are solid," the young private replied crisply. "The next three release hundreds of razor-sharp fléchette rounds. The last shell in the clip is high-explosive, armor piercing." He grinned. "In case an invader is also wearing body armor."

"Very wise. Carry on," Shen-wa said, walking around a corner. Just a few words now and then, a touch of courtesy, and the troops would die for him. It was a good investment.

An iron gate closed off this section of the corridor, and the major again pressed his hand to a sensor plate. The gate unlocked with a clang, and he went through, closing it tight behind. Electronics were all well and good, but he would always put his real trust in simple cold steel.

An unmarked door was at the end of a short corridor, and sitting at a plain wooden desk nearby was a mature woman in a long civilian dress, the flowing black fabric decorated with colorful flowers. A plate on the desktop had her name in both Mandarin and Cantonese. She was industriously typing away on a computer keyboard, and looked up at his approach.

"She's waiting in the office," Wu Cassandra said without any preamble, not pausing in her work.

"Thank you, Miss Wu," he said, walking past and opening the door, which gave a musical chime.

Across the office, a tall woman in a tan outfit looked up in surprise at the noise, then jumped to her feet and gave a salute. "Good evening, sir!" she cried out.

There was a canvas duffel bag on the floor near her chair, along with a nylon travel bag locked with a red security seal. Shen-wa recognized it as a weapons kit. "At ease, Zhang," he said, closing the door.

"Yes, sir," Lieutenant Zhang Meiron replied uneasily, but stayed erect. It had been a long flight from Taiwan, and she was more than a little tired. However, she was also grimly determined not to show any weakness before the dreaded old man.

A veteran of numerous wars, the major had helped create the Red Star, and had personally terminated over a hundred enemy spies during his long career. It was rumored that he had even helped design the August 1st Building, the headquarters for the entire Chinese military. The only reason Major Shen-wa held so a low rank, instead of being in charge of the CMC, was that he was a maverick, a loner who hated politics, and disliked obeying the rules, being much more interested in getting results.

Just like me, Zhang thought proudly.

Six feet tall, and built like a professional weight lifter, Zhang found that nothing in the world easily accommodated her. Beds were too short, doorways too low, shirts too tight, and romance was mostly a matter of finding somebody drunk at a bar, and leaving quietly in the morning before finding out his name. Only the military had accepted her with open arms, in spite of its many reservations to a woman serving in combat.

Automatically cycling closed, the armored door to the office shut with a muffled boom.

"Why are you out of uniform and dressed like a civilian?" Shen-wa demanded.

"Sir, I...I was told to remain inconspicuous in my travel here," she replied.

"Logical and reasonable," he agreed, starting across the office.

Resembling a research library, the metal walls of the domed room were lined with bookcases stuffed with bound technical manuals. There were no personal effects anywhere in sight. No sports trophies, family pictures, knickknacks or executive toys. It was neat and impersonal, a place of work, nothing more.

The single humanizing aspect was a small black lacquered cabinet set under a large flag of China. The cabinet was made in the style of the Hung Dynasty of the fourth Century BCE, and whatever had been its original purpose, it was now well stocked with liquor bottles, glasses, an automatic ice dispenser and a tobacco humidor.

"So, how much do you know about this project?" Shen-wa asked, going to the liquor cabinet.

"Nothing, sir."

"Then why did you agree to the assignment?" he asked pointedly, making a stiff drink of whiskey, then taking a seat behind a large redwood desk. Covered with piles of reports, and computer monitors, the desk was set kitty-corner to the rest of the room, so that his back was protected by the plain steel walls.

Zhang paused uncertainly. "Because I wish to work with you, sir," she replied honestly. "You're a living legend!"

"No matter what the project is?"

"My faith in you is absolute!"

"How touching," Shen-wa whispered, almost smiling. "Make yourself a drink, Lieutenant. Relax."

"Not while on duty, sir."

Taking a sip from his glass, Shen-wa said nothing.

Suddenly, Zhang realized that she was being tested, not merely interviewed, and wondered what would happen if she failed.

"You're smarter than you look," Shen-wa said, turning on a monitor. "Very good. I suspected as much. You hide your intelligence to catch an opponent by surprise."

"It is a man's world," Zhang stated, keeping the emotion from her voice. "A woman is either smart or pretty. Nature made my choice for me."

Clearly, that confused him. "But you are both," he said hesitantly.

She scowled, but said nothing. Did he really mean that?

"Ah. I see that we disagree." He smiled, typing briefly on the keyboard. "Good! I like that. Now sit down. I prefer to talk at eye level."

She wavered, wondering if this was another test.

"That was a direct order, Lieutenant."

"Yes, sir. Thank you, sir," she replied, sitting down and stretching her long legs. She was in traveling clothes of a loose tan jacket, white blouse, pleated tan skirt and flats. High heels made her long legs look good, but the additional height only served to alienate her more from the rest of scurrying humanity.

Briefly, Shen-wa glanced at her legs in frank appreciation, then went back to the monitor.

Pleased with his controlled reactions, Zhang warily studied the officer behind the desk. Major Shen-wa Fen was old, but clearly in excellent health, his face and hands braided with muscle. Her guess was that he was a student of kung fu, probably Southern style, from the appearance of his fingers. The bent pinkie was a dead giveaway to those who knew what to look for. Old, but fast and accurate. That would make him a very deadly opponent, indeed. It would seem that the major also liked to attack with surprise. She liked that and felt a growing warmth in her stomach. She liked that a lot.

In spite of the outside environment, Shen-wa had a deep tan, and his thick black hair had natural wings of silver at the temples. There was no other word for it but dashing.

Then she saw his eyes looking directly at her face in mild disapproval, and felt a chill. Oh yes, she knew that look well enough. She had seen it a thousand times before in combat zones across the world. It was the face of a killer, as cold and merciless as an open grave. Briefly, Zhang wondered what he would be like in bed.

Thinking along similar lines himself, Shen-wa grinned as a report scrolled on the monitor about a drone attack on the Tokyo computer complex that controlled the coastal defense guns for Japan.

"Sir?" Zhang asked.

"One moment," he replied curtly. Ah, the backup computers in Osaka had also been destroyed, along with a busful of technicians racing to effect emergency repairs. More food for the demons of hell, he thought. There could never be enough dead Japanese, but it was merely the beginning. France would be next, then Russia again, followed by the United States.

"Ahem, sir?"

He looked up with a broad smile. "Yes?"

"When did Colonel Weng die?" Zhang asked, crossing her legs at the ankles.

"How could you possibly know that he..." Shen-wa scowled. Was *she* testing *him* now?

"Weng is—was—the head of security for the Three Gorges Dam," Zhang stated with a neutral expression. "If you need another, then he must have failed in some gross manner involving your private project, and now you require a replacement. Why else would you summon me?"

Templing his fingers, he openly smiled. "Publicly, he fell out of a Z-8 transport."

"And actually…?"

"I slit his throat and threw him out alive. The man acted foolishly, and may have alerted enemy forces to my plans long before I was ready to openly act against them."

"Is the project compromised?" she asked, leaning back in the chair. Her jacket spread wide, exposing a holstered 9 mm Norinco pistol and spare ammunition clips.

"Not at the moment. But for want of a nail…" He made a vague gesture.

She dismissed that with a wave of her hand. "I know the allusion, sir. Will my first duty be disposing of the body?"

"Already taken care of by Sergeant Ming. You will meet him later at the general staff meeting tonight. However, at the moment I need you to take over all matters involving security for Project Keyhome."

"I accept," she said.

"Excellent!" He rose to offer a hand.

She stepped closer and they shook, maintaining the hold for much longer than necessary. They could each feel a bond start to form between them that was more than just impersonal business.

"Do I need to know what Sky Tiger is?" Zhang said, reclaiming her chair. "Or would it be better for me to work in the dark?"

"It would probably facilitate matters if you were fully informed," Shen-wa said, reaching for a thick security folder. He was starting to like this bold woman more and more.

Pressing his thumb to the metal clasp, Shen-wa waited until it hummed twice, announcing that the explosive charge was deactivated, then tossed it onto the desk.

Uncrossing her legs, she leaned forward to pick up the massive folder, and started riffling the pages. As her fingers touched the paper, it turned bright red at that exact spot.

"Let me summarize," Shen-wa said, excited, and slightly embarrassed, by the brief glimpse down her blouse. Her breasts were small but firm, and the lieutenant was obviously not wearing any sort of undergarment.

"Not necessary, sir," she replied, speed reading through the pile of reports and documents. "Is…is this already in operation? Wait…yes, I can see that it is from the dates the cargo boxes were shipped." She looked up, her eyes bright with excitement. "I gather the drones are a success."

"Eminently so!" Shen-wa beamed proudly. "Every few hours a new flight is unleashed to secure a critical bridge, destroy a vital airfield or assassinate a potential troublemaker. In two days, we will be ready to move."

"And then…?"

Tapping the keyboard, he started the printer humming, and said nothing in reply.

Sexy or not, he was a reticent bastard, Zhang thought. "What about the CMC in the August 1st Building?" she asked, spreading her legs on impulse to see if the major would notice.

Privately, she was sexually excited by the sheer force of the man and didn't care in the least about the vast difference in their ages. Zhang had no objection to going to bed with a superior officer. She did that often, but only after being assigned to a project. Never before. She didn't trade sex for advancement, as some female officers did. That was an insult to the uniform.

"The August 1st Building?" Shen-wa muttered, slowly returning his gaze to her face. This time he didn't seem embarrassed in the least. "Once I inform the Central Military Command of these events, the fat occupants of the August 1st Building will have no choice but to comply with my plan and attack at full force in all directions!" He gave a cold grin. "Soon, the West will be crushed, and China will finally be the dominate military force on the entire planet!"

"As we should be," Zhang acknowledged, placing the folder aside. "However, sir, there will be opposition."

"And that is where you come in, Lieutenant," Shen-wa whispered, the strobing light of the monitor highlighting his craggy features in stark relief.

"Sir?"

The printer stopped humming and Shen-wa passed her a photograph. "After the staff meeting, have Sergeant Ming find this enemy agent. He was nearly apprehended in Hong Kong by one of our operatives working as a cabdriver, but we both know what he will do next."

"Of course. The obvious choice is Macao, so he will not try there. I would think that a clever man would attempt to sneak into China through the city of Guangzhou, what they call Canton. The heavy industry there will offer good cover," she replied, then frowned. "No, that is the location of Red Star field office. There will be agents everywhere. Instead, he'll try for...Fufa, on the coast, where there will only be the harbor patrol and a few police to worry about."

Debating the matter, she gave a nod. "Yes, Fufa. The heavy industry there would offer good cover for a stranger. It is the more logical location."

"He would have no reason to check Fakkah?"

"None, sir."

"Good. And not even an American would be bold enough to go anywhere near Guangzhou," Shen-wa said, making a short note on a sheet of sticky yellow paper with a stubby pencil. "Have Ming find the man, and detain him."

"Kill him?"

"Not until he talks first," Shen-wa said, gesturing with the pencil. "If he is CIA, I wish to know everything about all the other CIA operatives in mainland China—who they are, locations, specific goals and such."

"So that we can remove them."

"So that you can, Lieutenant," he said, attaching the note to the side of the monitor.

Slowly, she smiled.

CHAPTER FIVE

Kowloon District, Hong Kong

Thick greasy water slapped listlessly against bare rocks along the jagged coastline, and liberal amounts of broken glass sprinkled along the weedy beach seriously discouraged any potential swimmers.

Situated on a rock jetty, the old warehouse was isolated from the rest of the busy dockyard by a sprawling junkyard of smashed cars. The huge mounds of rusting metal and cracked fiberglass effectively hid what happened at the private warehouse from the view of the general public, and the police. A tall wooden fence topped with razor wire kept out the curious, while hidden security cameras and teams of armed guards kept out everybody else.

The Amsterdam Import-Export Company was a well-known cover for Leland Ortega, the largest arms dealer in all of Hong Kong. Half Spanish and half Chinese, Ortega specialized in relaying a wide assortment of death dealers back and forth between Asia and South America. The Chinese street gangs loved the Imbel 12-gauge pistols from Brazil, possibly the strangest weapon Bolan had ever encountered. The soldier had been planning on visiting Ortega sometime to shut him down permanently. However, this day he was at the warehouse for a different purpose: supplies. And he was there to help himself.

As Tsai Adina had promised, Bolan had acquired almost everything he wanted in the warehouse, along with a few wholly unexpected items, such as a brand-new Martin. That had been his first acquisition, the second being an old friend, a .44 AutoMag. The monstrous pistol was a real man stopper, the staggering recoil so difficult to control that the weapon was no longer in production.

Unfortunately, he didn't locate any ammunition for the gargantuan weapon, but he brought it along anyway, just in case he passed by a heavy machine gun on the way out. Only a handful of shells for the AutoMag could make a real difference in any fight.

There also weren't any Beretta 93-R machine pistols to be found, his preferred sidearm. But he had located several brand-new Glock 18 pistols. Identical to a semiautomatic Glock 17, the 18 was a true machine pistol, and discharged all thirty-two 9 mm rounds contained in an extended clip in just under two seconds. The recoil was bone-jarring, but a lot worse for anybody on the receiving end of that metal storm.

However, Bolan had been able to load only a single clip for the weapon when Ortega unexpectedly returned.

"Guards! Guards!" Ortega shouted, triggering a spray of 12-gauge cartridges from the big Atchisson autoshotgun cradled in his hands.

Dodging between tall stacks of crates, Bolan got hit in the back by the spray of double-0 buckshot, but his ballistic vest easily stopped the pellets from reaching flesh. However, the brutal impacts still felt as if he were being pounded by a rain of hammers. Rolling behind another crate, Bolan was startled to see an open briefcase full of .44 ammunition boxes. Quickly, he grabbed several to stuff into his war bag.

Wisely deciding it was time to go, he activated a remote-control unit attached to his belt, and pressed the detonator button. The muffled bang sounded from the direction of the utility room, and every light in the warehouse winked out.

"Son of a bitch!" Ortega bellowed even louder than before, blindly firing the autoshotgun into the darkness.

Ricochets bounced off the nearby concrete wall, and Bolan grunted as a spray of buckshot again hit him in the back.

Activating his night-vision goggles, Bolan stood and poured his last four rounds from the Glock pistol directly into the chest of the fat man.

Wildly firing back, Ortega grunted at the arrival of the 9 mm rounds, but didn't fall.

Dropping the spent magazine, Bolan ducked behind a crate of G-11 caseless rifles. Quickly, he thumbed loose rounds into the clip. Clearly, the arms dealer was also wearing a bulletproof vest under his clothing. Or maybe even some of that military body armor Bolan had discovered on the second floor of the old warehouse.

The waterproof war bag slung across his back was heavy with a set of the armor, along with several blocks of C-4 plastic explosives. Bolan had known this third trip to the warehouse was pushing his luck, but the chance to get some plastique had been too good to pass up. Unlike Ortega, the agents of Red Star were famous for being excellent shots.

Slamming in the clip, Bolan jacked the slide and reached around the crate to put several rounds into a fire extinguisher attached to the far wall. As the pressurized container exploded, a cursing Ortega staggered into view, trying to wipe the stinging foam from his face.

Without remorse, Bolan fired twice more. Gushing blood, Ortega staggered backward, dropping the Atchisson to grab his ruined throat with both hands. Mercifully, Bolan put another round into the forehead of the dying man, and Leland Ortega finally paid the ultimate price for his life of crime.

Just then a door was slammed open and out ran five large Asian men wearing body armor, night-vision goggles, and carrying mini-Uzi machine pistols. The boxy weapons were equipped with coffee-can-size sound suppressors almost as large as the machine pistols themselves.

Grunting at the sight of the weapons, Bolan shot one of the guards in the armpit, So, they wanted to keep things quiet, eh? Bad for them, good for him.

As the guard fell, red blood arched away from the ruptured artery, and the rest of the guards quickly pulled back the arming bolts on the top of their weapons.

"Lu ta!" a large man with a mustache commanded, hosing the dark warehouse with a stream of small-caliber rounds.

The other men did the same, and ricochets filled the darkness, splinters flying off the wooden crates in every direction.

Quickly, Bolan thumbed more loose rounds into a magazine, then eased it into the Glock 18. Standing, he emptied the entire magazine, and one of the guards was slammed backward by the hellstorm of 9 mm rounds. All eighteen rounds cycled in under two seconds, and two of the guards were nearly torn to pieces. Dark blood splattered the concrete wall, and the Executioner ducked out of sight again as what was left of the men slumped in stages to the dirty floor.

Someone called out over the chattering of the weapons.

It sounded like the man with the mustache again, and

Bolan now marked him as the new boss. The king was dead; long live the king.

Another man answered, a touch of nervous laughter marring the response.

Staying safely behind the heavy crate, Bolan opened the war bag and rummaged among the assorted weapons and high explosives. Locating what he wanted, he pulled out a couple of squat canisters. The British stun grenades were relatively harmless, only making an extremely loud explosion when detonated, along with a brief brilliant flash. They were designed to incapacitate an enemy, not kill. Humane weapons, if there was such a thing. However, in the right hands…

Pulling the pins, Bolan flipped three of the canisters high and wide over the crate, then charged for the exit.

Instantly, the guards started shooting, but a heavy wooden workbench prevented the .22 rounds from reaching him.

Moving low and fast, Bolan took out two of the guards with leg shots under the workbench. As they fell into view, he ended their lives with a single 9 mm round to the forehead, then hopped over the still body of the first guard he had killed upon entering the warehouse, and hit the exit door at a full run.

As he burst through, an alarm went off, but it made no difference now. Zigzagging across the junkyard, Bolan tasted fresh salt air and saw the shimmering harbor a split second before the stun grenades detonated.

Thunder and light filled the interior of the warehouse, and Bolan heard the guards cursing in surprise. Then the screaming began, as they continued to blindly fire their weapons into one another. Charging through the gate in the wooden fence, Bolan noted that no professional soldier would have made such a classic mistake. These men were merely street muscle, thugs for hire.

Sprinting down the curving road, the soldier soon reached a wooden dock, and almost dived into the water when he saw a small speedboat lolling in the waves alongside the pier. He changed the dive into a jump, and landed on the moving deck of the boat in a crouch, alongside a large wooden crate.

"Thought I told you to stay out near the breakers," he growled, his gun sweeping the shadows of the craft for any sign of intruders. But only Tsai Adina was on board.

"And I thought you might need a fast escape," Tsai countered, tucking the pearl-handled S&W .38 revolver into a black nylon holster at her hip. She was wearing a black scuba suit, her long hair braided into a ponytail.

Just then, an explosion came from the direction of the warehouse, followed by the long chatter of a machine gun, and then another.

"What the hell did you do back there, start World War III?" she demanded, tilting her head.

"Damn near," Bolan countered, going to the helm and shoving the throttle all the way. In a growl of controlled power, the speedboat moved away from the pier and headed toward the breakers and the harbor.

However, they got only halfway there when the lights returned to the warehouse and a searchlight exploded into operation on the roof, the brilliant beam sweeping across the water.

"Take the helm!" Bolan commanded, pulling out the Glock.

As Tsai grabbed the yoke, he cradled the weapon in a two-handed grip and fired. The Glock almost seemed to explode from the rapid-fire discharge, the continuous muzzle-flash extending for nearly three feet. With a crash, the searchlight died.

"That was close." Tsai sighed in relief, relaxing her stance slightly.

"Too damn close," Bolan replied, sliding in his last clip.

Then he saw the front door open and out stumbled a large man with a mustache, cradling what appeared to be a Carl Gustav multipurpose rocket launcher.

Instantly, Bolan aimed and fired in a single smooth motion.

Riddled with bullet holes, the man stumbled backward and the Carl Gustav flew straight upward. The fiery wash blew off the legs of the dying man, and a moment later the roof of the warehouse violently exploded. Windows were shattered on both levels, and roiling flames filled the interior, spilling over the assorted crates, barrels, boxes and pallets of military ordnance.

"Sweet Mother of God," Tsai whispered, making the protective sign of the cross. "Do you think that the place is going to—"

"Down!" Bolan snarled, dragging her to the deck.

For an entire minute it seemed as if his caution was unnecessary. The boat was coasting past the breakers into the harbor when there came a flash of light from the shore, closely followed by a mind-numbing explosion.

A roiling fireball rose from behind the piles of junk cars, slowly forming the standard mushroom pattern of any sufficiently hot detonation. Black clouds laced with flame extended across the rock jetty as smoldering pieces of broken concrete, smashed weapons, busted machinery and human bodies rained across the landscape. The dark water of the harbor churned from the falling debris, and

Bolan grabbed the yoke to steer the speedboat farther away from the dangerous shoreline.

Everywhere across the Kowloon District, lights appeared in windows, and somewhere a fire alarm began to clang, then an air raid siren cut loose with a long, pronounced howl.

Burning out of control, the destroyed warehouse continued to explode irregularly from the tons of military ordnance that had been stored there. Bullets crackled like strings of firecrackers, land mines thundered, and as the remains of the warehouse began to collapse in upon itself, something flared white-hot for a long moment in the heart of the inferno, then died away, making the rest of the blaze seem pale and inconsequential by comparison.

"Well, that certainly put Ortega out of business!" Tsai laughed, shakily rising to her feet.

"Almost certainly," Bolan said, giving a half smile.

"Almost? Damn, you're a hard man to please." Tsai started to say something else when somewhere in the darkness ahead there came the warning siren from a Red Chinese gunboat. It was promptly joined by another, and then countless more. Then an aircraft rumbled by overhead, the hot wash buffeting them both and rocking the speedboat.

"How did a jet fighter get here so soon?" she asked with a frown.

"It doesn't matter. Time to go," Bolan said, angling away from the open harbor and heading back toward the rolling waves cresting nosily on the rocky shoreline.

"I'm ready," she announced, tucking the mouthpiece of her rebreather into place.

"Change of plans," Bolan said, lowering their speed to avoid attracting unwanted attention. "You're not going crash the boat as a diversion so that I can hijack a gunboat."

She yanked out the mouthpiece. "We're going to charge across Victoria Harbour and into up the West River in this old thing?" she demanded askance. "We'll be slaughtered!"

"True." He glanced at the large wooden crate in the rear of the craft. "Which is why we're going back to the boathouse. I'll need some time to get ready."

"Get ready for what?" Tsai asked, looking over the crate. It had been the first thing the big American had hauled out of the warehouse, and even though he had used a hand truck, judging from his expression at the time, it had to weigh a ton. There was no company logo, manufacturer name or even a description on the packing slip, only a string of numbers.

"Okay, what is it?" she demanded, loosening the ponytail to let her hair billow in the wind. "A miniature submarine or something?"

"Better, if it actually works," Bolan answered, throttling down the engine to head for the shore.

CHAPTER SIX

Pushing open the swing doors, Sergeant Ming walked into the Ichi Ban restaurant radiating death the way a furnace radiated heat.

Instrumental jazz was playing over the wall speakers mounted in the corners of the sushi bar, nearly masking the steady sound of traffic from the busy street outside. A pretty waitress with a solemn expression was working the cash register, the punching of the keys and the rattle of the old machine sounding almost like music itself.

"We're closed!" a short fat man announced from behind the counter, both hands busy washing crystal wine goblets.

"Not anymore," Ming snarled, firing the Norinco from the hip.

Across the room, the waitress looked up just in time for her face to be removed, then the bartender jerked backward from the arrival of a .50-caliber hollowpoint slug, his brains blowing out the back of his head to splatter across a gilded mirror and the neat rows of imported liquors.

The noise of the shots echoed throughout the restaurant, and seconds later the wooden lattice of the pass-through was slammed aside and two Japanese men shoved out double-barrel shotguns.

Already safely behind a bubbling stone fountain, Ming fired a fast five times, and one of the sushi chefs staggered backward, blood everywhere, his face bristling with splinters from the ruined lattice.

The other chef bellowed in rage, spittle flying loosely from his distorted mouth. The double-barrel 12-gauge boomed like thunder inside the restaurant, and the stone fountain exploded into rubble.

Water gushed high from the shattered pipes, and Ming answered back with the Norinco, the big pistol blowing hellfire and doom from his scarred fist.

The first shots went into the faux-bamboo wall just under the pass-through. The chef cried out as the steel-jacketed rounds punched through the flimsy material and sent him tumbling away. The next shots took out a video camera in the corner of the ceiling.

For a long moment, a ringing silence filled the restaurant, disturbed only by the bubbling of the destroyed fountain.

Slapping a fresh magazine into the gun, Ming looked over the sea of linen-covered tables and chose a large one that had no decorative cloth. It was older than the others, made of dark wood and situated directly under a hooded vent.

Keeping low, he was scuttling closer when the rear fire door slammed open, and in strode three Japanese men carrying boxy MAC-12 machine pistols tipped with elongated sound suppressors.

Ming dropped behind the table just as the men opened fire. Crisscrossing streams of 9 mm rounds chewed a path of destruction across the table, sending plates, bowls, chopsticks, silverware and napkins flying everywhere.

A ceramic shard from a sake bottle nicked Ming's cheek, the fermented rice wine burning in the cut like liquid fire. Ignoring the minor distraction, he pulled out a second gun and fired four times, the big-bore weapon sounding louder than doomsday. Quickly turning off the gas lines that lead to the burners, Ming stayed exactly where he was.

Half a heartbeat later, the big table shuddered violently and Ming grunted as the bottom bulged outward, shiny metal showing through the array of dark splinters. Apparently, he had chosen well. This was a grilling table, something the Japanese cooked stir-fry on in public for reasons beyond his understanding. The sheet of stainless steel that served as a grille bulged in several spots, but the 9 mm rounds from the MAC-12 machine pistols didn't quite achieve full penetration. The major often said that brains beat brawn every time, but seeing the axiom proved correct less than an inch in front of his face was a more sobering dose of reality than Ming normally cared to experience. He would have to end this fast, no matter the cost.

Listening intently, Ming heard the men push aside the ruined pieces of furniture, their silenced weapons sputtering softly in short, controlled bursts. The sheet of metal dented in several more spots, then the decorative wooden edges of the table started breaking off in chunks as they tried to catch him on the rise. Clearly, they had done this sort of thing before.

Breathing slowly, Ming charged his body with oxygen. The old Norinco pistols felt responsive and alive in his hands, and he expertly eased two pounds of pressure on the six-pound triggers, calmly waiting for the chance to strike. Then the barrage stopped and he heard a series of subdued metallic clicks. The idiots were all reloading at the same time. He grinned. Big mistake there. An empty weapon was a useless weapon.

Surging upward, Ming fired both handguns, the big-bore weapons bucking as stilettos of flame extended from the barrels.

Caught in the act of working the arming bolts, the three men jerked as the hollowpoint rounds hit them like sledgehammers. Stumbling backward, they slammed against the wall, one of them going out the exit to land sprawling in the parking lot. However, Ming heard only dull thuds from the hits, not meaty smacks. The gunners were wearing body armor under their clothing. He grinned. Excellent.

Moving fast around the battered table, Ming kept firing the heavy guns, concentrating on the machine pistols and not the operators. The battered weapons were torn from their grips, startled cries of pain announcing the breaking of several fingers in the process.

Suddenly, the kitchen door swung open and there stood an elderly Japanese man wearing a very nice suit, his hands working the arming bolt on an American-made M-16 assault rifle.

The man yelled something, the weapon riding up in his hands to pepper the ceiling with 5.56 mm rounds.

Firing both handguns, Ming put a pair of bone shredders into the knee of the manager, which no body armor usually covered.

The manager screamed as his leg exploded. Dropping the assault rifle, he fell in a heap, cradling the wounded limb.

Turning fast, Ming caught two of the other men in the process of drawing sleek .22 pistols from ankle holsters. Coldly, Ming executed both of them on the spot with a single round to the temple.

Snarling a curse, the third man awkwardly struggled to haul out a revolver from inside his waiter's jacket with a broken hand. Ming slapped the gun away, and the man cried out in agony. Skittering across the floor, the weapon went into the far corner, near a restroom.

Striding to the fire exit, Ming quickly moved to the side of an open doorway, and stayed safely behind the brick wall to listen for traces of a backup team getting ready to move. But there were no slamming car doors, squealing tires, running shoes, hushed whispers, or anything like that, only the sounds of traffic.

Easing back the hammers on his pistols, Ming risked a quick glance around the wall. The parking lot was empty aside from the hulking shape of the large garbage bin squatting like a cubist toad amid the rows of chained bicycles. On the corner, a traffic light changed colors, and in the distance he could heard a train clatter along the elevated tracks. There was nobody in sight. Even the homeless people were gone, wisely departing at the sounds of a pitched battle. Everybody knew what the Ichi Ban restaurant really was, even if the local police pretended otherwise.

Satisfied for the moment, Ming closed the door and locked it with a dead bolt. Crossing to the front door, he pulled out a string of firecrackers, lit the fuse with a match and tossed them outside, then closed and locked the door.

The fireworks began to crackle and bang away, sounding oddly similar to machine guns. It was highly unlikely that anybody in this neighborhood would call the authorities. But just in case some tourists did, when the police drove by they would spot the tattered paper residue on the sidewalk and simply assume that some nervous fool had mistaken the bag of firecrackers for a machine-gun fight.

Now that the battle was over, the sushi bar seemed preternaturally quiet. Soft jazz still played from the hidden stereo speakers. The plasma screen TV above the counter had a line of holes across the front, a crackling short circuit mixing with the soft curses of the wounded men. The air was thick with the taste of gunsmoke.

Reloading his guns, Ming looked down at the two wounded men amid the scattered corpses. The manager was trying to wrap a handkerchief around his leg just above the shattered knee, using it as a tourniquet to try to stem the blood flow.

"Don't waste your time, old man," Ming whispered, aiming a gun at his face.

Going pale, the manager backed away, leaving behind a contrail of red on the floor. "Take it!" he panted, raising a bloody hand. "Take it all! Everything in the cash register is yours! But please, leave us alive!"

"And what makes you think this is a robbery?" Ming asked in amusement, then cuffed him across the face, knocking him unconscious.

Grabbing the two men by their collars, he hauled them into the kitchen, then down a short flight of stairs into the basement. Off to the side was a storage room, and Ming checked inside to make sure it had no windows, and much more important, that it had a drain in the floor. He almost smiled. Yes, this would be perfect for what came next.

Kicking the door shut, Ming dropped the men on the concrete floor. They both grunted from the impact, fresh blood welling from their wounds. Locking the door, Ming turned around just as the waiter slashed at his face with a straight razor. Dodging out of the way, Ming actually saw his own reflection in the polished steel. Damn, the man was fast! As the waiter tried again, he grabbed his arm and twisted hard. There came an audible breaking of bones, and the man yelped loudly, the razor clattering to the floor.

Kicking it aside, Ming pulled out a pistol to keep both men covered, and did a proper search for any more weapons. But the razor appeared to have been his last defense. Ming hated to admit it, but that had been a bold move, and might have worked if he'd used a gun instead.

Leaning against the locked door, Ming clicked back the hammer on the huge gun to get their undivided attention.

"Waiter, do you speak English?" Ming asked.

Pale and sweating, the man slowly shook his head.

"Mandarin?"

Another negative.

"Then you're useless to me." Ming fired his gun point-blank into the man's face. The nose disappeared, and the back of his head exploded across the room in a horrid spray of bones, brains and blood.

"Stop! In the name of God! Stop!" the manager pleaded, inching into the corner. "Whatever you wish, I can get it for you! Money! Lots of money! You have no idea what resources I command!"

"Yes, I do," Ming replied, crouching. "You are Yee Toshario, special agent for the Japanese National Police Agency."

"What?" Yee cried. "Utter nonsense! Who told you these outlandish lies?"

"Everybody knows that the Ichi Ban restaurant is really the local safehouse for some Japanese spy agency," Ming said with shrug. "I do not really care which of them it is—Division 22, Military Intelligence, the PSIA...." He made a vague circular gesture.

Sensing a possible chance at negotiations, Yee forced himself to smile. "So, what do you care about?" he asked with a respectful bow of his head.

A true Communist, Ming was disgusted at the actions of

the slave. Holstering the gun, he started cleaning his nails with the razor and said nothing for a very long time.

"Sir, I need medical help," Yee pleaded, a hand pressed tightly to his knee, the blood welling between his fingers. "Tell me what you want, and perhaps we can come to some arrangement."

The wound had started bleeding again on the way down the stairs, which was just fine by Ming. He wanted the spy weak, humiliated, dirty and scared. Yee was close, but not quite there yet.

"Well?" Yee asked hopefully.

Not bothering to reply, Ming took a can of lighter fluid out of his pocket and popped the top. Squirting some of the contents on the concrete floor, he then struck a match and dropped it into the puddle. The liquid ignited with a whoosh, the writhing blue flames rising high for a moment, before dying away as the fuel was consumed.

"N-no p-please," Yee whispered hoarsely. "Our nations are not at war! You cannot…must not—"

Yee stopped talking when Ming squirted him in the mouth with the lighter fluid, then put some into his hair until it ran down his face like tears. Next, Ming soaked the wounded leg, and finally the crotch of his pants, until the flammable liquid seeped way down deep where he could really feel it.

"Stop, please!" Yee sputtered. "Okay, I'm not an agent for the Japanese government. I work for Mr. Tanaka. Tanaka!"

That caught Ming by surprise. Tanaka, the Yakuza boss? How very interesting. Tossing away the empty can, he struck a match and let Yee see the pretty dancing flame.

"Tell me more," Ming said in a monotone, bringing the match closer. "Tell me everything…."

EXTENDING INTO THE HARBOR, the wooden boathouse was old, built during the time of the British occupation. The exterior desperately needed painting. Dead barnacles on the side showed the rise and fall of the tides. The windows were securely covered with steel grating against would-be thieves, and the glass itself was so dirty that it was nearly impossible to see through.

The interior was bright and clean, freshly scrubbed and painted, the walls neatly lined with tools for the repair and maintenance of the speedboat.

Upon their arrival, Tsai used a remote control similar to that used with an ordinary car garage to lift the huge front door and gain them access, then closed it tightly in their wake.

Expertly guiding the speedboat to a gentle stop in the slip, Bolan securely lashed the mooring lines to a massive wooden pylon lined with old car tires. Then he got some tools from the wall and went to work opening the big wooden crate.

"Are you sure that thing is going to work?" Tsai asked, removing the cumbersome rebreather to hang it on a wall peg.

"Sure hope so," Bolan replied, prying off a stubborn slat. A wad of excelsior packing puffed out, and he brushed it aside to reveal a gleaming white metal surface that shone like a polished mirror.

"Damn. Got any paint?" he asked, working the crowbar under the next slat and starting to apply pressure.

"Sure. Pink, and I think some dark green."

"I'd prefer black, but green will do."

"Not into pink, huh?"

"Not as camouflage, no." Originally, his plan had been to crash the speedboat, then board a harbor patrol gunboat and force the crew to carry him to the mainland. But that plan had been quickly scrubbed when he found the Martin. If it worked as advertised, it would save him a lot of time, which was a very valuable commodity at the moment.

Though he put his back into the job, it still took Bolan most of an hour to unpack the contents of the big crate. He painted the white fuselage a dark hunter-green, then immediately started going through the preflight checklist. He charged the batteries, filled the double gas tanks and made sure that everything was secure for the maiden journey.

"What is that again?" Tsai asked, crossing her arms.

"Martin jetpack."

"Is it really a jetpack, like in the movies?"

"Close enough." He flipped a series of switches to activate the internal gyroscope.

Even out of the crate, the Martin was huge, and oddly resembled a refrigerator with wings. The main assembly stood five feet high, and the two wing engines extended an additional five feet. The curved cowling covered the complex internal machinery. There was a fairly standard safety harness in the front, along with two cushioned horns to go under the pilot's arms and help him stay in place during operation.

To the left was a small control panel showing direction, speed, height. On the right was another panel showing electrical power, fuel level and engine temperature. Normally, the pilot would be wearing a parachute in case of emergencies. Bolan had passed on that in order to carry an extra war bag strapped to his chest, with additional clothing, weapons, cash and medical supplies.

Depressing the main master control switch, he breathed a sigh of relief when the Martin quivered to life.

Tsai walked over to the window. Using the ball of a fist to rub a clean swatch on the glass, she looked out.

In the distance, the burning warehouse dominated the night. Muffled alarms clanged and hooted from a dozen locations, and a score of fireboats were moored along the shoreline like an invading flotilla. The busy crews struggled with deck cannons to hose down the flaming structure with steady streams of salt water, which moved in a steady rhythm back and forth.

"The harbor patrol is going to be busy until dawn," she noted, stripping off the scuba suit to reveal very brief undergarments. "How soon do you plan on leaving?"

"The moment it starts to work," Bolan replied, detaching the battery cables. "In the dark, I'll just be something odd moving in the sky. In daylight, I'm a dead man."

"Not very fast then, eh?"

"About 30 mph, but with all that I'm carrying, I'll be lucky to reach half that speed."

"Is that all?" she scoffed, crossing her arms. "I would have thought a jetpack would do a lot faster than that."

"As I said before, it's not really a jetpack," Bolan answered, busy checking the fuel lines. "The Martin company of New Zealand merely calls it that for advertising. Actually, this machine is propelled by a balanced pair of turbofans."

"Ever flown a Martin before?"

Closing a hatch, he frowned. "No, not really. But I have used a jetpack."

He knew that the Martin should be good for thirty miles, and at this point the harbor was only eight miles across. So there was a healthy safety margin for him to maneuver through the collection of little islands and swing northward to reach dry land. Which was good, because if he ran out of power over water, the five-hundred-pound machine would drag him down to the bottom like an anchor.

"By the way, this is for the boathouse," he said, pressing a stack of large-denomination currency into her hand.

"I thought you were low on funds," she commented suspiciously, zipping up the side of the red dress she'd just donned.

Bolan shrugged. "I was, but Leland wasn't. There was a safe in his office. I'm a little hazy on the conversion rate, but I think a hundred billion yen should be enough for a new boathouse."

"More than enough! Better keep some for yourself. Communists or not, hard cash has a way of helping folks make lots of new friends in most countries."

"There are no friends where I'm going," he stated, declining the offer, and strapping on the .44 AutoMag. The massive weight settled right into place, as if the weapon had been made for him.

Accepting that, she tucked the cash into a purse. "I just wanted to say that..." She stopped, flustered.

"Time for you to go," he stated, stepping into the safety harness and cinching it tight.

Tsai walked over to Bolan and gave him a brief hug. Then she turned and went out the side door of the boathouse without saying a word.

As he performed a final check of the Martin, Bolan listened to the slap of the waves against the boathouse walls, trying to attune himself to the night. Then he raised the AutoMag and fired once, and the skylight exploded into pieces. The soldier waited until the twinkling shards ceased coming down, then twisted both hand controls.

For a long moment, nothing seemed to happen. Then in a low growl of controlled power, the twin turbofans rapidly revved to full speed, and a hurricane of warm air washed over his legs, sweeping the planks clear of any loose items.

Testing the play on the controls, Bolan rose slowly to the empty skylight. Hovering just below the opening, he pulled the pin on a high-explosive grenade and tossed the bomb into a pile of greasy rags situated in the corner, alongside the fuel tanks. He then twisted the controls to full power and rocketed straight up into the night.

From that vantage point, he could see most of the Kowloon District, the building and busy streets spread out before him like a diorama at a museum. The sensation was like that of parachuting out of a plane, only in reverse, and cold adrenaline flooded Bolan as the dockyard below vanished into the night. A few seconds later, he heard a dull thud, and then the boathouse erupted into flaming debris.

Shifting his pitch and yaw experimentally, Bolan started to move across the sky, when something vaguely shaped like a battered rebreather shot past. Quickly, he swerved to the right to get out of the way of any possible shrapnel.

Out on the harbor, a dozen Hong Kong patrol boats swung sharply about and headed toward the inferno. Warning sirens blared and more searchlights swept across the bay.

But not up here, Bolan noted in grim satisfaction. So far, so good.

Flying past the vessels, he swooped down to move low across the harbor. As Kowloon disappeared behind him, Bolan checked the fuel reserves and settled in for a long flight. The twin turbofans rumbled softly on either side of him, the vibrations penetrating deeply into his muscles.

Moving past Hong Kong Island, he avoided the lighthouse on Soho Island and started flying in a northerly direction. As he streaked by Neilinagding Island, a dark shape appeared directly ahead. Bolan swung wide to avoid flying into a fishing trawler. When he saw the nets hanging from the mast, he squeezed the hand controls hard. Shooting straight up into the air, he felt the mast of the trawler smack into the AutoMag at his hip. The flap snapped open, but the gun stayed in place. That had been close.

Closing the flap again, Bolan rose slightly higher and headed on across the harbor. The sooner he was over dry land, the better.

CHAPTER SEVEN

Tel Aviv, Israel

"Falafel!" a vendor sang out, pushing a wheeled cart through the park. "Homemade falafel! Best in Tel Aviv!"

"You mean the worst on the planet," Soshanna Fisher retorted without looking up from a book on tarot cards. The young woman was sitting on a wrought-iron bench near a wooden tier of assorted flowers, the vibrant spectrum of colorful blossoms rivaling a summer rainbow.

"Strange lady, why do you insult me so?" he demanded, stopping the cart near a splashing fountain. A broad umbrella rose from the cart, casting both man and machine in cool shadow. Wisps of steam rose from the vented steel hood.

"I was insulting your lousy falafel," she replied, closing the book with a snap. Gilded earrings sparkled from within her cascade of dark curly hair, a Star of David on the right side for luck, and a pentagram on the left for love. Although in her opinion, neither seemed to be doing much lately.

It was a beautiful day, and the park was full of families enjoying the lush greenery. Young couples were strolling along holding hands, students were hunched over books, children flew kites in the azure sky, a young mother breast-fed her infant, and old men were playing deadly seriously games of chess on the wide grass lawns.

The shining skyscrapers of downtown Tel Aviv rose just over the border of trees, the low roar of rush hour traffic only a background murmur almost completely lost in the happy sound of the splashing water in the fountain.

"Lousy? How dare you say such things about my mother's homemade falafel?" he asked, spreading his arms so wide that his hands touched sunlight.

"Because, Neil McShane, you were born in London!" she declared, rising from the bench and walking closer. "You're Catholic, your mother works at a bank, it's frozen falafel mix, and that fake Israeli accent is making my ass ache!"

"Bloody good for business, though," McShane whispered, lapsing back into his real voice for a moment. "Eh, what, ducky?"

Just then, with a hiss of pneumatic brakes, a tour bus braked to a halt at the nearby curb.

"Fa-la-fel!" McShane bellowed, making it three separate syllables. Eagerly, the German tourists surrounded the vendor, their waving hands full of cash.

"God help us if that man enters politics," Fisher muttered, shaking her head in dismay. Tucking the book into her shoulder bag, she headed away from the noisy crowd toward the nearest exit. So much for a quiet afternoon in the park. Time to go back to work.

It was a relatively cool day in the city, the temperature only in the midnineties, so she was conservatively dressed in a loose T-shirt, khaki shorts and sneakers. Aside from the earrings, her jewelry consisted of a necklace carrying a silver ankh, the ancient Egyptian symbol of life, along with several rings adorned with much more obscure occult symbols. A black nylon bag was slung across her chest as protection from purse snatchers, and a cell phone was clipped to the strap for ease of access in case of trouble.

At the moment, everything was relatively quiet in this part of the world. As much as it could be, she amended privately. But things were always a little tense in any desert nation. Always had been, always would be. She didn't blame politics, God or ancient feuds, but the endless, sizzling heat. It drove a sane person crazy. Cool the whole area down thirty degrees and there would be peace overnight. Unfortunately, knowing how to solve a problem, and implementing that solution, were two entirely different matters.

As she moved through the crowd, numerous men watched her progress with marked interest, but their gaze rarely reached past her chest to her face. Ignoring the lustful glances, Fisher looked over the throng of business executives, students, tourists and soldiers for anybody holding a book. She was rewarded with failure. A handsome face didn't guarantee a good heart, and rarely did it ever seem to come attached to a working brain. Sad, but true.

Leaving the park, she caught a cross-town bus and let the familiar sounds flow over her in reassuring comfort. Tel Aviv was a city of life, with people laughing, talking, singing and praying, and shouting into cell phones. Dogs were barking, babies crying, radios blaring, and a thousand people used a dozen different languages to haggle in the marketplace, as if bargaining were an Olympic event. Old cars sputtered by, trailing blue clouds of exhaust, while sleek modern vehicles ghosted along as silent as a midnight prayer. Swarms of children on skateboards darted in every direction as orderly lines of rabbis shuffled along, more attentive to the next world than this one. Trucks rumbled, cabs rattled, motorscooters sputtered, and the ting-a-ling bells of countless bike messengers merged in musical counterpoint to the muted roar of an Israeli jet fighter streaking by overhead. The choir of life.

The strident cacophony was jarring to most newcomers, aside from New Yorkers, but she found it as relaxing as a babbling brook. The only times the great city ever became still was when a disaster hit. Silence meant that death stalked the land, so the louder and the nosier things got, the better Fisher liked it.

Hopping off the slowly moving bus at her corner, she bought a fried chicken sandwich and a soda at a fast-food restaurant, and ate while she walked the last few blocks to her apartment building. Wolf whistles greeted her along the way, and one man yelled out a phrase in Hebrew that was borderline obscene, but she remained coolly aloof.

Reaching the apartment building, she bypassed the front entrance and went around the back. Unlocking a steel door, she took a long flight of concrete stairs to the basement.

It was much cooler in here than outside, and at the bottom of the stairs she unlocked another steel door to enter her home. The apartment was long and narrow, occupying exactly half the basement. A painted cinder-block wall separated her side from the water pumps, furnace and such used by the upstairs tenants. A rabbit's foot hung from a sump pump that had been giving the woman some trouble lately, and an Eye of Horace was painted over a small mouse hole to keep out unwanted visitors.

Her quarters were rather small, consisting mostly of bookcases packed with ancient texts and papyrus scrolls, a single bed, bathroom, a closet and a computer console, but no kitchen, which was why she always ate out at restaurants. The rest of the apartment was hermetically sealed behind a double-thick wall of Plexiglas, and lined with redbrick over the concrete for additional thermal shielding. Softly humming in the icy mist stood a blinking array of the monolithic servers that composed the central data processor of a Cray supercomputer, a gift from her current employer.

Although massive, the Cray was over two decades old and thoroughly obsolete, almost a dinosaur. There were easily a dozen other types of supercomputers available on the market that were cheaper, easier to maintain and much faster. However, the old mainframe served her well, and offered something that none of the next generation of supercomputers could: functionality. Once it was modified slightly, she could run the goliath machine entirely alone. As long as the servers were kept cold, the Cray would run forever.

Her mother had disappeared five years earlier, and eventually her father had died of a broken heart. After sitting shivah for them both, she'd taken the insurance money, sold his electronics business, acquired this small apartment building and bought some time on the Tel Aviv University supercomputer, a Dell Thunderbird, the fastest computer in existence.

After learning how to hack into other computers using the Thunderbird, Fisher began offering her services to local corporations. Then she started doing the odd job for private individuals who wished to hide their true wealth from the tax collectors. After that it was a small step to dealing with criminal organizations, and finally the Red Star. She would have much preferred to work for the Mossad, but since it wasn't interested in her skills, and the Chinese were, like any freelancer, she simply went to where the work was. As simple as that.

These days, Fisher mostly patrolled the internet erasing any evidence of the existence of the Red Star, deleting photographs, posting false or conflicting data, arranging for alibis for their agents in jail, and so on. Occasionally, the Communists would ask her to skim funds from some major project in China, and funnel the money through several overseas banks to finally arrive in their secret Swiss accounts. She really had no trouble stealing money from the Central Committee. What possible difference could it make in the big picture? In her opinion, Cervantes had been absolutely correct when he said that stealing from a thief wasn't a crime, merely irony.

It was also extremely lucrative, she added smugly, taking a scrunchy from a pile inside a small bowl. A tenth of one percent of what she stole for the Red Star went into her private Cayman Island bank account. A mere pittance to them, but a small fortune to her. Soon, she would be able to purchase her own supercomputer, and then she would be free from the odious control of the Red Star.

Bunching her hair with a fist, Fisher used the elastic ring to hold her explosion of bouncy curls in place before sliding on a bulky turtleneck sweater. Then she removed the scrunchy and her hair sprang back into place, shooting out in every direction.

Sliding behind the console, she slipped off her sneakers to pull on knee socks, and then put the sneakers back on again and wiggled her toes. The Plexiglas wall kept out most of the cold needed to operate the Cray at peak efficiency, but some always seemed to leak through no matter what she did.

"Advanced technology is so primitive," she muttered, stroking a touchpad to check her email. There was the usual load of unwanted advertising to delete. Spam was the technological equivalent of a cockroach, constantly coming back no matter how hard you tried to stomp it out.

There were a couple of emails from some relatives in Jaffa—that was nice—and some correspondence from internet friends around the world…along with a webcam transmission from China. Time to go to work.

"Receiving you, Grendel, this is Beowulf," she said in perfect Mandarin.

The screen blurred into random colors, then cleared in a picture of Major Shen-wa.

"Good morning, sir," she said, giving a salute. "What can I do for you today?"

"I simply wanted to thank you for the excellent work in tracking down suitable targets, and erasing all evidence of where the eggs were shipped from," he said stiffly. "Your work has been exemplary, and of the highest value to the project."

She preened under the unexpected praise. "Why, thank you, sir. I was just doing my job."

"Not at all. I only wish that you hadn't stolen so much money. I really was hoping that we could continue to work together rebuilding China after the nuclear war. Such a pity."

As her stomach tightened, Soshanna blanched at the remark. "Steal… Sir, I can assure you that—"

"Goodbye, thief," he said, and the screen went blank.

Jumping out of the chair, Fisher made it halfway across the apartment before the tons of C-4 high explosive hidden inside the Cray supercomputer violently detonated.

The blast took out three blocks of downtown Tel Aviv, including an experimental weapons laboratory working on stealth drone countermeasures for the Israeli government.

Outside Canton, China

DROPPING OUT OF THE SKY as fast as possible, Bolan landed in a small clearing surrounded by tall willow trees.

Even before the turbofans of the Martin slowed to a halt, he slapped the release on the chest harness and twisted hard. The straps came loose, and he shrugged out of the machine to hit the ground in a roll. He came up in a sprint and reached the trees a moment before bright lights appeared, bobbing about in the darkness and coming this way.

Terse voices muttered in Chinese, and two guards appeared from the trees on the other side of the clearing. Each was carrying a long halogen flashlight and a Norinco pump-action shotgun.

Warily, the prison guards approached the softly ticking jetpack, their weapons sweeping the darkness. The guards were wearing dark gray uniforms unlike anything else in the Chinese military, and as well as shotguns they were carrying compact stun guns, and several cans of pepper spray.

Screwing a sound suppressor onto the barrel of the Glock 18, Bolan waited until the guards moved a little closer together, then he stroked the trigger twice. They fell without a sound.

Going over to the splayed bodies, Bolan grabbed them by the collars and dragged the guards into the bushes. Usually he wouldn't have burned down a prison guard any more than he would have a police officer. And that would have also been true if these were regular guards. But Xiban Prison was divided into several buildings, each separate and unique. The Block was the main part of prison, a massive structure used for the general population of regular criminals: bank robbers, counterfeiters, smugglers, rapists and such. Then there was the High Mountain, a small building with central heating, soft beds, good food and private showers for the rich prisoners who could afford such luxury.

Then there was the Castle, the special section of Xiban reserved solely for the private use of the Red Star. Prisoners who entered the Castle never came out again, and every guard assigned there was a criminal himself, a professional killer and psychopath, many of whom were wanted by China's government for multiple crimes against humanity. It was only their absolute allegiance to the Red Star that kept the guards from being summarily marched in front of a firing squad and executed.

Staying low, Bolan paused a moment to make sure that nobody else was coming to investigate the strange noise, then he quickly checked their uniforms for keys, pass cards or identification badges. But their pockets were empty of anything except some personal items.

Impressed at that, Bolan grunted. He had heard the Castle was deliberately kept as low-tech as possible, making it not only cheap to operate, but also invulnerable to computer hackers. The guards knew one another personally, so infiltration wasn't possible. Strangers would be shot on sight, no questions asked.

Briefly, Bolan debated flying away to land on the roof, but decided to save that as a last resort. The roof was certainly rigged with proximity sensors against a rescue attempt by helicopters or paratroopers. He might get into the prison that way, but leaving would be out of the question. Flying was the only way in, and the only possible way out.

Reviewing his options, he returned to the clearing and followed the tracks of the two guards back to a small brick kiosk set inside the gate of a razor wire fence. A third guard was inside, scanning the sky through night-vision goggles.

Moving low and fast, Bolan covered the few yards of open ground separating the trees from the kiosk before the guard could turn. Reaching through the window, he slammed the heavy steel barrel of the .44 AutoMag against the rear of the guard's head. Giving a low groan, the man buckled and dropped out of sight.

Going around to the door, Bolan eased inside and checked the guard's pockets. Removing a set of keys, the soldier reached into his war bag to remove a pint bottle of whiskey. He poured some of the contents into the mouth of the guard. Sputtering and coughing, the unconscious man managed to swallow a little before starting to choke. Reluctantly, Bolan stopped and simply sprinkled the rest of the liquor over the man's uniform. With any luck, if the guard was discovered, it would be assumed that he had simply gotten drunk on duty and passed out.

Recovering the night-vision goggles, Bolan checked the immediate area and saw nothing coming his way. Everything seemed peaceful and quiet. Just then a muffled scream came from the second floor of the Castle, the horrible noise trailing away into anguished silence. Somebody was being tortured. He only hoped it wasn't the man he'd come for.

Keeping to the shadows as much as possible, Bolan bypassed the front entrance of the building and went to the side door. Unfortunately, there was no lock set into the seamless slab of steel. With the numbers falling, Bolan pocketed the keys and pulled out an EM scanner. Checking for internal sensors, he found nothing active, which meant the door was simply bolted closed from the inside. A dead end.

Trying around the back, he found a similar door and

accepted that he'd have to go in through the roof or the front door. Both could be death traps. That was when he noticed a garbage bin near the door. Experimentally, he kicked it, and the metal box gave a nice hollow boom. Almost instantly a fat raccoon scurried out of hiding underneath it to race away into the night.

Nodding his thanks to the animal, Bolan kicked the bin a few more times. Suddenly, there came the sound of hurrying footsteps from inside the building, a bolt slid aside and the door swung open a crack. A thin strip of light illuminated the garbage bin, and then a frowning guard stepped into view with a Norinco .45 pistol clenched in his fist.

Muttering something, the guard squinted into the darkness for the raccoon, and Bolan clubbed him hard across the back of the head. He heard the telltale crack of breaking bone, and the guard shuddered and limply crumbled. Lifting the man, Bolan eased him into the piles of garbage filling the bin and lowered the lid. Where technology failed, guile prevailed. But this would only buy him time. The moment the guard was noticed missing, and somebody checked the kiosk, all hell would break loose.

After slipping inside the prison, Bolan let his eyes adjust to the bright lights. There was a bare wooden bench against the wall, directly underneath a gun rack full of 5.56 mm assault rifles and Norinco shotguns. Boxes of ammunition were stacked neatly inside a locked cabinet with a glass door. Nearby was a plain wooden desk, the top covered with a lewd adult magazine and a partially eaten meal of noodles and a bottle of beer. Excellent. The guard had to have been on his break. That just purchased Bolan a few more minutes, but not much more.

Closing the door, he slid the bolt into place, then felt a surge of adrenaline as he spotted a hidden security camera set into a corner of the ceiling. Swinging up the Glock, he almost fired, then decide to check with the scanner first. Thankfully, the camera had no power. It was a fake, just there to keep the guards alert, and nothing more.

Reaching under the desk, Bolan slapped a wad of C-4 plastique into place, activated the detonator, then drew both his weapons and started down a long corridor. His crepe-sole shoes made no sound on the concrete floor, and Bolan strained to hear any noises. But there was only the gentle rush of warm air coming from a wall vent. It smelled of coal dust, and that gave him an idea.

Checking the side corridors, he located the door to the basement. It was also locked, and none of the keys recovered from the two guards outside fit.

Pulling out a key-wire gun from a miniholster at the small of his back, Bolan wiggled the flexible tip into the lock and squeezed the handle to fill the mechanism with stiff wire. When he heard a click, he turned the gun and the lock disengaged.

Removing the key-wire gun, Bolan holstered it again and slowly opened the door. A short flight of stairs led to a basement, the darkness banished by the dull red glow of a coal-burning furnace. There came a steady scraping sound of something being shoveled, punctuated by the occasional crack of a whip and low grunts of pain.

Softly, Bolan closed the door.

But as the lock clicked shut, a voice called out in Chinese and a guard stepped into view at the bottom of the stairs. A coiled bullwhip was clenched in his fist, his other hand resting on a holstered pistol. His eyes went wide at the sight of the man dressed all in black, and the guard hesitated for a vital instant, torn between using the whip or the gun.

Moving down the stairs, Bolan stroked the trigger, and

the Glock gave a hard cough as a 9 mm hollowpoint round removed the guard from life. Gushing crimson, his body staggered backward to trip over a shovel and fall into a pile of coal chunks, scattering them loosely about.

The shoveling stopped.

Proceeding to the bottom of the stairs, Bolan looked the basement over for more guards. But there was only a handful of scrawny prisoners in sight, everybody so covered with coal dust it was impossible to tell their race.

Barefoot and dressed in rags, the wretches were dripping sweat, shackled with leg irons and holding shovels. Behind them was a huge pile of coal, before them the open doors to a furnace, the blazing fire filling the basement with waves of heat and snaking tendrils of thick smoke. The ceiling overhead was a complex maze of water pipes and heating conduits, with tiny puffs of steam hissing from a few of the joints.

"Anybody speak English?" Bolan demanded, lowering the gun.

"I…I'm British," a thin man said. "Justin Richards… MI5. Are you American?"

"Close enough," Bolan lied, trying to make the man think he was Canadian. "Where are the keys to the chains?"

Wordlessly, a small Chinese woman pointed at the corpse.

Moving quickly, Bolan recovered the keys and tossed them over. Richards made the catch and knelt to start on the lock.

"Why are you here? Did my boss, Mr. Tanaka, send you?" a bald man asked in a Japanese accent, his scarred shoulders hunched as if to ward off a blow. His powerful body was covered with Yakuza tattoos, showing his rank and position in the criminal organization. "I am Hiakowa Wellington, his nephew."

Wellington?

"Never heard of you. I'm looking for an American prisoner, Eugene Snyder," Bolan said bluntly. "Anybody know his cell number?"

The man at the end of the chain gang looked up at that, but said nothing.

"Cell nineteen, on the third floor," the Chinese woman said, stepping slightly in front of the man. She had a strong accent, but spoke English perfectly.

"Nice try, miss," Bolan answered, and nodded to the man. "Nice to see you again, Ice Tea."

"Hi.... What's your name these days, old pal?" Eugene Snyder whispered, as if the words were being torn from his flesh.

"Matt will do," Bolan replied.

"Any...chance you're..." Snyder broke into a ragged cough.

Looking around, Bolan found a wall spigot and filled a plastic bucket. He pushed it over with a shoe, and the prisoners descended upon the tepid water.

"Better." Snyder sighed, wiping his mouth dry on a ragged sleeve. That left a clean swatch across his face, showing a heavy layer of beard and skin darker than the coal soot. "You here to blitz this particular shit hole? Be more than glad to help. Just give me a piece, old buddy." He held out a hand.

"I came to get you out," Bolan said, placing a Norinco .45 into his palm. He started to add something about the Red Star, then decided it could wait. Now was not the time or the place for a debriefing on the internal politics of the Communist government.

"Sounds good. But everybody comes along, right?"

Snyder asked, dropping the magazine to check the rounds, then slapping it back into place and working the slide. "I'm not going to leave anybody behind in this cesspool."

"They'll have to find their own way home," Bolan countered. "There's only room for you and me in my… plane." Wisely, he decided that trying to explain the Martin jetpack would be close to impossible. It had to be seen to be believed.

Stubbornly, Snyder shook his head. "Then no deal. Everybody leaves, and Li comes with us, with me."

"Ziu Li-Quin," she stated proudly, stepping closer to the man, a coal shovel balanced in her hands as if it were a quaterstaff.

Bolan could see what the man liked. She had real guts.

"There's only the four of us," Richards muttered, as the lock disengaged. The chain slithered through and dropped away.

"There was another, a Russian agent," Snyder added, looking upward at the ceiling. "But a few minutes ago we heard him… I mean, he's never made a sound before. Not a word!" He stopped talking, then started again. "There's only the four of us now."

"They took him to the Garage," Ziu added in a dull voice.

Bolan felt his stomach tighten. He knew what the slang meant. A garage was where a prisoner was taken to be disassembled while still alive, slowly cut into pieces until he either talked or went insane.

"We can hold on to wings," Hiakowa said, jerking the chain out of his shackles. "Just get us past the land mines. We will run the rest of the way to Hong Kong, and swim back to Japan!"

The big Yakuza enforcer looked as if he actually meant

it, but the hard truth was that the more people Bolan tried to get out, the less of a chance any of them had of reaching freedom. However, there really was no choice in the matter. Anybody left behind would be hauled straight to the Garage for questioning. That was completely unacceptable. Bolan would put a bullet between the eyes of a good friend before damning him to that monstrous form of interrogation. He had once before.

"Okay, everybody goes," Bolan stated, pulling out a spare Glock and giving it to the British agent, along with two magazines.

"Now you're talking." Snyder grinned, his smile a flash of lighting in the night.

"There is an abandoned cement factory 120 klicks to the northeast of here," Ziu said, going to the dead guard and pulling off his gun belt. "Get us that far, and my people will protect us the rest of the way."

"Your people? And exactly who are they, miss?" Richards asked curiously.

Draping the belt across her chest like a bandolier, Ziu said nothing as she worked the slide on the 9 mm pistol.

"She is a member of the White Lotus Society," Hiakowa said. "I came here as a representative for Mr. Tanaka to sell her military weapons."

Respectfully, Ziu bowed to the man, and Hiakowa returned the courtesy.

"The enemy of my enemy, and all that jazz," Snyder explained with a shrug.

Passing out some grenades, Bolan nodded. He knew what the White Lotus was. A couple thousand years ago, China was being persecuted by a mad emperor, so a group of people got together to plot his execution. The group called themselves the White Lotus Society, and wore the flower as an identification badge. Unfortunately, in spite of every safeguard, the emperor discovered their plan and captured every member of the society alive. He tortured them for months, and finally killed them—along with every member of each of their families, and their neighbors on every side of the house. Nobody in China even spoke the words "White Lotus" again for more than a century. But now, it seemed, under the communist regime, the ancient freedom fighters were staging a comeback.

"All right, what's our first move?" Richards asked resolutely. Then he suddenly went pale and slumped against the stone wall.

Reaching into his war bag, Bolan pulled out a medical kit and extracted a loaded hypodermic syringe.

"Benzedrine?" Richards asked weakly.

"NATO hotshot," Bolan stated, cracking the seal. Ripping off the raggedy sleeve of the man's shirt, he injected the entire contents directly into an artery.

Almost instantly, Richards began to breathe easier, and some color returned to his face.

The so-called "NATO hot shot" was a strictly emergency measure, the hypodermic filled with a devil's brew of painkillers and stimulants specifically designed to get even a mortally wounded soldier up and moving so that he or she could reach the evacuation helicopter. For the next hour Richards would feel normal, then he'd collapse. But an hour should be enough.

"Better," the man muttered, rising to his feet and taking a few deep breaths.

"Glad to hear it," Bolan said, sliding off the bag and giving it to Snyder. "There are six more shots in the med kit, along with more ammo and a few stun grenades. Get to the roof, barricade the door and wait for me to arrive."

"On the roof?" Hiakowa asked with a scowl. "But I thought you had a plane?"

Bolan drew both his handguns. "I'm going to exchange it for a helicopter."

"Matt, the prison airfield is twenty miles away!" Snyder countered, slinging the war bag across a shoulder. "Surrounded by as many land mines, guards and dogs as this damn place! Even if you do make it back, it will be dawn by then."

"We'll never last that long against the guards with only a couple of handguns," Richard added grimly, the veins in his neck throbbing.

"There are plenty of assault rifles and shotguns near the back door," Bolan stated, starting up the stairs at a full run. "Just hold out for fifteen minutes!"

"Fifteen…how is that even possible?" Ziu demanded.

But Bolan was already out of sight.

"What is he going to do, fly there?" Hiakowa asked scornfully.

"Knowing Matt, I wouldn't doubt that in the least," Snyder grunted, shifting the bag. "Okay, double-time, people! We got a bird to catch!"

"First let me leave a little present for the guards to find," Richards countered, going to the control valves of the furnace and turning off the feed and safety.

As the group raced from the basement, the main pressure gauge began to loudly thump as the quivering needle started to slowly creep into the red zone.

CHAPTER EIGHT

Executive Suite, Project Keyhome

The misty air of the room was sweet with the smell of marijuana and wild honeysuckle. Their lovemaking over, Zhang Meiron tucked another joint between her lips and applied the flame. She paused to draw the dark smoke deep into her lungs, and let it out slowly. "So far, Ming has discovered nothing about the mystery man in Hong Kong," she stated.

"Nothing at all?" Shen-wa Fen queried.

"No, sir."

"Now that is significant," the major replied, accepting the joint. He inhaled for a long time, then let the sweet smoke out slowly. "There was a report about a warehouse full of weapons that burned down…is still burning, in fact."

"So?"

"It was operated by one of my agents, Leland Ortega. He was half Chinese, but looked Spanish."

"A half-breed?"

He gave a shrug. "I use what is available."

"Perhaps the fire was a diversion," she suggested, tapping some loose ash off the end onto the linoleum floor. Reaching the ashtray would have required her moving, something that was quite impossible for the next few minutes. If her bladder called, it would just have to wait until the strength returned to her shaking legs. The man was only average size below the waist, but his extremely talented tongue more than made up for that minor deficiency.

"Or more likely, somebody covering their tracks," Shen-wa said, rolling onto his back and putting both hands behind his head. "What better way to disguise what you stole than to destroy everything else?" Briefly, he smiled, thinking about the hacker in Israel.

"Anything important stored there, sir?" she asked, taking another long drag.

"No drones, if that is what you mean, Lieutenant," Shen-wa replied. Then he frowned and thoughtfully chewed a lip.

"Something wrong, sir?" she asked, trying not to exhale, then finally succumbing to the biological need for fresh oxygen.

"Double the exterior guards, and have a team set some land mines in any forest clearings for ten miles in every direction."

"Lands mines?" she asked, putting aside the tiny nubbin of the leafy joint.

"Make sure they're equipped with proximity triggers."

"Yes, sir. Within the hour." Then she added, "Sir, what about any civilians that might wander into the area?"

"There will always be breakage," Shen-wa said with a shrug, running a palm along her muscular stomach.

After a moment, she accepted that hard reality. Breakage. The slang made good psychological sense, just as in a prison, where the guards only referred to the prisoners by their numbers. Remove their names and you remove their humanity, thus making it much easier to treat them like animals. Unimportant and disposable.

"Yes, sir. They'll be installed within the hour," she

repeated, grabbing a beer bottle to moisten her palm, then running the cold hand down his hairy chest and across his smooth stomach. Without clothing, it was clear that the man was in excellent shape, a true student of the martial arts. His shoulders were broad and his chest stocky, with layers of muscle.

"No need to hurry, my dear," Shen-wa muttered, his amorous intentions clearly rising.

"Then we have a few minutes, sir?" she asked, turning over to encircle his softening manhood with her cool fingers.

"At the very least," Shen-wa whispered, then inhaled sharply and went perfectly still.

Unexpectedly, someone pounded frantically on the locked door.

"This better be important!" Shen-wa panted, his face drenched in sweat.

"Sir… Major! There has been an incident at Xiban!" His assistant called through the door. "A helicopter has been reported stolen!"

"What? Impossible!" Zhang stated. "Nobody escapes from that prison!"

"What kind of helicopter?" Shen-wa demanded, feeling the ethereal rush of passion fading away.

"I was told an English word…a Gazelle? I do not know what that means, sir."

"A gunship," Zhang whispered, her voice fading away.

Snarling a curse, Shen-wa pushed the lieutenant off and climbed out of the bed. None of the common criminals in the Block would have any idea how to operate that sophisticated piece of advanced military equipment. And the privileged fools in the Mountain had no real desire to leave their gilded cage. Which only left the foreign spies inside the Castle.

Cursing, Shen-wa strode toward the door. After witnessing the rape and death of his mother, he had been reluctant to torture any woman, even a member of the White Lotus. He had hoped that giving Ziu Li-Quin enough time to know the other prisoners before they went screaming into the Garage would break her resolve. Clearly, that had just been a dream. Now the entire operation was in danger because of his weakness of character. Furious beyond words, Shen-wa felt something inside him grow cold, wither and die. So be it! Never again would he ever show anybody mercy. He flung the door open.

"Have the squad warm up the Mi-8 transport helicopters!" he commanded. "I want them armed with everything possible, and a full tactical assault team ready to go in five minutes!"

"Yes, sir!" Wu replied, trying to avert her gaze as she turned to hurry away.

"You're going into combat, sir?" Zhang asked, surprised.

"Of course not," Shen-wa snorted. "The transport and troops are for you."

"Ah. Surely the warden of Xiban can handle a simple escape attempt—" Zhang started, brushing back her damp hair.

"Attempt?" Shen-wa snarled, reaching for his pants. "If the prisoners have a Gazelle, then they are halfway home by now!"

"We don't know for certain that it is a prisoner."

"And who else could it be, the CIA agent from Hong Kong?"

"No, of course not," she said, sliding off the bed and stepping into a skirt. "That is impossible."

Buckling on a gun belt, Shen-wa frowned. She was starting to use that word more often than he liked. Had he made another mistake, choosing her as his chief of security?

"Perhaps we should alert the CMC," Zhang said, buttoning the blouse over her bare breasts. "The August 1st Building could activate the national Skynet and—"

"Never!" Shen-wa countered, pulling on a T-shirt. "We must handle this privately! I am not ready yet for those fat fools in Beijing to find out about Sky Tiger!"

She arched an eyebrow. "Surely they must know by now, sir."

"They suspect, nothing more," he replied, bending to pull on shoes. He stomped them into place, then scowled. "Well, Lieutenant, what are you waiting for? You are the chief of security for the project. Get to the helipad and find those prisoners! Bring them back alive or in pieces. But you bring every one of them back to me. Understood?"

She gave a crisp salute. "Sir, yes, sir!"

"Afterward, you will find me in the control room," Shen-wa stated, his dark eyes narrowing into thin slits of raw insanity. "Advancing the schedule to the next level."

IN A POWERFUL RUSH of warm air, the SA-341 Gazelle lifted off the roof of the Castle just as the access door was smashed aside and out charged a squad of guards, their assault rifles firing in every direction.

As the soft-lead rounds slapped against the bulletproof windows, Bolan swung the gunship about and pulled back on the joystick. The 590 horsepower Turbomeca Astazou engine roared with power, and the sleek French-built helicopter angled away into the night.

Jammed into the rear seats, Ziu and the others shoved their stolen Norinco shotguns out the gunports and began shooting at the guards. Several of the men staggered from the barrage of buckshot, but there was no blood and nobody fell.

"Hey, Matt! Is this piece of crap really the best you could steal?" Snyder said jokingly while shoving his pistol out a gunport and slowly firing at the dwindling guards. "There's four of us in three seats!"

With a cry, a guard grabbed his perforated throat, blood spurting out high in a hellish red arch.

"Only thing available without a reservation," Bolan snapped, flipping the safety cover on the main coaxial machine gun.

Leveling the gunship, Bolan pressed the red button, and a volcano stream of 7.62 mm rounds exploded from a side-mounted weapon. The hell storm of high-velocity lead tore the guards apart, punching through their body armor as if it wasn't there. Jerking about like mad puppets, the tattered bodies flew off the roof in gory pieces to fall into the darkness.

"Any second now..." Hiakowa said, racking the pump-action on his weapon.

As if it had been waiting for those words, the entire Castle visibly shook as the basement windows exploded. Smoke and flame engulfed the building as the stone walls cracked open, and the crumbling masonry fell away to reveal the inner frame of riveted steel girders. Steam and flames rose up the core of the structure, boiling along the stairs and elevator shaft to blow out the roof in a geyser of parboiled bodies and assorted debris.

Instantly, alarms began to howl over at the main prison, and searchlights crashed into operation to sweep across the ground, searching for any escaping prisoners.

"Wrong direction, boys," Snyder chuckled. "But a nice try, nonetheless."

Swinging about fast, Bolan headed southwest, in the exact opposite direction from the cement factory. Soon he lost sight of the destruction, but continued to hear the noise for several moments even over the steady pulse of the big engine.

"Rigged the furnace?" he asked over a shoulder.

"Well, it's not polite to leave a party without thanking the hosts," Snyder said, forcing his hands to lower the smoking weapon. "By God, that pays a lot of debts!"

"We're not safe yet, my love," Zin reminded him, yanking open the breech of a 7.62 mm Giat machine gun. "We still have over a hundred klicks until reaching safety!" With a snort, she recoiled from the hot metal and rubbed her singed fingers, using a strip of cloth from her tattered clothing in lieu of gloves to lay in a fresh ammunition belt.

"At least we're out of that hellhole," Hiakowa muttered, setting aside his weapon. He was jammed in a corner, trapped between the hull and a jump seat. Something was stabbing into his back, his head kept hitting a stanchion, and he had never been more delighted to be so thoroughly uncomfortable. Free, they were actually free!

"Li, how are you doing back there?" Bolan asked, swooping down to treetop level to try to avoid the prison radar. There was nothing on the screen yet, but then the Chinese had some of the most advanced anti-intruder systems in existence. Something called Skynet. The British had invented the system, and the Chinese simply duplicated it, ignoring such minor considerations as treaties, patents and international law.

"Locked and loaded," Ziu replied, closing the access hatch. "You've got a standard belt, a hundred AP rounds, every fifth a tracer."

"Good to know," Bolan said, swinging wide around

some power lines. In the Martin, he could have simply flown between the cables without undue concern. But now, if one of their rotors even brushed a cable, the blades would snap off and the Gazelle would spin out of control to violently crash.

Off in the distance, the prison searchlights were sweeping upward, and Bolan could see numerous flickers from the direction of the airfield as heavy-caliber machine guns blindly raked the sky.

"Anybody familiar with Chinese countermeasures?" Bolan asked, glancing at the complex controls to his right. The board resembled something out a science-fiction movie, all blinking lights and digital readouts. He had flown enough with Jack Grimaldi from Stony Man to know how most of the equipment worked, but not everything.

"Allow me," Hiakowa said, wiggling into the copilot seat. His hands moved across the controls like a concert pianist's, flipping switches and adjusting dials.

"There we go," he announced. "The running lights are now...off! I've jammed every band of radar the scrambler can handle, and the emergency transponder is... Damn! There's no off switch!"

Without a word, Bolan passed over the AutoMag.

Impressed, Hiakowa could only stare at the colossal weapon for a moment, then he held on tight with both hands and squeezed the trigger. Inside the tight confines of the gunship, the muzzle-blast sounded louder than doomsday. The dashboard shattered into pieces, bits of circuit boards, microchips and wiring spraying the cabin.

"There's no way the CMC can track us now," Hiakowa said confidently, returning the weapon.

"They still find us on infrared," Richards panted, pressing two fingers to the carotid artery in his throat.

"No, the defuser is active," Bolan replied, checking the

controls at his side. "Our engine exhaust is as cool as an autumn breeze."

"What about the engine itself?"

"Shielded."

"Fair enough," Richards wheezed, lowering his hand. "Look, chaps, I...I'm going to crash soon. Already starting to feel rather..." Without another word, he slumped over in the jump seat.

Pulling the man upright, Ziu checked the pulse in his throat and peeled back an eyelid. "Just asleep," she announced. "They beat him more than the rest of us combined. Because he was British, you understand?"

"Sure, lots of old grudges between the nations."

"Exactly. But he should be fine once we get him some proper medical care."

"Which is hours away," Hiakowa stated grimly.

Just then, something rumbled overhead, the wash rocking the speeding Gazelle hard.

"That was a jet fighter," Bolan snarled, trying to urge a little more speed from the laboring engine. Damn, the Chinese military was fast on the job!

"If they spot us, we're dead," Ziu declared woodenly.

"Matt, how long is the defuser good for?" Snyder asked, leaning forward between the two front seats.

"An hour, maybe less," Bolan replied, reaching out to tap the pressure gauge. He knew there was some form of liquid air cooling the baffles over the exhaust, but not what it was. Probably liquid nitrogen. Hackers used the stuff to keep their supercomputers operating at peak efficiency.

"An hour," Hiakowa repeated, putting a wealth of meaning into the words.

"Yeah," Bolan said, flying around the bright lights of a shopping mall. "Li, anyplace closer than the factory that I can drop you folks at?"

"Sadly, no."

"Actually, there is," Hiakowa stated. "There is a Yakuza safehouse near the People's Glorious Sports Arena. We can get a car there, and drive the rest of the way."

"Better make that a truck," Snyder said, tugging on his filthy shirt. "Something without windows."

Hiakowa nodded in agreement. Unshaven and unwashed, the four of them resembled refugees from Tibet, illegal aliens who would be arrested by the police, and probably shot on sight by the military.

"Okay, where can I drop you off?" Bolan asked, spotting the smokestacks of the Canton city incinerator, and heading that way. "Landing this ship in the middle of a soccer field would be like setting off a flare inside an elevator."

"I'm not sure," Hiakowa said hesitantly.

"There is a railroad yard near the arena," Ziu said. "Lots of open space and no power lines."

Smart lady, Bolan thought. "Sounds good. I'll dump this somewhere and meet you at the cement factory."

"There's a swamp to the north," Ziu said. "That should serve you well."

"Any gators to watch for?"

"Gators?" she asked, furrowing her brow.

"Alligators," Snyder explained. "No, nothing more dangerous than some rats. It's a runoff for a rice farm. Biggest paddy in the district. Good enough?"

"Good enough."

Just then, a touch of rose brightened the eastern sky.

"Dawn soon," Ziu said unexpectedly. "We better hurry."

"We'll wait for you until noon," Hiakowa said, brushing back his hair. "But no later. Then you must find your own way."

"You may do whatever you wish," Ziu replied stiffly. "But my people will wait until he arrives, or we hear of his death on the radio."

"Want some company on this, brother?" Snyder asked, pulling out the Norinco pistol to jack the slide.

"Thanks, but I'll move faster alone," Bolan said honestly, maneuvering around a tall block of apartment buildings. Straight ahead was the railroad yard, a long span of darkness surrounded by a sprinkling of golden streetlights. "Just take care of the lady," he continued, "and put a beer in the fridge."

Patting him on the shoulder, Snyder gave a chuckle. "Consider it done!" Then he leaned closer. "Eventually, you are gonna cut the shit and say why you actually busted me out of prison, right?" He paused. "Does this have anything to do with Major Shen-wa Fen of the Red Star and some kind of an armed drone?"

Giving the man a hard look, Bolan started to answer when another jet zoomed overhead, closely followed by two more. Buffeted by the wash, the Gazelle actually shook from the combined turbulence.

"Later," he growled, easing the power to the engines.

Almost silently, the gunship descended, to land with a hard bounce in a weedy field behind an old brick roundhouse. Even before it stopped moving, Snyder had Richards over his shoulder in a fireman's carry, Ziu threw open the side hatch and everybody piled out.

The bedraggled people were still limping into the shadows when Bolan lifted off again and quickly angled away into the night. The numbers were falling, but the mission had been a success. The enemy now had a name: Major Shen-wa Fen of the Red Star.

Now all I have to do is find the bastard, Bolan mentally

noted, checking on the fuel tanks and the defuser. Still minutes to go. Plenty of time.

Suddenly, an alarm began to beep, and a whole bank of controls glowed alive. A split second later, something flashed past the Gazelle to slam into a billboard and violently explode. The roiling fireball illuminated a busy street corner full of cars and shocked pedestrians.

Screaming loudly, the people scampered for cover.

Quickly spinning the gunship around to block any further strikes from reaching civilians, Bolan cut loose with both air-to-air missiles, and a full salvo from both of the side-mounted rocket pods.

As the missiles curved after the departing jet fighter, the 57 mm rockets streaked away to blow up another billboard and a water tower. That should confuse the sensors of the jet long enough for him to make an escape without endangering the mob of innocents below.

Releasing flares and chaff as additional protection, Bolan then shoved the joystick all the way forward. At full speed, the Gazelle slammed down in the middle of the intersection between a car and a van. Bolan heard the crunch of bending metal as he slapped the release on his safety harness, and actually felt the tail rotor assembly break loose as he yanked open the escape hatch.

Bolan hit the ground running, and charged for a nearby alley. Half a heartbeat later, something fiery darted out of the lightening sky to slam into the crippled Gazelle, and a thunderous detonation filled the intersection. Red pain filled his world as the brutal concussion hit, and the soldier went flying helplessly into the cold darkness.

CHAPTER NINE

Washington, D.C.

Reaching across the desk, the President of the United States solemnly picked up a picture of his wife and children. Using a thumb, he pressed a small stain on the chrome frame. Softly, the disguised sound scrambler built into the frame began to vibrate as it scrambled every known type of recording device and audio microphone. The Oval Office was swept daily for such illicit devices, but the first thing any new President learned was to never take anything for granted.

"First things first," he stated in a deep, cultured tone. "Please allow me to apologize. You were right and I was wrong. Completely wrong."

"Thank you, sir. But we've no time for recriminations," Hal Brognola said, sitting down in a wing chair. "What do we have?" he asked without preamble.

"Posing as Red Cross relief workers, a CIA team investigated the incident in Oskemen Valley and discovered the source of the attack. They sent a message to Homeland Security, which the NSA decoded and personally delivered to me only an hour ago." He placed the folder on the desk and pressed a thumb against the small metal clasp, holding it closed. After a moment, the clasp recognized his thumbprint and gave a low beep as it disarmed.

Brognola grunted. So much for interdepartmental cooperation. "Any chance it was al-Quaeda or Hamas?"

"See for yourself," the President said, sliding the folder across the desk.

Accepting it, Brognola flipped past the security notices to find several dozen photos of varying degrees of clarity. He recognized the style as surveillance shots taken from a spy satellite in a low Earth orbit.

"The CIA found an empty shipping container in an abandoned railroad yard. It was one of the big ones, the kind that are carried on trucks and cargo ships," the President replied.

Tall and dapper, the man possessed the voice of a natural orator, and more closely resembled a university professor than the leader of the free world. Then again, Brognola remembered that before getting elected, the President had been a university professor. Unlike so many other politicians, with this man, what you saw was what you got. That was nice for a change.

"The container wasn't made of cheap steel, as most of them are, but a modified form of Chinese tank armor. Extremely durable and highly resistant to corrosion," the man continued. "That's what first caught their attention."

"The rust looked fake?"

"Exactly. Further examination showed that the lid was rigged to blow off with low-yield black powder charges."

"Clever. We've had trouble with similar containers, terrorist organizations using them to smuggle people and weapons into the country," Brognola replied, flipping through the report.

"So I recall. That problem with a neutron cannon." The President sighed, brushing a hand along his brow. "Nasty business. Yet this is potentially worse."

"What was inside?"

"A lot of sound suppressant padding, hydrogen fuel cells for electrical power, and some rather advanced equipment for the long-term storage of six winged machines, roughly two yards across, weighing approximately a hundred pounds, and heavily armed with missiles, rockets, gas, and Lord knows what else."

"Drones."

"A new form of stealth drones, to be exact," the Man stated.

"Any chance of tracing the radio signal that triggered the release of the drones? Or were they activated by a timer?"

"There's no way to tell. Something in the container was melted down to slag from a small thermite charge. The bad news," the President said, "is that the container was shipped to Kazakhstan slightly more than five years ago."

Brognola looked up from the folder. "These bastards have been planning these attacks for five years?"

"If not more," the President stated grimly. "Because the company that shipped the container went out of business six years ago."

That information hit hard, and Brognola started to speak, then stopped from a sheer effort of will. Putting aside the report, he rose from the chair and strode over to a sideboard near the fireplace. An antique gold tray held a pile of gourmet sandwiches, along with a Steuben crystal water decanter that was probably worth more than his house, and a sterling silver coffeepot made by Paul Revere.

"There's whiskey in the cabinet," the President offered. "Fifty years old, single malt, from Selkirk."

"No, thanks," Brognola replied, returning to his chair.

"Okay, so the terrorists, or whatever they are, have been using dead companies as fronts to ship out armored containers packed full of the armed drones across the globe."

"Apparently so."

"That's smart, and unbelievably patient," Brognola stated, his face darkening with a frown. "These are first-class professionals, Mr. President. And this is old school."

"Meaning they'll be that much harder to stop?" the President said as a question.

"Exactly."

Inhaling deeply, the Man glanced out the nearby window at the Washington Monument, rising tall and graceful in the distance. The sight made him feel proud of the nation, and gave him new strength every day to face the challenges of the office. Unemployment, pollution, the crumbling infrastructure, war, terrorism, and now this. He fully understood why every President finished his term of office looking much older than when he started. The responsibility was staggering.

"Out of curiosity, sir, how many of these type of containers does Red China ship out in a year?" Brognola asked, cradling the steaming mug in both hands.

"We have no accurate figures. Most of China isn't on the internet, and many of their businesses don't have computers. But at a rough estimation, about seventeen million of them."

"Million?"

"Easily. America does twice that amount, so it is not unusual, or even suspicious."

"How many just to us, the U.S.?"

"Five million, give or take a hundred thousand."

"Wonderful," Brognola growled, loosening his necktie.

"Compounded over five years…sir, there is no way we can check that many containers in time to stop the next wave of attacks. It would require a concentration and orchestration of every military and police force combined!"

"On top of which," the President added, "I feel quite sure that the enemy has several other containers stashed away in prime locations in case of trouble. We start looking, and drones would appear out of nowhere to start hitting civilian targets in retaliation. Shopping malls, schools, hospitals… The death toll would be staggering."

"You're probably correct."

"It's what I would do."

Surprised, Brognola arched an eyebrow.

"The Joint Chiefs have informed me that the best way to catch a terrorist is to try to think like them," the President said with a hard expression.

"You're right, sir. Just didn't expect you to catch on this fast."

"Thank you, Hal…I think."

"So, we have to do this on the q.t., as covertly as possible. Or else."

"Unfortunately, yes." The president rose from his chair to pace about the office. "And until they make some demands, or start bragging about the destruction, there is no way that we even try to track down the people responsible."

"Which raises the question, what do these people want?" Brognola demanded. "Is this some lunatic group merely sowing the seeds of random destruction, or is China actually planning to expand its borders as a preliminary move toward world conquest?"

"Lord, I wish I knew. Hal, I reread your original report," the President said slowly. "Do you honestly think this is being done by the Red Star? They're supposed to be counterintelligence."

"Yes, sir. But in their opinion, there's no better way to stop an enemy from attacking than by slitting his throat the night before."

"That's quite draconian of them."

"Fanatical would be a better word. There's a certain major in the Red Star who is believed to have tried several times to incite a nuclear war between China and Japan."

"Major Shen-wa Fen. Yes, I have heard about him. A borderline psychopath, but incredibly capable. Could the major be the person behind these drone attacks?"

"If not, then he certainly knows who is," Brognola replied bluntly.

"The CIA could go ask him."

"They would if they could, but Shen-wa dropped off the face of the Earth about a week ago. Nobody knows where he's located at the moment."

"Interesting." Going to his desk, the President glanced over the piles of reports. "I don't see anything here about the major," he said, fanning out the folders like playing cards. "Doesn't the Theoretical Danger Team have a specialist on Red Star operations?"

"They used to, a man named Eugene Snyder, Ice Tea to his friends. But the TDT reported that Snyder died in a car crash last week."

"Just when Shen-wa vanished." The President frowned. "Hal, I don't like that timing."

"Me neither, sir. That is why I asked somebody to look into the matter."

"Good. Has there been any news from...Colonel Stone?"

Finishing off the coffee, Brognola heard the brief pause and understood what the politician was not saying out loud. “Not yet, sir,” he replied, setting aside the empty mug. “But there have been several reports of explosions in the Kowloon District of Hong Kong.”

“And those are significant because…?”

“That was the colonel’s last-known destination.”

“I see.” Placing his hands behind his back, the President looked out the window at the Rose Garden below. His wife and children were busy with the gardener, pulling weeds and planting sunflowers. There was no press corps in attendance; it wasn’t a photo op. His wife simply liked to make things grow. She was his rock, and sometimes all that kept him sane in this insane job.

“If Shen-wa is hidden somewhere in China, then why did the colonel go to Hong Kong?”

“Actually, he’s headed for Canton. The Red Star has a maximum security prison there. If Snyder was taken alive, that’s were he is.”

That made the president frown. “Why would Shen-wa want Snyder alive…ah. So that he’ll know what we know about the Red Star, and can make preparations against our responses in advance. Clever.”

“And Snyder might know if Shen-wa is the person behind these attacks, and possibly even his location,” Brognola stated.

“Striker certainly has courage, breaking into a Red Chinese maximum security prison just to ask a man a question.”

“Whatever gets the job done, sir,” the big Fed stated, as a dark shadow swept past the window.

As a second shadow appeared, Brognola dived forward and tackled the President to the floor just as something exploded outside, the titanic force of the blast rocking the entire building. Glass shattered, a woman screamed and an alarm began to howl, as a second drone slammed into the side of the White House.

Outside Canton, China

SLAMMING ON THE BRAKES, Bolan sharply banked into the turn, the tires of the stolen car squealing in protest. Racing along behind, the four men on motorcycles bent into the turn, somehow managing to accelerate around the bend.

Two of them opened fire with boxy machine pistols, the 9 mm rounds slapping into the rear of the old sedan to the sound of a hard rain. Then the back window shattered, and Bolan made a fast decision.

Bracing himself against the steering wheel, he hit the safety barrier at full speed, smashing through the wood in a deafening crash. The headlights shattered, the windshield cracked into a crazy mosaic and both front tires blew. But he made it through, and was airborne for a lot longer than he expected before the hood nosed down and he slammed into the soft ground. Everything went dark.

With a jerk, Bolan regain consciousness, and it took him a moment to recall the frantic escape through the back alleys of Canton. He had managed to ditch the jet fighters by hijacking a car idling in front of a newsstand, then driving pell-mell into a rain culvert. The car barely fit, the bumpers scraping loudly along the concrete walls and generating sprays of bright sparks.

A few minutes later, five men on sleek racing motorcycles had appeared, to continue the chase. They were wearing tinted biker helmets, black leather jackets and blue jeans, civilian clothing. However, they openly carried 9 mm Norinco machine pistols, which clearly marked them as government agents. Bolan had grunted at the sight.

Obviously, his capture had been elevated to the highest possible level. The matter was no longer in the hands of the military. That was both bad and good news. These men would be professionals, trained to hunt down fugitives. On the plus side, Bolan seriously disliked killing soldiers.

Coming out of the culvert, he had sideswiped some garbage cans and sent them rolling wildly about. The bikes were forced to slow down at the obstructions, and Bolan had taken out one of the riders with the AutoMag, the big-bore round plowing through the tinted visor of his helmet and blowing out the back.

With the corpse still sitting in place, the bike gradually slowed to a stop, then toppled over. However, the others had learned their lesson and stayed far away from the sedan, weaving steadily back and forth, and making it very difficult for Bolan to target them again. One grenade would have done the job, but he had given all those to Snyder and the others. Bolan was down to his two handguns, a few spare clips and a pocketknife. However, now he was stuck in the mud, and he could hear the throaty sound of the bikes getting rapidly closer.

As the front hood was buckled like an accordion, Bolan wasn't surprised when the engine wouldn't start. Accepting that, he turned on the ignition and switched on the radio to full volume. Bizarrely, country music blasted out of the speakers, the singer warbling away in Mandarin.

Squeezing out from behind the wheel, Bolan forced open the door, the hinges protesting loudly. Feeling the pressure of the numbers ticking down, he carefully walked along the tire tracks left by the crashing vehicle until he was close enough to a small cliff to jump down into a muddy creek. He was annoyed that it proved to be only waist deep.

Wading downstream, Bolan realized that the Glock

was gone. No help for that now. The AutoMag would have to do.

Crawling up the opposite bank, the soldier took refuge in the weeds and stayed very still as the four riders arrived, their motorcycles purring like jungle cats on the prowl. The bright headlights cast a swatch of illumination across the muddy field, but the riders didn't open fire on the sedan. Instead, they stayed on their machines, clearly conversing with one another. They probably suspected a trap. Bolan almost smiled. They were right, but not in the way they thought.

Even if he had been close enough, there was no way that Bolan could have heard what they were talking about. The radio in the sedan was blaring away, dominating the night, the twangy song echoing across the muddy field.

From this angle, he could now see that the motorcycles were big BMW Imperials, which explained the lack of noise. That model of BMW used a transmission instead of a drive chain, and thus operated as quietly as a motorcycle could. Ghost bikes, some riders called them. The machines were a favorite of Navy SEALs, the SAS, the Mossad and the Red Star. This wasn't a favorable sign. Grabbing a fistful of mud, Bolan smeared it across his face in broad stripes to lower the reflection factor of his skin. The stripes would also help him merge into the weeds. Hopefully.

Suddenly, a large black Hoover-TT appeared through the gap in the safety railing. Sort of a Chinese version of a Hummer, the enormous vehicle jounced and bounced down the side of the embankment and stopped just behind the purring bikes. The headlights were off and the windows were heavily tinted, so there was no way for him to see who was inside.

Then all the doors opened. Out stepped four men wearing full body armor and carrying pneumatic rifles.

Spreading some of the mud along the shiny steel barrel of the AutoMag, Bolan scowled at the sight. Those were tranquilizer rifles. The bastards wanted him alive for questioning...in a garage somewhere for a turkey doc to experiment with, taking him apart like a jigsaw puzzle.

Moving deeper into the weeds, Bolan eased back the AutoMag's hammer. That scenario was never going to happen.

Unexpectedly, a fifth man got out of the Hoover-TT. Bald with a mustache, this man wasn't wearing body armor, only a bulging shoulder bag, and was cradling a massive Atchisson autoshotgun. Bolan could guess that was filled with spare ammunition drums for the Atchisson. This was backup, in case the others failed to take him alive.

Lifting a monocular, the driver swept the field, then spoke into a throat mike. The other men nodded and spread out in a search pattern. Bolan ducked as the team swept past, hoping they hadn't spotted his footprints. Then the night exploded into silence as the radio was turned off.

"You there, CIA!" a man bellowed through cupped hands. "Surrender! There is no need to die! Our nations are not at war!"

Oh yes, they are, Bolan thought, standing to fire a single round.

As blood erupted from the man, everybody turned to look, and Bolan used the opportunity to throw himself sideways and roll down a steep embankment into a rocky crevice.

Snarling curses, the bikers sprayed the darkness with their machine pistols, the weeds shaking from the passage of the 9 mm rounds. Using the noise as cover, Bolan quickly crawled along the crevice, ignoring the sharp rocks that ripped at this clothing and flesh. One man dead, eight to go.

Reaching the bottom, he moved low and fast along the muddy bank, making sure that he stayed out of the turgid water. The reek of chemicals and human waste was strong down here, almost overpowering, so Bolan tried breathing through his mouth, but that only made it worse. Now he could almost taste the filth.

Reaching the culvert on the other side, he crawled up the embankment, listening for any sounds of pursuit. Softly, there came a clatter of loose rocks tumbling into the creek. Risking a fast peek, he saw the men standing in an arch along the reeds, only three of them in sight, plus a body lying still near the ruined sedan.

Easing off his shoes, the soldier padded across the fifty yards of open space, and stopped in a crouch on the lee side of the sedan. Listening to their muffled conversations, he waited a minute, and as their voices faded away, he jiggled a piece of broken mirror out of the frame. Looking through the smashed windows, he could see that none of the men were in sight any longer. Apparently, everybody had gone into the creek after Bolan. Bad for them, good for him.

Easing around the sedan, Bolan grabbed the machine pistol from the dead man and shoved the barrel into the soft earth. Then he brushed off any trace of soil from the barrel, put it back into place and moved toward the Hoover-TT.

However, Bolan got only halfway there when the driver with the mustache appeared from the crevice, his pants torn and bloody, but the Atchisson still expertly balanced in both hands.

"Get him!" the man roared, triggering the Atchisson. The chattering shotgun vomited flame and noise, a cloud of fléchettes chewing a path of destruction along the sedan, then stirring the ground into a muddy hurricane.

Diving behind a motorcycle, Bolan heard a score bounce off the metal frame even as the tires went flat, the windshield shattered and the gas tank sprang a dozen small leaks. Dodging the sprinkle of flammable fuel, the Executioner aimed through the spoked wheels of the bike and fired. The Atchisson was torn from the hands of the bald man, several of his fingers bent at crazy angles.

"Kill him!" he bellowed, pointing with a ruined hand.

Circling around to keep the wounded man between him and the others, Bolan checked inside the saddlebag of the BMW and unearthed some spare magazines for the machine pistols, and two grenades. Using his teeth, he ripped off the safety tape, yanked out the ring, flipped off the handle and stood to toss the grenade through a broken window into the sedan.

With a gasp, the bald man started to back away.

Just then, the other Red Star agents appeared from the crevice, their weapons chattering nonstop, the streams of lead hammering the sedan and motorcycles.

Priming the second grenade, Bolan then tossed it over the crashed vehicle to land among them.

For a horrified moment, they did nothing. Then one of the men dived back into the crevice, another reached for the grenade and two more turned to run away. At that moment the grenade inside the sedan detonated, the fiery blast lifting the car from the ground and igniting the gas tank.

A halo of broken glass and loose parts sprayed outward, tearing the Red Star agents into screaming hamburger, their weapons briefly discharging at nothing, then ominously going silent. Cut nearly in two, one of the agents was still standing, blood gushing from his legs, then he toppled over to join the others in death. That was when the second grenade cut loose, spattering the body parts wide and far.

Pausing briefly, Bolan tossed some spare magazines from the Norinco machine pistols into the burning wreckage of the sedan, and went straight to the Hoover-TT. As the ammunition began to cook, the rounds began smacking randomly into the motorcycles, ground and weeds. It sounded like a major firefight.

The door to the Hoover-TT was locked, but Bolan soon got it open and climbed inside. As he started the engine, a wild round zinged off the windshield, leaving a tiny starburst pattern. That was close. Exhaling in relief, he began to back away, just as the last surviving Red Star agent lumbered into view.

Covered with filth, the man was bleeding from several small wounds, but his face blazed with uncontrollable anger. Raising the pneumatic rifle, he tried to squeeze off a shot, but the barrel was bent. Tossing it aside, he reached down to grab a Norinco machine pistol from the bloody mud.

"Don't do it," Bolan yelled, shifting into gear.

Shrieking something in Mandarin, the agent aimed and pulled the trigger. Instantly, the weapon exploded, the back blast tearing through his unprotected chest and blowing his organs across the field.

Continuing up the embankment, Bolan reached the main road and started back toward town. It was cool and clean inside the colossal Hoover, the air smelling faintly like pine. Several weapons cases were in the backseat, along with several military-style war bags. Driving with one hand, he reached back to flip one open, and out fell an assortment of grenades, ammunition clips, sealed boxes of ammunition and a thermos. But no weapons.

Opening the container, he found it full of hot soup, and drank directly from the thermos as he drove along. Even if a police officer could see through the tinted windows, nobody in China would ever stop this vehicle.

Traffic was sparse on the highway, but Bolan wisely kept to just below the speed limit. Avoiding the wreckage of the Gazelle, he kept to the side streets until locating the railroad tracks. Backtracking along them to the weedy field was relatively easy, and using that as his starting point, he headed north-by-northeast again.

Dawn was cresting the horizon when Bolan crossed into the city of Canton, and realized that he was being followed.

CHAPTER TEN

Canton, China

Starting to pull a credit card from his wallet, Sergeant Ming stopped to blink in confusion. "Out? What do you mean, you're out?"

"Sorry, sir."

"How can you be out of butane?"

"Nobody smokes anymore," the clerk behind the counter of the convenience store replied laconically.

Tucking away his wallet, Ming scowled but kept his temper. The clerk wasn't being disrespectful, merely uncaring. Across the aisle he saw a display of outdoor grills, stacks of charcoal briquettes and several cans of lighter fluid. Bah, useless. Lighter fluid was too flammable and hard to control. Ming knew exactly how far he could go with butane. It was extremely difficult to intimidate somebody if the person was already on fire.

"How about some kerosene?" the clerk suggested, trying to be helpful. "We have lots of that, sir."

After a moment, Ming shrugged. "Thank you, but no. I'll just take the sledgehammer."

Leaving the store, Ming walked along the empty streets, listening to the click of the traffic lights. He had read that a black American invented the device. Amazing. Naturally, the Chinese government claimed that a Communist scientist invented it, but he had slowly learned over the many years that not everything the government stated was precisely accurate. A certain flexibility was involved in their brand of reality. The yin and yang of contemporary politics.

The neighborhood around the People's Sports Arena was rather poor, and slightly run-down, but coming back strong as downtowners flooded out along the highways, buying anything they could that offered easy access to work, and a vague suggestion of suburban life.

Surrounded by neatly trimmed trees and facing the river, the old apartment building was elegance in decline, standing on the edge of urban squalor like a suicide on a cliff. Not there yet, but poised and ready to take the final plunge.

Hefting a canvas duffel bag, Ming walked toward the building, noting that the windows were blocked with iron lace, lovely and strong, to keep out intruders, while coils of military razor wire decorated the roof. There had also been security cameras, but they had obviously been stolen, and now only bare wires dangled from the mounting brackets. He did love irony.

The front lawn was green and freshly mowed, the air redolent with the rich smell of nature beheaded. There were flower beds, but no flowers, and a pair of winged gargoyles stood guard on either side of the front door, their grotesque faces oddly reminiscent of two of the senior members of the CMC. Ming could only assume that ugliness was universal.

Pausing at the front gate, he calmly watched as a patrol car rolled into view from down the block. The pretty young policewoman behind the wheel gave him a hard once-over, recognizing trouble at first sight.

Just for a moment, Ming thought she was going to stop, and surreptitiously eased a hand closer to his .45 Norinco pistol. But then her older partner grabbed the hand mike off the dashboard, said something into the radio, then frantically gestured forward. The woman hit the light, and the police car raced away with the siren howling.

Returning to his work, Ming used a keywire gun on the lock, and was soon inside. The floor of the foyer was made of tiny black and white tiles, and one wall was composed entirely of mailboxes.

The door to the lobby was unlocked. He found that the room was surprisingly spacious and in better condition. Well, it was cleaner, anyway. The walls had been painted sometime this decade and the tile floor recently washed, the smell of pine-scented disinfectant still lingering. Ming always found it amusing that police stations, churches, schools and whorehouses all smelled exactly the same. Disinfectant, the tie that bound.

Heading down the terrazzo stairs to the lower level, Ming casually walked along a well-lit corridor to a plain wooden door located at the far end. Clearly, the resident liked privacy. Bad move. There was always more safety in numbers.

Gently setting down the duffel, Ming knocked hard, finding the door deeply resonant. A steel plate had to be hidden inside the wood. With decent hinges and a fancy lock, this door would be exceptionally difficult to get through. Unless, of course, you simply knocked.

"Yeah, who is it?" a thin voice demanded, a quaver of fear marking the challenge.

"You don't know me," Ming said, "but you've got a relative who is in big trouble. Stupid bastard has lost a fortune to some gamblers and desperately needs your help. Call him right now. Goodbye."

That was the clincher, the key to success—saying goodbye. That removed any threat from the presence of a stranger, and most folks opened the door on the spot, nine times out of ten.

Turning his back to maintain the illusion that he was leaving, Ming heard the lock slide and the door swing open.

"Wait a second," a voice commanded.

Slowly, Ming turned and acted surprised to see a short, fat man in a bathrobe, brandishing an Uzi machine pistol. Now, that was real trouble.

"Don't shoot!" Ming gasped, raising both hands in surrender. "Please..."

"Oh, put those down!" the man muttered.

Doing as he was told, Ming slipped his hands into his coat and grabbed both his Norinco pistols.

Suspiciously, the fat man glanced up and down the corridor. But there was nobody else in sight. "Okay, tell me again, who did you say was in trouble?"

"Your cousin," Ming lied. But it was a good one, rock solid. Nearly everybody on Earth had a cousin.

Blinking a few times, the fat man raised the mini-Uzi with both hands, assuming a firing stance. "I don't have a cousin," he growled, working the arming bolt on top. "I'm an orphan!"

Now, that was a genuine surprise. After so many years on the job, Ming had finally encountered an orphan. Incredible.

"Tajkemine?" Ming asked, leaning close, as if looking at his face. "Tajkemine Yoritomo, right?"

"Tajkemine Hideyo," the fat man corrected with a snort, slightly lowering the Uzi's barrel. "You got the wrong—"

Triggering both guns, Ming fired through the fabric of his coat, the flames extending for over a foot. The Uzi was slammed into the man's chest, and Tajkemine went flying backward, hitting the wall hard enough to crack the plaster.

Grabbing the duffel, Ming stepped into the apartment and closed the door.

Wheezing for breath, Tajkemine fumbled behind his back and pulled a compact derringer into view. Ming slapped it aside, then gave him a prolonged taste of a military stun gun. Tajkemine gasped, then crumpled to the floor.

Beating out a small fire in his coat, Ming shrugged off the badly singed garment and kicked it aside. The coat had done its job for the night, and there was nothing to connect it with him or the Red Star.

Removing the spent magazines from his guns, Ming tucked them into his back pocket, then reloaded the weapons. Next, he removed the other man's body armor and lashed him to a wooden chair, using lots of duct tape. Then Ming did a quick sweep of the apartment for any hidden witnesses or webcams, but it proved to be clean.

There was some cold fried chicken in the refrigerator, and Ming helped himself to a snack before continuing down into the basement. That was where all the fun stuff should be hidden.

Sure enough, behind the furnace Ming found a riveted steel door painted to resemble the wall. The door was sealed, and a nearby keypad took him a full ten minutes to get past. Inside was a large room, extremely well illuminated by halogen tubes, the floors, walls and ceiling covered with gun racks full of automatic weapons of every description, size and caliber. Pallets of grenades stood in a corner, and a stack of crates was marked in English. Ming checked inside to find Stinger antiaircraft missiles. It was a small fortune in illicit munitions.

There were also several printing presses, including a

Gestetner, an old-style Xerox machine, a newspaper linotype machine, shelves of typewriters, a dozen computer printers, a humming computer flanked by state-of-the-art blade servers, and a long row of steel cabinets. Each drawer listed what it contained: different types of paper, government watermarks, federal seals, college diplomas, medical licenses, pardons, death certificates, passports, and so on. There were even some fake identification cards for Red Star agents.

Hatred boiled inside Ming at the insult, and he returned to the living room. Tajkemine was still unconscious, so he used the opportunity to drag over a heavy wooden table from the kitchen. Arranging both of the man's hands on top, Ming taped them securely into place, then went to the kitchen to make some coffee. He also got a bottle of cold water from the refrigerator and a small can of air freshener.

A few minutes later, Tajkemine gave a low moan and awoke sluggishly. Trying to touch his face, the man suddenly realized where his hands were. Panic filled his eyes and he wildly jerked about, trying to get loose. But this wasn't the first time Ming had used duct tape on a prisoner, and he remained firmly in place.

"Stop that, or you'll make a mess," Ming said from the doorway.

Blinking in confusion, Tajkemine looked down to see the steaming mug of fresh coffee only a few inches away from his splayed hands. Licking dry lips, he tried to say something, but all that came out was a low croak.

Sauntering closer, Ming held out the bottle of water and let the other man see him break the seal around the neck before he offered him a drink. It was gratefully accepted.

"Thank you," Tajkemine croaked, then swallowed hard.

"So, who are you, and what do you want? If it's money, I can assure you that—"

Lifting the sledgehammer, Ming swung it hard and fast. The coffee mug on the table disintegrated under the blow, the heavy steel hammer continuing through the table in a splintery explosion and leaving behind a ragged hole.

Tajkemine screamed, his shirt covered with broken pieces of mug and stained dark with coffee.

Allowing the monster to peek out a little, Ming smiled as he raised the sledgehammer again. Tajkemine went pale, and suddenly there came a strong reek of urine. Putting the hammer aside, Ming sprayed the air freshener under the table.

"As I was saying," he repeated, hefting the sledgehammer again, "I want information on the Yakuza operations in China. Who you buy from, sell to, everything and anything. If you don't talk, I'm going to have to insist. How badly I insist will depend entirely upon your wish to keep functioning hands."

Wiggling his imprisoned fingers, Tajkemine whimpered at the threat. Ming struggled not to smile. He had thought hands would be the weak point for the forger. Some men were as tough as iron, and wouldn't tell you the time of day if you removed their dick and balls with a chainsaw. But threaten their dog, and they spilled their guts. The major had taught him that. Everybody had a weakness, some key that would unlock their deepest, darkest secrets.

"My files are in the office...." Tajkemine said hesitantly.

"Wrong answer," Ming said, swinging with all his strength. The sledgehammer thundered through the table again, leaving a massive hole less than an inch from the man's thumb.

"Basement!" Tajkemine screamed, struggling once

more to get loose. "There…there's a hidden door in the basement! The place is stacked with guns, money, drugs, anything you want!"

"But all I want is some information," Ming replied, hefting the hammer once more. "Who is Tanaka's contact in Canton? Who are your biggest customers for weapons? Do you sell information to the CIA?"

Breathing heavily, Tajkemine darted his eyes about, obviously trying to desperately find some way out of the predicament.

Annoyed at the delay, Ming swung again and the table exploded. Split asunder, the sections fell away, leaving Tajkemine with his arms taped to the chair, and big pieces of table stuck to his splayed hands. Loose strips of duct tape hung off his fingers like dirty bandages.

"Now things get interesting." Ming smiled, setting down the sledgehammer. "No more table means no more chances." Spitting into his palms, he rubbed them together vigorously. "Last chance."

Gulping air, Tajkemine said nothing. He seemed paralyzed with fear.

"Your choice," Ming said with a shrug, raising the sledgehammer.

Bursting into tears, Tajkemine began to babble names, data and places.

When he was done, Ming used the sledgehammer one last time. Leaving it jammed in place, he went to the upstairs bathroom and removed the lid to the toilet tank. Unscrewing the rubber flotation bulb from a threaded brass rod, he carefully dried it on a towel. Dimly, he saw old scars from where the rubber had been previously cut and then resealed with epoxy. It was a masterful job, barely discernible even when Ming knew exactly where to look, but then he would have expected no less from a pro like Tajkemine.

Using his pocketknife, Ming carefully sliced open the bulb and extracted a plastic bag containing a film canister sealed with electrical tape. Safety first! Inside the canister he found another plastic bag, but this one contained a dozen strips of old-fashioned microfilm.

Holding the strips up to the light, Ming found a series of alphanumeric codes, along with what could only be latitude and longitudes showing the locations of the banks were the money had been deposited. If the total was correct, he would never have to work another day in his life. Retirement. It was a word he had never taken seriously before. But now the key to it was resting comfortably inside his shirt pocket.

Ambling cheerfully back down the stairs, Ming departed to find a restaurant and get some breakfast. It had been a long day, and there was still a lot of work to do. The fat little Yakuza forger had talked, of course. They always did. However, Ming disliked using such crude devices as a sledgehammer. That wasn't dignified. A hammer was something a German would use, or an American, not an artist like himself. Pity about that butane.

Once outside, Ming pulled out a cell phone and used the speed dial. "Hello, Major…yes, sir, the White Lotus Society is hidden inside an abandoned cement factory along the waterfront. Give me ten minutes, and…yes, sir, right away."

Closing the cell phone, Ming tucked it into a pocket and smiled. "You poor bastards." He chuckled, leaving the apartment building to find a cab. With luck, he might get there in time to watch the fireworks.

Afterward, Ming was going to retire to Luxembourg, or perhaps New Zealand. Someplace very far away from here. Major Shen-wa could have China, and then go conqueror the rest of the world, if he wished. Ming was going to become a gentlemen of leisure, have meat at every meal and open a school for professional assassins. Something small and elite, for only the best of the best. After all, everyone needed a hobby.

THE GAS GAUGE of the Hoover-TT was flickering just above the empty mark, so Bolan pulled the vehicle into a gravel parking lot to brake to a halt alongside a small Shinto shrine. Rolling hills of the darkest green extended to distant mountains frosted with mist. There were several different types of temples and houses of worship, including a Tashan temple, and stone drums dotted the landscape like granite kettles. They looked real, but he knew these were merely duplicates of the actual stone drums made a couple of centuries ago. Bolan wasn't a particularly religious man, but he felt a great sense of peace here. Which seemed proper for a cemetery, the abode of eternal peace.

A graveyard wasn't the ideal location for a fight, but he really had no choice in the matter. Out of fuel and out of cash, Bolan had to stop somewhere to face the people following him, and this would do as well as anything else. At least there were no civilians in sight.

Searching everywhere while driving, he had finally located another weapon in the car, a Webley .445 revolver hidden under the front seat. Until only a few years ago, the Webley had been the official sidearm of the British Secret Service. It was a top-break revolver, allowing for easy loading the massive rounds, and was a perfect counterpart to the titanic .44 AutoMag. There was only one speedloader for the Webley, but it was filled with high-explosive, armorpiercing, tracers—HEAT—rounds. The rounds wouldn't be able to penetrate level four body armor, but the explosive impact should incapacitate a man for quite a while.

Getting out of the vehicle, Bolan caught the aroma of fresh coffee on the breeze, but banished that from his mind. He had been on the move since the previous afternoon and was nearly exhausted. The soup had helped some. There was a small medical kit in the glove compartment, but everything was written in Chinese, and there was no way for him to tell what was a stimulant, and which was a sedative, or vitamins, or whatever. It would be playing Russian roulette with loaded hypodermics.

Aware that he was being watched, Bolan sauntered to a random gravestone. He was surprised to see the Star of David carved into the granite, and took a small rock from the ground and placed in on top. Jewish mourners did this for the first year instead of bringing flowers.

Looking around the peaceful green cemetery, Bolan found a massive backhoe parked near a freshly opened grave, and headed that way. The cottonwood trees and weeping willows added small islands of shade from the morning sun, and sprinklers created small rainbows.

A lot of graves were marked with headstones. Only a few had a statue of some sort, or an elaborate obelisk. Oddly, there were quite a few mausoleums—squat, white tombs with black iron gates, the granite lintels carved with the family name. Dominating the cemetery, the mausoleums were situated on top of the hillock, surrounded by a lush array of flowering bushes, cherry trees, willows, stone benches and splashing fountains.

Walking along the sloping hillside, Bolan suddenly caught a movement at the bottom of the hill, near the entrance. Three black Polarsun cargo vans rolled through the stone archway of the cemetery to stop in a fan formation in the parking lot, neatly blocking any attempt by the other cars to leave.

"Here we go," Bolan whispered, pulling out the revolver and pistol.

The windows of the vans were darkly tinted, so it was impossible to see inside the vehicles. But then the front doors of the Polarsuns opened and out stepped six large men. Bolan blinked. Correction, five men and one woman.

She was very tall for an Asian, well over six feet, with broad shoulders and a powerful build that spoke of years lifting weights and working in a gym. Her face was too stern to be called pretty, but her black hair hung in a ponytail down her back, almost reaching her waist. Her mouth was wide and expressive, and her skin had a golden tone as if she were made of living bronze.

However, the fashion show stopped there. She was dressed in gray fatigues and combat boots, with a web holster strapped around her waist. A weapon was holstered on each hip, a sheathed knife on her left thigh, binoculars hung around her neck, and a wireless communication device was tucked into her left ear.

Bolan instantly marked her as the commander. His hand twitched to shoot her on the spot, but the distance was too great for either the Webley or the AutoMag.

The men resembled a street gang rather than the military. They were dressed in baseball caps, sunglasses, windbreakers and denims. Modern American chic. Four of them wore sneakers, and the fifth had on snakeskin cowboy boots. They seemed like civilians. However, the windbreakers were unzipped. As they walked, Bolan caught a glimpse of weapons holstered underneath. Mostly pistols of some kind, but the cowboy appeared to he hauling heavy artillery, although exactly what it was Bolan wasn't sure. Maybe a grenade launcher, or perhaps an autoshotgun.

These might be an undercover squad of the Canton police; there really was no way for him to tell yet. However, there were no oversize radio antennas on their vehicles. Cell phones were great, invaluable, but there wasn't a cop in existence who would go anywhere without a radio for emergencies. Bolan decided to test how good they were by standing there and doing nothing. He'd see how long it would take them to find the man in the cool marble shadows.

Without any conversation, the five men clustered around the woman, as if they had done it a hundred times before, their sneakers and boots raising little clouds of dust. Looking around the graveyard, she maintained a neutral expression, until locating Bolan near the top of the hill. Then she smiled and started his way, the five men fanning out behind so that each had a clear field of fire.

Their hands swinging at their sides, their faces masked by their hats, the five strangers maintained a tight formation and marched straight over the graves, old and new.

"You there, freeze!" the woman shouted, pulling out a folded piece of paper. "Interpol! You are under arrest!"

She said it with conviction, but Bolan still didn't see any badges or commission booklets, which sealed the deal for him. This was an execution squad, plain and simple. Diving to the ground, the Executioner came up behind a headstone with both weapons booming.

His first rounds slammed into an obelisk, rock chips flying out in every direction. One of the men cursed as his sunglasses shattered, and he staggered backward, fisting both eyes. But the other men only flinched and rapidly took cover behind headstones and statues.

Putting two rounds into the blinded man, Bolan hastily

rolled to a new position just as the hit squad came back into view, their hands full of weapons.

Cursing in Chinese, a man crouched behind a winged statue of an angel, and triggered a huge revolver three times.

Even in the morning sunlight, Bolan could see the bright muzzle-flash, and the bullet hummed through the air as it went past. That was at least a .50-caliber round.

Firing both his handguns, Bolan sent back a couple of thundering man stoppers. The battered headstone cracked in two, but the hit man was already gone. Once the balloon had gone up, they constantly stayed on the move.

With a snarl, the man dressed as a cowboy cut loose with both barrels of a sawed-off shotgun. The double report boomed louder than imprisoned thunder, and the grass on the hill seemed to boil from the arrival of the buckshot.

Then Bolan saw something shiny sticking out of the forehead of a stone statue. The sawed-off wasn't packing buckshot, but fléchettes, steel razor blades designed to cut a man in two. His ballistic shirt was good, but it wasn't body armor, and against a swarm of fléchettes it would offer about as much protection as positive thinking. Time for a new plan.

Firing randomly to make them think he was panicking, Bolan wasted only a moment looking at their vehicles. The Polarsun vans were probably full of weaponry, but it might as well be on the moon for all the good it would do him now. There was no way Bolan could even get close, so he banished that consideration from his mind, and concentrated on killing these people, which was the best way to stay alive. If possible, he would save one of them for questioning.

Crawling backward, he took refuge behind a flowering

rhododendron bush, and reloaded the AutoMag even though the magazine was still half-full. In a few minutes, he might not have the opportunity. Spend the brass and save your ass, that was his motto for the day.

Tucking his sunglasses in the fork of the bush as a diversion, Bolan now aimed at the Star of David on top of a fancy headstone and blew it to pieces. There was no reaction, so he walked the guns along the edge of a granite headstone, trying to catch the man with the shotgun on the move. But the hit man remained hidden as his associates shook the bush with concentrated volley fire, trying to hit him amid the dense greenery. His reflective sunglasses were quickly annihilated, but Bolan was already yards away, safely behind a large stone drum, using the cover to move backward again, heading for a copse of blossoming cherry trees.

"Delta fourteen!" the woman yelled in English, firing controlled bursts from a Steyr machine pistol. "Delta fourteen!"

Staying low behind the brickwork of a tiered fountain, Bolan grimaced at the phrase. Coded battle phrases; okay, that was trouble. He burned a lot of guys who shouted stupid things in the middle of a fight, such as, "Everybody head for the ladder!" Then Bolan would aim for the ladder, and wait for them to arrive like lambs to the slaughter. But now he was getting the flip side of that.

Darting from headstone to statue, always on the move, two of the men headed for the backhoe, while the others went for the stand of willow trees. They were trying to circle around the hill in a flanking maneuver. Watching the headstones, Bolan leveled his guns and waited for the woman to appear, but she stayed amid the marble and granite.

Reaching a wrought-iron bench, the soldier eased

behind it and risked a fast look around the shaded grove. There was a wrought-iron table to match the benches, a couple of basins to hold candles, plus, and a small painted metal box at the base of a tree. It was locked, so Bolan smashed off the tiny padlock with the butt of the Webley, flipped open the door and twisted the handle inside.

Suddenly one of the men pointed and shouted. A split second later, the leaves of the little arbor rained down as a maelstrom of lead converged on the area. The pistols banged, the machine pistols chattered and the sawed-off shotgun boomed. Bolan knew there were only four of them now, but it sounded like the Normandy invasion.

"Come on, come on," he said impatiently, restraining himself from shooting. If there was no response, then the only way for them to know he was still alive would be for them to go and see. Unless they planned to flush him out of hiding with a…

There was a rustle in the cottonwood tree as something hard bounced from branch to branch, and a metallic sphere landed on the iron table with a hard clatter.

Swinging behind the tree, Bolan braced for the concussion, and seconds later his feet left the ground for a long second before he dropped, sprawling into the flowering bush. Unhurt, the soldier clawed his way free.

With lead starting to fly in his direction, Bolan reloaded the Webley as the sprinklers came to life, misting the entire hillock with a fine spray.

Caught by surprise, the men vehemently cursed, and Bolan charged forward, firing both guns on the run. With a startled cry, one opponent fell, dropping something round. Rolling away, the grenade violently detonated in a flower bed, blowing the roses skyward.

Shoving in a fresh magazine, a man with a Beretta was caught in the corona of the explosion, and he staggered backward, both arms ending in tattered strings of flesh dangling where his hands had just been. Shrieking, he stared in disbelief at the red blood gushing into artificial rain. Bolan paused to put a mercy round into the temple of the dying man.

Then something hard slammed into his belly, throwing Bolan to the wet grass. The Webley went flying and disappeared down the hill.

Rolling to the side, Bolan barely got out of the way in time as the sawed-off shotgun boomed once more, the passage of the fléchettes actually visible in the downpour. Holding the wet AutoMag with both hands, the soldier knelt to steady his aim, and emptied the entire magazine at the dimly seen shape of the other man. At first there was no response, then the Steyr chattered as the woman darted between a pair of stone drums.

Slamming in his last magazine, Bolan stayed low, moving to the blast crater in the flower bed. His guts hurt and breathing was a chore, but the soldier was still alive, and that was good enough for the moment.

Ducking behind an obelisk, the woman shouted something. A man replied, then they all popped up and fired, to blow off the top of a tiered fountain.

Reaching the churned earth, Bolan fumbled amid the plants and mud until finding the dead man. Lifting him as a crude shield, Bolan checked his pockets and found some spare magazines for the Beretta, and another grenade. Placing the AutoMag on the warm corpse, Bolan pulled the grenade's safety ring and gave a low moan of pain, then a few weak coughs.

"Yang?" a man asked in a worried tone, coming closer.

Mumbling incoherently, Bolan released the arming lever, lobbed the grenade gently forward, then ducked.

The woman screamed, then abruptly stopped as a fireball thundered into existence, the heat flash briefly overwhelming the gentle waterfall.

Hugging the earth, Bolan heard the awful sound of body parts smacking into the damp grass. There was no sign of the guy with the shotgun.

Recovering the AutoMag, Bolan did a quick check of himself for any wounds, but between the water and the mud it was impossible to tell.

Slowly standing, he let the cool water wash away the dirt as he listened intently for movement from the missing man. A low groan sounded from his left, and the soldier swept wide to approach that area from a different direction.

Sitting with his back to a tree, the cowboy was fumbling with his left hand to load the sawed-off shotgun, his right arm hanging limply at his side. No bones were visible, but it was clearly broken.

Stepping in close, Bolan pressed the barrel of the AutoMag against the man's temple. He went motionless, then ever so slowly raised the shotgun and let it drop.

"Very smart. You get to breathe for another couple minutes," Bolan growled, thumbing back the hammer. "Now, who sent you?"

"Not...telling you...shit...Yankee," the cowboy hissed.

There was a medical kit in the Hoover, but Bolan wasn't feeling quite that generous to a guy who just had tried to splatter his brains across the countryside. Considering the situation for a moment, Bolan chose a different tactic and probed the broken arm with his toe.

The high-pitched scream seemed to fill the universe, and the cowboy slowly slumped over. Bolan thought he had fainted, but the man started to curse wildly in English, Chinese and Spanish.

"Now, let's try this again," Bolan said, placing the barrel of the AutoMag against the guy's neck, and digging in deep. "Who sent you?"

Clutching his arm, the cowboy stopped cursing and trembled slightly. But Bolan could see that it was from frustration, not fear or pain.

"Go ahead...shoot me," the cowboy said with a guttural laugh. "I don't know anything. Jade-Lee hired us on the docks, and she's dead now. Go...ask her."

These were dockworkers? Just hired muscle then, street soldiers using borrowed guns. No wonder they were such bad shots. "And who does Jade-Lee work for?" Bolan asked.

"Bitch..." he muttered softly, then added something in Chinese. But it was barely audible, the man clearly nearing the limits of his strength.

Did that mean Jade-Lee was a bitch or the person she worked for was? Bolan needed more intel, but it wasn't going to come from this man. He could tell that the guy was running on pure adrenaline at this point, and would soon crash.

To be honest, Bolan felt pretty much the same, his thoughts slow and murky. It was becoming hard to make fast decisions. The cowboy was about to pass out. Jade-Lee was a dead end. That grenade had done too good a job. She was sprawled in a shallow reflection pool, what remained of her head lolling back and forth in the pink waves. Bolan might have retrieved some phone numbers from the communication device in her ear, but the blast had partially embedded the device into her skull. Now it was just loose wires and smashed plastic covered with brains.

"Okay, you can live," Bolan said, holstering his piece and turning away.

Walking as if he was in no hurry, the Executioner counted to three, then spun in a low crouch. The cowboy was just pulling a .38 derringer from an ankle holster.

Bolan fired first.

Walking back to the arbor, the Executioner turned off the sprinklers and searched for the Webley. He discovered it submerged in a muddy puddle, along with an empty boot. Shaking off the dirty water, Bolan holstered the gun, knowing that it couldn't be used again until thoroughly cleaned.

In going through the pockets of the dead woman, Bolan found nothing of interest. He checked the black vans. They were unlocked, and also empty of anything interesting. One vehicle held a steamer trunk containing more guns and some ammunition, but that was it. This had been a real bare-bones operation. It would seem that Jade-Lee and her employer had been overly confident about this being an easy job.

Transferring what little there was into the Polarsun van took only a few minutes, then Bolan climbed in and started the long drive back to Canton.

CHAPTER ELEVEN

Central Command, Project Keyhome

The room was large and filled with the low hum of hushed voices, along with the steady tapping of fingers on keyboards.

The sterilized air was flat and tasteless, automatic scrubbers having removed every trace of the outside world that might contaminate the vital machines. Uniformed guards stood on either side of the only door, a massive slab of truncated steel more suitable for a bank vault. The guards were wearing body armor, QBZ assault rifles were slung over their shoulders, and pistols were holstered at their sides.

In the center of the room a row of control consoles sat in a sweeping arch, the scrolling monitors and flashing lights washing the faces of the technicians with a rainbow of colors. Directly in front of the consoles were three huge monitors that spanned the wall. The left monitor showed an orbital view of the current location of the drones, the middle was blank, and the right showed the ready status of China, everything from ground troops and submarines, to military satellites.

"Show me California," Major Shen-wa commanded, taking a sip from his cup of jasmine tea.

He was in full dress uniform this day, freshly shaved, with his hair slicked back and his boots polished to a mirror sheen. Such foolishness meant nothing to him, but his appearance always had a noticeable effect on the demeanor of the technical staff. But then, scientists weren't truly soldiers, even if they wore a uniform and learned how to shoot, and march in formation. They were merely support staff, not his brothers in blood.

"California coming online right now, sir!" a corporal replied crisply, adjusting the controls on her console.

The center monitor swirled in bright colors that dissolved into a thick gray fog. In the background were murky shadows and indistinct objects. There was a low whirring in the background.

"Going to UV," a private announced, flipping several switches.

Impatiently, Shen-wa grunted but said nothing out loud.

The middle screen flickered through several settings as it switched from the visible spectrum into the ultraviolet. Then the picture became a stark black-and-white that clearly showed piles of garbage, rusty bathtubs and the general effluvia of a city dump—along with the startled face of a homeless man spooning something from an open tin can.

Wiping his mouth on a sleeve, he squinted into the fog and started to rise.

"Kill him," Shen-wa commanded, sipping his tea.

Giving a nod, a private pressed a red button and from the screen came a brief hiss as the 4.45 mm caseless machine gun of the drone cut loose. The startled man was thrown backward into a pile of rubbish, his life splattering across the mounds of garbage.

"Radar?" Shen-wa asked.

"Clear, sir!"

"Infrared?"

"There are no other civilians in the immediate area, sir," the corporal reported.

"Proceed to the bridge," Shen-wa commanded, holding out the teacup for a refill.

Typing away on the keyboard, the staff relayed his commands, and the drone flew into the fog. Hugging the mounds of garbage, it circled around a sewage processing plant, and suddenly was flying low and fast across open water. In the distance the sound of a foghorn warned away commercial traffic, and numerous buoys clanged loudly as they rocked back and forth on the waves, informing the ships of shallow water.

A fishing boat of some kind appeared out of the fog, and the drone arched away fast before any details became discernable.

"A hundred meters," a private called out, studying a vector graphic. "Fifty, ten…"

Something huge loomed out of the fog—the famous Gold Gate Bridge.

"Go to automatic," Shen-wa said. "Let's see how well the programs work."

"Yes, sir!" the corporal replied, and flipped a switch.

Instantly, everything began to move extremely fast, the waves almost becoming a blur as the Sky Tiger drone rapidly accelerated. Swooping low across the bay, the drone did a fast sweep around one of the support towers of the bridge, checking for any other boats in the area. But the concrete island around the tower was empty aside from a few seals barking at the strange machine as it went zooming past.

Just then, the view from the video cameras on board the drone inverted as the machine flipped over, then rose vertically. Soon the underside of the bridge could be seen, then there was only girders and cables. The swift motion eased, then stopped completely as the belly of the drone pressed against the riveted steel plates with a soft click. There was a brief flash of sparks as magnesium charges in the drone ignited to permanently weld the machine to the bridge.

Through the swirling fog, Shen-wa could see the next drone do the exact same thing, and then the next. After that, the fog was too thick, and all that could be seen on the monitor was the brief spray of white-hot sparks from the welding charges.

After a few minutes, those also stopped, and the soft whirring noise faded as the drone turned off its turbofans and went completely silent. With a crackle, the view faded to black.

"All drones in position and ready, sir," the corporal announced.

"Are you sure they are in the correct locations?" he asked. "The drones carry only six kilos of thermite."

"Absolutely, sir!" she replied, working the console.

The center monitor converted into a graphic of the suspension bridge, the location of the hidden drones shown as blinking triangles.

"These are all critical stress areas. When the thermite charges are ignited, they will soften and melt, shifting the dynamics of the cables. They will snap, and then gravity will do the rest, sir. The Americans will die by the thousands."

"Excellent, well done. Now, show me the George Washington Bridge in New York."

"Yes, sir!"

With a click, the center monitor came alive again, and the scenario was repeated, this time without the loss of civilian life.

"Well done, Corporal," Shen-wa said, finishing his

tea. "Have you already done the Zhivopisny Bridge in Moscow?"

"Yes, sir."

"Excellent. How about the Sydney Harbour Bridge in Australia?"

"Just finishing now, sir. London Bridge is next."

"What did you say?" Shen-wa whispered dangerously, slowly rising from the chair. "I specifically instructed to have you ignore London Bridge, and instead mine—"

"Tower Bridge, yes, sir," the corporal hastily interrupted, giving a fast salute. "My apologies. I misspoke. We will be mining Tower Bridge in London next. Sorry, sir!"

After a long moment, Shen-wa gave the slightest of nods. "Very well, continue the operation. Has there been any interference?"

She glanced at a scrolling submonitor on her console. The numbers were in the low hundreds. "Nothing significant, sir," she reported. "Everything has proceeded smoothly in Japan, Greece and Russia. The drones at the Howrah Bridge in India were discovered by a family having a picnic. They were removed, and the bodies dropped into the Ganges River."

Shen-wa frowned. "A family…with children?"

"Yes, sir. Two boys and a girl."

Expectantly, Shen-wa waited for a twinge of guilt over the deaths, but nothing happened. Good. It seemed that he was over such nonsense now. "How many bridges have been done?"

"One hundred and ninety seven, sir."

"How many to go?"

"Fifty-six."

"Giving us a total of…?"

"Two hundred and fifty-two bridges."

"Yielding a theoretical death toll of…?"

"One million on the bridges, and six times that number from rioting in the city streets." She smiled. "More than enough to effectively throw the enemy nations into chaos, crippling their ability to respond to our military advance."

"Very good. Here are some new targets," Shen-wa said, removing a folded piece of paper from a pocket and passing it over. "The Vasco da Gama Bridge in Portugal, the Ponte Vecchio in Italy, the Bosphorus in Turkey, and switch from the Akashi-Kaikyo in Japan to the Alamillo in Spain."

"Why the exchange, sir?" a private asked. "We have enough drones to mine them both."

"Because we'll need the bridge in Japan when our army invades," Shen-wa explained patiently. "One does not lock a door before you enter the house, eh?"

The private heard the controlled tone of impatience in the major's voice, and realized she had crossed some line of decorum. "Ah, of course, Major. Very wise. China forever!"

"China forever!" everybody in the room chorused.

Just then, the buzzer to the main door sounded.

Going to a monitor set into the wall, one of the guards pressed his thumb against a sensor pad. The monitor cleared to a view of Lieutenant Zhang.

"The tiger walks," she said. Nodding, the guard pressed another button.

With a series of dull thuds, the armored portal unlocked and slowly cycled open to the sound of working hydraulic pumps.

"Yes, Lieutenant?" Shen-wa asked with a scowl.

"Good news, sir!" she announced with a salute. "Sergeant Ming has discovered the location of the headquarters for the White Lotus Society!"

All the typing stopped as excited faces were raised from the control boards and low murmurs filled the room.

"Excellent! Attack at once," Shen-wa instructed. "Burn the place to the ground."

"At once, sir. Do you wish any of them taken alive for questioning?"

"But there were no survivors," Shen-wa said with a thin smile. It was as pleasant a sight as an open grave.

Zhang smiled back. "Absolutely correct, sir. No survivors. I'll send two full wings."

"Send ten wings of drones, and pound their base into the ground," Shen-wa corrected. "I want to make an example of the fools, one that will be remembered for a thousand years."

Canton, China

DRIVING SOUTH, Mack Bolan avoided the main roads and kept strictly to the side streets. There were always cameras at tollbooths these days, and he certainly wasn't going to use the electronic pass clipped to the visor. That would be tantamount to suicide.

Feeling the lack of sleep, he pulled into the parking lot of a shopping mall to catch a much needed nap before continuing on to the city. His mouth was starting to taste like burned gunpowder, and there was a faint smell of sour sweat in the van that he could assume came from him. The last time he'd washed was in Hong Kong, which now seemed years ago. Two hours later he stopped at a convenience mart and used some of the money recovered from the would-be killers to purchase supplies. As there was no coffee, he got an energy drink, baby wipes, bottled water and a steaming cup of sesame noodles.

One sip from the energy drink, and Bolan almost poured the rank-tasting brew out the window. But he drank it anyway, out of necessity.

The noodles were delicious and put some strength back into his body, and the baby wipes did a fairly good job of removing the smells of blood and gunpowder from his clothing and hair.

Finishing the noodles, Bolan next took apart the Glock and washed it thoroughly with the bottled water, then lubricated it with a few drops of hot oil from the engine, using the dipstick. It wasn't homogenized gun oil, but seemed to work fine.

Afterward, Bolan got back on the street. Retracing his route to the sports arena, he meandered into Canton and finally located the Pung-Yin cement factory.

The description of abandon had been kind. The place looked as if it had been firebombed. The decorative front gate was in pieces on the cracked pavement, and the parking lot was strewn with leaves and weeds. The main building was overgrown with ivy, the walls covered with layers of graffiti. Heavy steel chains secured the front door, and rusty grates covered every window.

Pulling to the side, Bolan parked the van behind a massive delivery truck without windows or tires. Turning off the engine, he listened to the sounds of the city traffic, and the slap of the waves of the nearby river on the rocky shoreline. If this actually was the location of a safehouse, then Ziu Li-Quin and her people had to have him under observation by now. All he had to do was wait until they showed.

With the low squeal of rusty hinges, a louvered steel

door on the loading dock rolled up, revealing the dark interior of the factory.

Starting the engine again, Bolan rolled the van over the trash and broken beer bottles and straight up the concrete ramp of the dock into the darkness. Dimly, he could see a dozen other vehicles, mostly tiny Chery econo cars, and a few Great Wall trucks. Before he stopped the van, the door rolled back down, cutting off the morning sunlight.

Leaving the engine running, Bolan pulled the AutoMag and slid out of the van. Silently, he eased away from the vehicle and moved behind a huge machine of some kind that smelled of dust and decaying rubber.

There came the sound of footsteps, then a muttered curse. "He not here," a man muttered in heavily accented English.

"Well, what did you expect him to do, wait for an invitation?" Snyder asked, flicking a butane lighter alive to apply the flame to a cigarette. "Come on, Matt, we've got breakfast cooking. Let's shake a leg!"

Moving fast, Bolan appeared from the shadows to press the cold barrel of the AutoMag to the back of the man's head. Instantly, Snyder went completely still.

"Is this Istanbul or Bosnia?" Bolan asked in a tense whisper.

"Istanbul, Istanbul!" Snyder replied with a nervous laugh, trickling smoke out of his mouth. "This is not a trap like the bookstore in Bosnia!"

Bolan did nothing for a long moment.

"Honest, Matt, it's safe. By God, you're a suspicious bastard!"

"Only way I know to keep breathing," Bolan growled, staying alert. "Have them turn on the lights. Now."

"You heard the man, turn them on, people!" Snyder spoke loudly, taking another drag on the cigarette.

There came some hushed voices, hurried footsteps, and then a series of hard clicks. Slowly, fluorescent tubes in the ceiling flickered to life, bathing the interior with a cool white illumination. The cement factory was filled with jumbled piles of smashed machinery, stacks of corroded pipe and huge mounds of some loose material that resembled sand. The mounds reached all the way to a trapdoor in the ceiling. Bolan guessed the stuff was dried clay, the main ingredient for portland cement. Rusty chains hung from corroded steel beams, and the cracked floor was dotted with small puddles of oily water.

Ziu Li-Quin stood near the running van wearing loose black pants and a button-down shirt. A Russian AK-47 assault rifle was slung over her shoulder. Standing protectively nearby were several large men, their faces grim and their hands empty, but only inches from an arsenal of revolvers and pistols tucked into their belts.

"Hello again," Ziu said, bowing slightly. "I am glad to see that you arrived safely, and without being followed."

"Wasn't sure if this was the correct place or not," Bolan said, easing down the hammer on the massive weapon before sliding it back into a holster. "I've seen worse buildings, but not by much."

"As it should be! When hunting a tiger, one never approaches from the front," Ziu replied with a smile, then added something in Chinese to the other people.

The men laughed and relaxed their stances.

"I had to be sure," Bolan said to Snyder.

"Not a problem," he replied, massaging his neck. The man was wearing white pants and deck shoes, with a black T-shirt and a Hawaiian shirt with orchids so vivid they almost seemed to be exploding.

"Pretending to be a tourist?"

"Too damn tall to pass for anything else."

"Fair enough." Going to the van, Bolan turned off the engine. "Now, I heard mention of something about breakfast?"

"Bacon and eggs, double portions," Snyder said, exhaling a long stream of smoke. "I knew you'd be ready to eat the treads off a tank when you got here." Then he sniffed. "Do I smell baby wipes?"

"Better than nothing," Bolan said with a shrug.

"There is a proper shower downstairs," Ziu said, gesturing with an open hand. "Follow me, please."

Entering a shabby office full of moldy furniture, Ziu went directly to an open lift and stepped onto the wooden platform. Dangling loosely at the end of an insulated power cable was a control box with only three buttons, each bearing a faded Chinese symbol.

After everybody else took a place on the platform, Ziu pressed one of the buttons. Gears ground, then the lift started to descend.

"Those symbols are reversed," Bolan noted with a grunt. This close to the woman he could smell her perfume—gardenias and roses.

"I am pleased you know something of our language," she replied with a polite smile. "Yes, I pressed the button marked for upward traveling. Pressing the other brings swift death, and explosives close the shaft."

"You expect to be invaded?"

"No, but the wise person plans for what could happen, not merely for what is wished would happen."

"To achieve success, plan for failure." Snyder grinned, puffing away contentedly.

"Benjamin Franklin," Ziu said. "One of my favorite Western philosophers."

Bolan glanced upward as steel plates slid out from the walls to seal off the homemade elevator shaft.

The dilapidated old lift loudly rattled and clanked as it descended, giving plenty of advance warning to the people below.

"Where are Richards and Hiakowa?" Bolan asked.

"Richards is asleep in the barracks, and Mr. Hiakowa is being smuggled back to Japan," Li said, rubbing her thigh.

"Are you hurt?"

"It is nothing. A sprain."

After several minutes one of the men used the control box to stop the lift, then start it again, gradually descending along the shaft until stopping at a set of steel doors.

Ziu knocked on the metal door twice.

A single knock answered. She replied three times.

The doors parted with a rumble, revealing a brightly illuminated corridor full of grim men and women, all of them heavily armed. Most were in work clothing, a few were dressed as waiters and the rest wore business attire, suits and dresses.

"This way," Ziu said, starting off with a lurch.

The floor of the corridor was made of concrete, the curved walls of redbrick, reminding Bolan of a sewer system. In the bright lights, he noticed that Ziu had a slight limp, and wondered if it was something from her childhood, or from time as a prisoner in the Castle.

"Some giant son of a bitch broke her leg with a sledgehammer," Snyder muttered out of the side of his mouth. "Didn't even ask any questions. He just used duct tape to lash her to a chair, then broke it and walked away."

"Softening her up for the Garage."

"Yeah, I know," Snyder drawled, patting a .45 Norinco pistol in his belt. "I'm really looking forward to meeting him again someday."

"Be glad to lend a hand."

"Then bring a shovel, because it'll take at least two of us to bury the giant motherfucker."

If she heard the conversation, Ziu gave no outward notice. But afterward she walked a little closer to Snyder, and her fingers brushed against his hand just for a moment.

The corridor was lined with doors, most of them closed, and the open ones closed quickly at the approach of the group. Seemingly without apparent reason, the hallway curved every now and then, then ran straight for a long section.

Bolan recognized that the pattern was a design to slow down the advance of invaders, and then offer them nowhere to hide from defensive gunfire. He approved. The freedom fighters were obviously cash poor, and so made the best of whatever they could get their hands on. Even the sewers of Canton. They were smart and brave, but no matter how many people the White Lotus Society recruited, the Chinese army would outnumber them a thousand to one. The cause was hopeless, but still they fought. Just for a moment, he was reminded of his own war against the Mafia. Sometimes, impossible dreams did come true.

A set of double doors stood at the end of the corridor. Ziu pushed through and wonderful smells filled the air: fresh bread, hot coffee, frying bacon, and a host of others. Bolan felt his mouth water.

"Would you prefer food first, or a shower?" Ziu asked politely. "The communal bath is down that side corridor, and to the right. I will accompany you if you do not wish to be alone."

Bolan arched an eyebrow.

"Not in that way, of course!" Ziu rushed to say, actually blushing. "I only assumed that as an American you would not wish to disrobe in front of another man, even Eugene. You saved my life, so trust is not a factor...and you do not know us well to be unarmed and...I mean...that is..." She looked at Snyder for assistance.

He grinned widely, but said nothing.

"A shower would be great, but no company needed," Bolan said honestly. He caught another whiff of the delicious aromas wafting from the kitchen. "Then again, make that food."

Designed to carry miles of wire, empty wooden spools had been flipped over to serve as crude tables. The seating arrangements were a collection of folding chairs covered with the shiny welding scars of repairs.

Several people were talking and eating breakfast in the corner, their table covered with maps. A woman was field stripping an American M-16 assault rifle, each part laid reverently on a clean piece of white cloth. A group of men and women were reading aloud from books, trying to learn English, and a sullen man sat alone, poking at his food with a fork. He glanced up as Bolan took a seat at a nearby table, abruptly rose and walked away.

"He thinks you are British," Ziu explained as an apology.

"No offense taken," Bolan said. "Any chance I could get some of that gun oil?"

"Really? I prefer ketchup myself." Snyder chuckled, turning a chair around to sit in it backward.

Bolan noticed the odd maneuver, then saw Ziu do the same thing. Suddenly, he remembered the guard with the bullwhip at the prison, and the mystery was explained. Neither of them was showing any pain, but their backs were probably covered with raw cuts and welts.

A beefy young man in an apron was working at a stove covered with pots and pans, his arms covered with garish tattoos. A backward baseball cap kept the hair out of his face and the food. He was busy frying something in a wok, and moved with the innate grace of a born chef, tossing ingredients about almost casually. They always landed in a pot or pan, however. He never missed.

Ziu spoke to one of the men, who went around the counter to return with a tray loaded with covered dishes and an old-fashioned iron coffeepot.

"Eat," she commanded, and took a dish to dig in with chopsticks.

Bolan found his dishes were filled with scrambled eggs, linked sausage and bacon. There were also some steamed dumplings filled with spicy beans, and a bagel with cream cheese, of all things. However, he went straight for the coffee. There was no cream or sugar, so he drank it straight, searing away the aftertaste of the energy drink.

"They don't have much money, but you always go into combat with a full stomach," Snyder said, biting into a bagel.

"We do what we can," Ziu said demurely, her chopsticks a blur.

Finishing off the coffee, Bolan almost chuckled. The woman ate like a marine. "Well, there's cash and weapons inside the van," he said, jerking a thumb upward. "Take whatever you want."

"We already have," Ziu said, without any false modesty this time. "And your gift is much appreciated, Matt."

A small box set near the door chimed musically.

Instantly, everybody stood and drew weapons.

CHAPTER TWELVE

Tokyo, Japan

As the long day slowly faded into a velvet twilight, a loud burst of compressed air erupted from a long-term storage facility on the outskirts of the sprawling metropolis of Tokyo. Briefly, an ultrafast machine gun stuttered followed by the strangled cry of a startled man. Then the Chinese drones flew out of the facility trailing gun smoke, their wings splattered with blood.

Checking for any new orders, the drones found nothing recent in the databanks and so proceeded on their last command. Breaking into pairs, they swiftly spread across the bustling city toward their assigned targets. The first two drones used missiles to blast a path into the control room of a nuclear power station, then shredded the technicians and the control panels with streams of 4.45 mm caseless rounds.

Instantly, the main reactors started going critical and the automatic controls kicked into operation, scramming the reactor to prevent any chance of the dreaded China Syndrome. But that wasn't the goal for this night, darkness was.

As the generators stopped, whole sections of Tokyo went black, the millions of neon lights winking out in ragged stages. Emergency lights surged promptly into operation inside the main stairwell of most skyscrapers and office buildings. But in the streets, a wave of panic started to spread as the traffic lights died, and countless intersections soon became jammed solid with honking traffic.

Almost immediately, the national power grid switched feeds, and electricity flowed into the city from the outer provinces. But the other drones had already smashed vital substations, and the overburdened busbars of the relays exploded from the titanic surge of power. Short circuits crackled like insane lightning along the grid, melting power cables and setting hundreds of small fires. The end result was that the million lights of downtown Tokyo flickered and then died, the great city illuminated only by a crescent moon and the headlights of cars.

Continuing on their mission of destruction, the Sky Tiger drones flew along the major highways, riddling random cars with their caseless machine guns, killing drivers and causing hundreds of accidents. In minutes, the main thoroughfares were jammed solid, the firemen and police unable to respond to any of the thousands of calls for help.

Now the drones cut loose with their machine guns, shattering the glass windows on skyscrapers and letting gravity do the rest of the job, accelerating the shards into deadly shrapnel that exploded like crystalline bombs on the sidewalks and streets. Innocent bystanders were cut to bloody ribbons.

The drones flew openly along streets full of frightened people, firing short burst into the crowds, trying to wound as many as possible to maximize the terror. Human nature did the rest. Soon, panic filled the streets, rioting broke out and citizens began killing one another to get away from the things in the sky, to reach safety, to obtain weapons, to settle old scores, for revenge, for lust, for no reason at all other than the beast was unchained. The vaunted civilization of downtown Tokyo tottered on the precipice, and then fell.

Mobs of terrified people broke into fistfights, stores were set on fire, acts of brutal savagery filled the normally peaceful city. Hovering over the madness, the drones assisted in any way possible, firing their weapons into any orderly crowd, or sending a missile to blow a medical helicopter to pieces as it tried to lift off the roof of a hospital.

Howling alarms filled the city as the growing chaos became pandemic. Returning from their nightly patrols, a dozen police helicopters converged on downtown, their brilliant halogen searchlights crisscrossing the darkening sky. One of the pilots caught a glimpse of a drone, but before he could radio in a report, the machine attacked with both machine guns and missiles. In a violent explosion, the police helicopter ignited into a thundering fireball that plummeted downward to impact on the crowded street below, the crash killing a dozen scurrying people and setting several nearby buildings ablaze.

More police helicopters took to the air, SWAT teams striking back at the drones with assault rifles. But the black crafts were nearly invisible in the purple sky, and a single attempt was all that any police team made before the drones retaliated with surgical precision.

A local news helicopter tried to stay out of the way of the deadly firefights, the camera crew heroically recording the mounting scenes of unbridled horror. Several times the aircraft was detected by a Chinese drone and nearly destroyed, until the onboard computer recognized the helicopter as the civilian media NHK World News, and it was given safe passage. The drones were programmed to never harm a news crew, as the full dissemination of the monstrous slaughter on television, cable and the internet would only fuel further acts of madness and help to increase the rapidly rising death toll.

In the harbor, alarms began to sound on the deck of the USS *George Washington*. Part of the U.S. fleet assigned to guard the coastal city, the colossal aircraft carrier suddenly burst into frantic activity as searchlights crashed into operation, and the hurrying crew struggled to launch the wing of F/A-18E Super Hornets sitting on the main deck. As the deadly fighters taxied into position, the drones arrived to riddle the pilots with case-hardened rounds that punched through the resilient cowling as if it was ordinary glass. When the afterburners kicked into operation, one jet rumbled forward, only to veer to the side and slam directly into the command tower.

The explosion shook the entire structure, shattering windows all to the way to the bridge on the top floor. Screaming men tumbled into the night, and fell the ten stories to the deck to abruptly go silent forever.

Gushing blood from a ghastly wound, a lone airman attempted to operate one of the huge elevators and get an Apache gunship out of the hold and onto the flight deck. Registering a possible source of danger, a pair of the drones flew low and slow across the bow, dropping a load of tumbling cylinders. They hit the deck and exploded into flame, sending a tidal wave of sizzling napalm over the entire vessel.

Caught in the wash, the burning sailors blindly raced about, many going over the rail and into the cold water below. The pilot of the Apache tried to take off anyway, and actually lifted wheels before one of the missile pods on a wing cooked off. The blast obliterated the armored gunship, sending out a deadly halo of shrapnel that tore a dozen more burning sailors into merciful silence.

With his jet fighter covered in gelatinous hell, one of the Super Hornet pilots tried to eject. But before he could, the other jet fighter detonated. The combined blast of jet fuel and munitions cleared the flight deck of any remaining sailors, and sent out a stentorian blast of shrapnel and assorted wreckage.

The antiaircraft Phalanx guns activated, the computerized weapons swiveling about to locate a target. However, nothing was registering on their radar, and with the staggering heat from the burning flight deck scrambling their infrared sensors, the deadly pieces of advanced technology did absolutely nothing as the Sky Tiger drones flew past them at point-blank range.

Pausing to hover in the smoky sky above the burning ship, the drones launched a full salvo of missiles into the nearby city, targeting police stations and hospitals. When they ran out of ordnance, the Sky Tigers pivoted neatly to streak away and crash into the sea, sinking below the waves and out of sight forever.

Minutes later, a hastily scrambled wing of Japanese F-2 jet fighters and American F-17 Eagles streaked through the smoky sky over the decimated city, but their radar and infrared sensors were unable to locate any enemy targets. There was only the burning skyscrapers, and the growing carnage in the dark and bloody streets.

Pung-Yin Cement Factory, Canton

THE BOX CHIMED softly again.

"Alert! We are under attack," Ziu stated, touching her ear.

That was when Bolan noticed that she had a wireless communication device there that perfectly matched her skin and hair color. It was a masterful job. Until she touched it he never would have noticed it was there.

Suddenly, an explosion sounded from somewhere above, and a much louder alarm began to clang.

"Son of a... Nerve gas!" Snyder yelled, pouring his coffee onto a cloth napkin and slapping it to his face.

Moving fast, Bolan followed his example, as did everybody else in the room. Without comment, Ziu rushed for the door, Bolan close behind, with the AutoMag in hand.

In the corridor, she grabbed a wall phone and started punching buttons. Bolan could hear shouting from the direction of the lift, then screaming, the chatter of automatic weapons and the dull thud of a grenade. Two of the men ripped bricks away from the curved wall to expose a small cache of weapons. Grabbing AK-47 assault rifles, they slapped in ammunition clips, then thumbed 30 mm shells into the attached grenade launcher.

Without comment, Snyder held out a hand, and one of the men tossed him a loaded weapon. "Time to party," he growled, working the arming bolt.

Just then a staggering blast rocked the entire complex. The lights flickered and dust rained from the curved ceiling.

"That came from below," Ziu gasped, lowering the receiver. "But how... Nobody could get inside so quickly!"

"It's not men, but machines," Bolan said, taking her arm. "You can't fight them. Better get your people out of here."

"I would take his advice, babe," Snyder said with a frown.

Hanging up the phone, Ziu glared in open hostility at

the men, and for a moment it seemed as if she was going to refuse. Then her shoulders slumped.

"You are correct," she said. "Run today, fight tomorrow." Ziu touched her ear and spoke briefly in Chinese.

Nodding, the rest of the men took off in different directions, then she turned and started down the corridor at a brisk pace. "Follow me!"

Staying close to the woman, Bolan and Snyder passed several rooms where people were pouring gasoline into file cabinets, or attaching wires to a detonator. This place was about to go sky-high, and the soldier wondered if that would stop the drones. How exactly did you kill a machine?

As the three of them sprinted around a curved section of corridor, a pair of wooden doors parted to reveal a modern-looking elevator cage. Ziu shouted, then stopped and backed away as people stumbled into the corridor, coughing blood and weaving drunkenly, several of them shuddering as if being hammered by heavy machine rounds.

Instantly drawing the Glock, Bolan fired once, and a fire extinguisher on the wall became dented, then ruptured, and a roaring torrent of compressed carbon dioxide rushed out to wash over the dying men.

A startled Ziu began to reach toward them, then turned and raced down a side corridor.

"Okay, that bought us thirty seconds," Snyder said, glancing over his shoulder. "What now? Should we… Shit, I forgot about Richards. He's in the barracks!"

"Then he's dead," Bolan said truthfully.

Sweating profusely, Snyder slowed to a stop. "Not necessarily," he said, then made an odd face and violently sneezed, blood speckling the floor.

As Ziu quickly moved away, Snyder began to hack

and cough as he tried to say something, then began to convulse.

Without hesitation, Bolan brought up the AutoMag, but Ziu placed a hand on his arm. He stopped, and lowered the gun in understanding.

With tears in her eyes, she drew her 9 mm pistol and fired twice to end the man's horrible pain. As he fell, she tossed the gun away as if it were unclean, and turned away. Bolan did the same, his thoughts dark and private.

From numerous directions, they could hear screams and cries echoing along the corridor, then an odd machine-gun chatter that was so fast it sounded like a zipper.

"That's a caseless machine gun," Bolan growled, tightening his grip on the two guns. "The drones are inside."

Still running, Ziu said nothing, her face drained of all emotion.

More explosions rocked the base, and the lights flickered again, only a few coming back on this time. Passing another fire extinguisher, Bolan shot it on the run, and the corridor was briefly filled with another swirling cloud.

Charging through a brick archway, Ziu yanked open a metal box on the wall. Inside was a keypad and a lever. Quickly, she tapped in a long sequence. A small light turned green and she grabbed the lever…but then paused.

"Do it," Bolan said.

Inhaling deeply, Ziu closed her eyes and pulled the lever.

A wide steel plate slid out from the wall to seal off the corridor. Then another did the same thing only inches away from the first, closely followed by a third even thicker plate. A split second later, there was a staggering series of explosions from the other side of the barrier. The blasts continued for some time, each farther away, until there was only an ominous silence.

"The Red Star will never dig out the bodies to track down our family members now," Ziu stated, obviously taking some small comfort in the words.

"Then you're not out of business?" Bolan asked. "I thought this was the whole operation."

She almost smiled. "Oh no, the cement factory was not our only base, merely our largest and best equipped." Her face grew hard, her voice rough with anger. "And the Red Star took it out in only minutes, like...like we were children playing in the street!"

"You were hit by the most sophisticated drones in the world. They're incredibly tough to stop, and have already killed thousands of people around the world."

"I see," Ziu said thoughtfully. Going to a plain wooden box on the floor, she rummaged about and extracted several plastic tubes. Bending them in two, she shook the contents, and the sticks gave off a strong blue light.

Giving one to Bolan, she started down the rocky passageway. The walls were rough-hewn here, carved from the living bedrock. There were no fire extinguishers in sight, no ceiling lights, power outlets or air vents. Just a long, irregular tunnel extending into the dark.

"These machines...the drones," Ziu said, holding the chemical stick high. "These are why you wanted Eugene, to find the people behind their creation?"

"He already told me. It's the Red Star, somebody named Shen-wa."

She grimaced. "Yes, I know of this man, old and insane." Coming to a complete stop, she took Bolan by the arm again. "Your fight is now mine, Matt."

She said it with such conviction that Bolan knew there would be no way to stop her.

"Let us find this Shen-wa and have him join the ranks of the dead."

"Sounds like a plan to me," Bolan said, offering her the Glock.

Ziu took the weapon and stepped once more into the darkness. This time, Bolan took the lead, the glow stick held high and the AutoMag ready at his side. But in the back of his mind he kept replaying the death of Snyder, watching the man hack out his life as he struggled to say something to Ziu.

Bolan slowed. Or had Snyder been trying to say something to him?

"Something wrong?" Ziu asked.

"Is there any person, place, anything at all called..." Bolan tried to reproduce the coughing noise as a word. "Fakkah?"

"Why, yes," she said, sounding surprised. "Fakkah is a small town up north. But nobody lives there anymore. There was a chemical spill and the land is toxic. Very deadly."

"And when did that happen?"

"About five years ago."

Bolan looked back down the passageway. "Thanks, brother," he whispered, throwing a salute. Then he turned and started walking briskly.

It was very dark ahead, but there seemed to be a light at the end of the tunnel.

Baffin Bay

COVERED WITH glistening mounds of snow, the old German freighter *Glucksstern,* lay motionless, locked into a sea of ice that reached to the horizon. A bitter wind blew across the frosty gunwale, whistling through the array of icicles hanging from the ropes, and faintly stirring the tattered clothing of the dead crew, giving them a brief illusion of life.

Frozen blood stained the teakwood deck in the dining room and the lavatories, spent brass glittering everywhere on the decks like offerings to some pagan god. But all of it came from the weapons of the crew, bolt-action rifles and old-fashioned revolvers. The invaders had left nothing behind, no hint of their presence, aside from violent death.

Wearing heavy parkas, insulated boots and huge mittens, the men resembled stuffed toys as they lay scattered all over the freighter, frozen in their last position: stitching a wound closed, trying to hide under a bunk, struggling to load a rifle, or even crawling through the engine room seeking refuge inside the machinery, the massive steel shafts of the diesel engines only inches above the corpses. The mighty heart of the freighter was as inert and immobile as the slaughtered crew. Even the captain lay sprawled in his cabin, an ax still clenched in his bandaged hands, the blade dented from hitting one of the flying things that came in the night. His reward for the act had been a stuttering flash of lights, terrible pain and swift death.

Only one man had made it over the edge of the freighter and managed to hide inside a mound of fresh snow on the shore of the iceberg. When the slaughter was over, he crept back on board, discovered the truth, got very drunk and summarily took his own life with a pistol. With everybody else gone, there was enough canned food in the pantry to last him decades, but the radio had been smashed, and the engines were dead. The huge fuel tanks were riddled with bulletholes, their precious contents poured into the turgid waters of the sea like pale blood gushing from a hundred pinpricks.

Unfortunately, aside from a few books and blankets, there was very little on the *Glucksstern* that he could burn to try to stay warm, and the stove in the galley was electric. After getting very drunk on brandy from the medical stores, he'd made the hard decision that a brief moment of pain was better than the slow, agonizing torture of freezing to death. He desperately wanted to leave some sort of a message, a warning to others about the monsters in the hold. But who would ever have read it out here, beyond the edge of world?

The *Glucksstern* had been hired by a consortium of private investors from Beijing to haul scientific equipment to the outer reaches of the polar ice cap to search for new reserves of oil. The plan sounded insane, but the money was good, and the cargo was only a dozen of those big steel containers. There weren't even any outsiders coming on board to run tests. A representative of the consortium named Shen-wa had assured the captain that the equipment inside the containers would take care of everything.

As the diesel engines died, the heaters turned off and the cold immediately began to invade, heralded by the moaning polar winds. First a chill seeped through the steel hull and down the companionways, then frost crawled along the bulkheads, down the air vents and along the walls. Slowly, ice formed around the freighter, gradually thickening until it came over the gunwale to spread across the deck like an intractable disease of white.

But now, years later, a low hum sounded from the cargo hold, followed by a gentle wave of heat. The thick layers of ice covering the hatchway cracked, sounding like a breaking window. The snow began to melt tiny rivulets of warm water trickling away to freeze solid again after only a few yards.

Slowly, the temperature rose higher until the ice broke apart and floated away. Soon, bare metal was visible.

Windows shattered, rivets popped from the expanding steel, and a coiled rope sluggishly burst into flames. Incredibly, a bearded corpse abruptly sat up as the frozen muscles contracted for an instant, then the dead man opened his mouth in a silent repeat of his death scream. A moment later, his clothing ignited, and the ammunition in his gun belt cooked off, the rapid series of explosions tearing the body into grisly chunks, and the tattered corpse dropped flat again and began to smolder, the smell of cooking flesh filling the air.

With a tremendous explosion, the hatch was blown aside, and several dozen Sky Tiger drones rose gracefully out of the interior of the freighter. Most were standard size, only two yards wide, small enough to enter buildings and chase down individual targets. But accompanying them were five giant Dragonfire drones, rumbling Goliaths that had barely managed to fit into the forty-foot containers down below. Their wings were studded with weapons, the angular black hulls a smooth composite armor of layered ceramics.

Immediately, the small drones did a fast sweep of the area to make sure they weren't under any form of observation. But the machines were alone, with only the dead as company. Meanwhile, the Dragonfire drones did a full system check on their turbojet engines and allotment of tactical nuclear bombs.

Confirming their exact position with a Chinese mil sat in orbit, the big drones promptly flew away, their powerful turbofans murmuring low in the frigid arctic wind. Maintaining a tight formation, the winged machines soon were only dwindling specks on the horizon. Then the Dragonfire drones switched to their jet engines and abruptly changed course, each heading directly for its primary target—NORAD, Washington, London, Moscow and Beijing.

Dutifully, the Sky Tigers returned to the icy ship and landed in a protective circle around the remaining cargo containers in the hold. Turning their engines off, the drones quickly lost heat, and frost began to cover them.

Next, a tiny hatch opened on top of one of the containers, and a slim titanium rod extended upward, going all the way through the open hatch on the deck, to rise several yards above the warped metal plates there. Quivering in the arctic wind, the rod started to emit a high-pitched hum.

Long hours passed and nothing else happened. Slowly, the polar ice began to reclaim the *Gluckstern,* the hull ticking as it contracted once more, the old rusty freighter as peaceful and quiescent as an armed land mine.

CHAPTER THIRTEEN

Heathrow International Airport, London, England

"Hi, it's Jimmy, right? Can I have an iced tea?" Captain Zale O'Hara asked, approaching the counter.

"Sure thing, sir," the new bartender replied, both hands busy already filling a tumbler with ice. "You're Captain O'Hannon?"

"O'Hara."

"Sorry. Glad to meet you, sir."

"Skipper is fine, Jimmy."

"Whatever you say, sir!" The man chuckled, adding sugar to the mixture.

Spanning the wall behind him were unbreakable glass shelves filled with plastic bottles of liquor from around the world. But then, only the best of the best was available in the Excalibur Club. There was also a bubbling antique samovar for fresh coffee, and an ultramodern iced-tea brewmaster that would have looked more at home on board a starship.

Crafted by the best, or at least the most expensive, interior designers in the world, the Excalibur was a cozy haven of natural wood and cushioned leather that flowed around the smiling bartender like an ocean wave. Even the bar stools were heavily padded and had backs. But then, everything on the second deck of the luxury jetliner was all curves and cushions, offering no hard edges. Just a logical precaution against turbulence this high in the sky.

The Airbus 380 was one of the largest commercial jetliners in the world, with three full decks capable of carrying over five hundred passengers, plus the Excalibur Club, a private lounge on the second deck reserved just for first-class passengers. There was a full bar, dining room, a baby grand piano, a small dance floor, a gift shop, and even several exclusive cabins for the ultrarich among the passengers who wanted someplace private to retire during the long flight between continents.

"Here you are, Skipper," Jimmy said, passing over a frosty glass.

"Thanks," O'Hara said, removing the sprig of mint along with a tiny umbrella.

Jimmy smiled in apology.

"How c-come you a-ain't drinking? It's free up here, ya know," a blonde woman slurred, resting an arm on the counter. Her black dress was cut so low that it struggled to contain her inflated breasts and it couldn't have been any tighter if she had been shoved inside using a hydraulic press. She reeked of expensive perfume and was wearing so much jewelry there was a faint clinking that sounded like windchimes with every motion.

"Sorry, ma'am, we're not allowed to drink while on duty," the captain replied politely, reaching out a hand to help her straighten in the stool.

"T'anks." She smiled, then gave a hiccup.

"Duty. That's a flunny word...."

He recoiled at her breath. The woman wasn't just drunk, she was plastered. Which was rather impressive, since the flight was only an hour into the trip from London to Miami. She had to have started pounding down martinis the moment the wheels lifted off the runway.

"Yes, it is a funny word," Jimmy interjected, hopefully pushing a bowl of cashews her way. "Please allow me to introduce you to each other. Captain O'Hara, this is Mrs. Laura-Ann Gunderson of the South Bridgeport Gundersons."

O'Hara arched an eyebrow at the addendum, and Jimmy rubbed his fingers together. Meaning: she had more money than Satan and Croesus combined.

"Charmed, Mrs. Gunderson," he said with a forced smile.

"Yeah, me too." She gave a lopsided grin. "God, I love a man in uniform!"

Don't say it, he thought, bracing himself.

"But I like 'em more out of 'em!" she chortled with a wink.

"Never heard that one before," O'Hara said with a polite chuckle, and shot the bartender a hard look.

Jimmy nodded and started pouring black coffee.

"Well, back to work for me," the captain said, leaving quickly. "Enjoy the flight!"

She giggled in reply and rose to stagger along with him.

He tried not to groan, then inspiration hit and he removed his cap to display his complete lack of hair.

"Oh yes…I ad-dore b-bald men," she mumbled, attempting a sexy smile and failing utterly. "T-Telly Savalas, Yule Brynner, V-Vin Diesel…"

Just then a flight attendant came into view from the curving staircase. There was a standard smile on her face, but he saw the controlled worry in her eyes.

"Janet," O'Hara said in greeting, setting the iced tea on a nearby table.

"Code Four," she whispered, then said more loudly,

"You're wanted on the flight deck, sir. Something about the stormy weather."

"Of course." He smiled, tilting his head toward the drunk woman. "Stall her, shoot her, lock her in the lavatory if necessary, but get her off my back."

"Mrs. Gunderson!" Janet called out. "There's a phone call for you from the prime minister."

"The...who was that now?" she said in confusion.

"Well, I think he's the prime minister," Janet said, herding the woman toward the private cabins. "But we better go check, and see for sure, right?"

"Sure. Of course..."

Exhaling in relief, O'Hara hurried down the stairs and went directly to the front of the jumbo jetliner. Pressing his hand against a wall plate, he waited for the armored door to unlock and then stepped inside.

"Okay, what the fuck is wrong on my plane?" he demanded, titling back his cap.

"We have a hitchhiker in the hold," Lieutenant Connie Zabor said, passing over a Glock pistol.

Frowning, O'Hara checked the clip, then worked the slide. He wanted to ask how anybody had managed to sneak on board past all the new security, but that wasn't important right now. The Airbus was jammed full of VIP passengers, many of them richer than Mrs. Gunderson. There were even a couple of congressmen and a four-star general. If some bastard started to run amok with a box cutter, it would be the end of O'Hara's thirty-year career.

"Have they done anything?"

"Nope."

"Only the one guy?" he asked, tucking the weapon inside his jacket.

"We think so," Lieutenant Gary Hutching said, using

both hands to adjust the controls on the navigation console.

"Have you informed the air marshal? It's the little guy with the big mustache sitting in business class."

"First thing we did."

"Good to know. Got a stun gun?" O'Hara asked, taking a pair of handcuffs from a wall compartment.

"Fully charged," Zabor replied, proffering the device.

As always, Hutching flinched at the sight of the stun gun, half expecting Zabor to test the damn thing right here on the flight deck. But apparently the former U.S. Marine knew better than to unleash a burst of high-voltage static in a small room stuffed full of delicate electronic equipment.

"Then let's move," O'Hara said, straightening his cap before opening the door once more.

Strolling along the aisle, the two crew members nodded at the passengers, and touched their caps in deference when passing a VIP or politician. Reaching the crew compartment, they quickly closed the door, then opened the hatch in the floor. A short ladder lead down to the cargo deck. There was only darkness and silence below.

"I think our guest killed the lights," Zabor said, easing the safety off the stun gun. With a flick of her thumb, she upped the voltage from the medium setting to maximum.

O'Hara started to reply when brilliant lights filled the lower compartment, and there was a strange whirring sound oddly reminiscent of an electric fan.

"Was that a chainsaw?" Zabor asked, moving back a step.

"More likely some sort of an electric drill," O'Hara countered, trying to see into the gloom. "But I cannot recall anything down there worth stealing. We're not carrying any gold or jewels."

"Then what—"

A hard chattering cut loose from the darkness, and Zabor staggered backward, blood gushing from a dozen gaping wounds.

Snarling a curse, the captain dived to the side, the Glock banging away steadily. If he hit anything, there were no cries of pain, only that damn electric whir.

Then something black rose upward from the hatch in the deck, some sort of winged device carrying a pair of machine guns and four small missiles, or maybe rockets. It took him only a split second to recognize the machine as a UAV, a remote-controlled drone.

A chill went down his spine at the realization that this was a terrorist attack, but he lashed out a leg and kicked the drone as hard as he could. Knocked off balance, the craft moved sideways across the compartment to crash into the wall. Immediately, the sleek machine guns lurched into operation, the rounds stitching a line of holes along the inner wall.

Screams of pain erupted in the passenger compartment.

Snarling a curse, O'Hara rammed his pistol against a grill covering spinning turbofans and fired a fast five times. The flame from the muzzle extended inside the drone, even as the 9 mm rounds punched through the turbofans and out the bottom again.

Crackling with electric sparks, the Sky Tiger spun wildly firing both machine guns in every direction. The bullets slapped into the floor, ceiling and walls, invoking more cries of pain and surprise from the passengers in the VIP sections.

With a crash, the door to the compartment swung open,

and Mrs. Gunderson walked in carrying a .357 Magnum Smith & Wesson. Firing from the hip, she sent four booming rounds into the front of the drone. The dark ceramic armor exploded into pieces under the trip-hammer arrival of the steel-jacketed rounds, exposing the inner workings, wiring and circuit boards.

As if they had trained the maneuver for years, both O'Hara and Mrs. Gunderson converged on the UAV, emptying their weapons at point-blank range. The drone cut loose with another burst of 4.45 mm caseless rounds even while bits and pieces of the interior machinery were blown away. A rocket launched, smashing a hole into the lavatory, the exhaust filling the room with acrid fumes and incredible heat.

When his gun cycled empty, O'Hara flipped it over, grabbed the hot barrel and began hammering on the drone like a wild man. The damaged turbofan creaked and died, the drone immediately dipping low on that side. Then another rocket launched, punching through the fuselage of the jetliner. A howling wind buffeted the man and woman as the air inside the jumbo jet was sucked out, and they struggled to stay on their feet and keep fighting.

Alarms began to wail all across the aircraft, and breathing masks dropped, to flail about in the deafening hurricane. Ditching the empty revolver, Mrs. Gunderson pulled out a Remington 4-shot derringer and blasted the grill covering the second turbofan. The caseless machine gun whined into action as the drone attempted to circle around, but O'Hara blocked it with his body to keep the guns pointed away from the passengers.

Another rocket launched into the deck just as Gunderson fired the .44 derringer again, and the grill came loose. Yanking it aside, she then shoved the empty gun directly into the spinning blades. There came a screech of tortured metal as the turbofans stopped dead.

Powerless, the black drone dropped to the floor—only to launch one more rocket. Spewing smoke and flames, it skipped along the deck, slammed into the aft wall and disappeared. A moment later, a gush of drinking water sprayed out of the ragged hole.

Reaching inside the machine, O'Hara grabbed a fistful of random wiring and pulled it out. Electricity surged along his arm, searing pain shooting through his chest, then down both legs. Then something crackled loudly, there was a puff of dark smoke and the drone went inert.

Turning around, O'Hara grabbed a seat cushion and pressed it against the whistling puncture.

Fighting to catch their breath, he and Gunderson paused for a few moments, then reached down and ripped more wires out of the drone, just to make sure.

"That should do it," Mrs. Gunderson wheezed, cradling a bloody hand.

"Damn well hope so," he growled, massaging his aching back. "I don't know who you are, but thanks for the help."

"No problem."

Stiffly rising, he went to check on lieutenant Zabor, then removed his jacket to cover her corpse. "As for you," he said, turning to face the busty woman, "I'll bet you weren't actually drinking any of the martinis."

"As you said, not while on duty," she replied.

"Okay, who are you?"

"Sunshine Katz, U.S. Secret Service," she announced in a clear voice, flipping open a leather booklet to show her badge and identification card.

O'Hara arched an eyebrow.

"Hippie parents," she explained with a shrug. "The air

marshal informed me the plane had a stowaway, and I came to see if there was any danger to my charge."

"Charge?"

"That quiet guy in first class with the beard and sunglasses isn't the good senator from the fine state of Nebraska," she said, opening the cylinder to dump the spent shells from her weapon. "It's the Veep."

That took a moment to clarify in his jumbled mind. "The Vice President," O'Hara gasped, "of the United States of America?"

She started reloading. "That's my boy."

"B-but he always travels in *Air Force Two*!"

"Not always."

"Then why isn't the goddamn plane full of Secret Service agents?"

She snapped the cylinder shut with a jerk of her wrist. "It is," she said, and opened the door again.

Standing in a tight crowd were a dozen men and women carrying weapons, including Janet, the new steward and Jimmy the bartender.

"Report?" Janet demanded in a commanding voice.

"All clear," Katz replied with a half salute. "The enemy has been neutralized."

"Any breakage?" Jimmy asked, looking over the compartment.

"Nothing serious."

"Nothing serious?" O'Hara retorted, jerking a thumb toward the quivering seat cushion whistling softly against the fuselage. There was a ring of white frost around the quilted pad. "My copilot is dead, passengers are injured, we were almost sucked into space, and if that rocket had hit a fuel line we'd all be playing harps for sweet Jesus!"

"As I said, nothing serious," Katz stated, limping past

the crowd of Secret Service agents and dropping heavily into a seat.

Stumbling into the passenger section, O'Hara took another seat. The destruction here was nowhere near as bad as he had feared. Nobody was dead, or dying.

A few moments later a flight attendant brought them cold water and aspirins. Both were gladly accepted. The staff was getting the terrified civilians calm and under control, making hasty repairs for the couple of people who were wounded, while the Secret Service agents were already sealing off the aft compartment.

Soothing music was wafting down from the Excalibur Club, and at the front of the jetliner, a huge monitor had cycled in place and was showing the opening credits for a science-fiction movie about tall blue people who lived in the forest.

"Was this a terrorist attack?" a young girl asked, hugging a teddy bear.

"No dear, just a drill. We use tomato sauce for the blood. Sorry we frightened you. Have some cookies," the steward said.

"Thanks!"

"Cookies and aspirin," O'Hara muttered, rubbing his sore back. For some reason his kidneys hurt. He could only guess it had something to be with being mildly electrocuted.

"I'd rather have a drink," Katz said with a sigh.

"But not while on duty," he finished, almost laughing from exhaustion. "Okay, what do we do now, Special Agent?"

"Now we get an escort of jet fighters until we land at the nearest airport," she said, using a paper napkin to mop the blood off her fingers. "Then we haul that UAV to a lab, take it apart and find out where it came from."

Sheraton Hotel, Canton

IN THE MORNING, Bolan and Ziu stole an SUV from the hotel parking lot and departed before dawn.

"We'll need weapons to strike back at the Red Star," she said, binding her long hair in an elastic scrunchy. "And that means money, of which we have none."

"Money I can always get," Bolan stated, driving past a police car.

The police gave the mixed couple a hard look, so Bolan pointed at them and cheerily waved. Following his lead, Ziu did the same. After a moment, the police replied in kind, forcing artificial grins on their faces.

Still waving, Bolan drove around a corner.

"That was risky," Ziu exhaled, releasing her grip on the Glock.

"Nothing makes a cop more suspicious than a person who refuses to meet their gaze," Bolan explained. "But smile and wave, and nine times out of ten they'll think you're just a tourist, and ignore you completely."

"And if not?" she asked, slipping the gun back under a newspaper lying on the front seat. With the sound suppressor, the weapon was uncomfortably big, especially for somebody her petite size.

"Then we would have run," Bolan said, shifting gears. "I don't shoot police." He took a corner. "Unless they're a member of the secret police. No problem there. But not ordinary street cops. Most of them are honest men and women, just doing a job."

"And if you are trapped, and you must die, or them?"

"Then I die," Bolan said bluntly.

That declaration clearly took her by surprise, and Ziu looked directly at him for the first time.

"Now, about the money," she began, switching back to

the original topic. "I am hesitant about stealing from my fellow citizens. Perhaps we should wait until I can contact another cell of the White Lotus Society. Then we will have everything needed."

"How long would that take?"

"A few days. Maybe more. We are deliberately unknown to each other to prevent one cell from being captured and forced to reveal the rest of us."

"Days? By then it might be too late," Bolan countered, heading for an elevated highway. "I need to find Shen-wa fast, before those drones start World War III."

"This is an American joke?" she asked hopefully.

"No. The major has already killed thousands of innocent people, military and civilians, and the death toll rises every day. Soon all hell will break loose, and when the Pentagon learns that China is behind these terrorist attacks, what do you think will be their first response?"

Sitting very still, Ziu said nothing for a long time, then gave a sigh. "Then we have no choice. However, if we must commit a robbery, then I would prefer to rob a bank, as those are owned by the state, and thus part of the system that keeps the common people oppressed."

"They're also very well guarded," Bolan said, swerving onto the entrance ramp. "How do you feel about drug dealers?"

"They're vermin, the scum of the planet," she said.

"No problem stealing from them?"

"None whatsoever. But how would you find them? They are controlled by the Tongs, a secret society of criminals, even more hidden than the White Lotus. I do not know how to contact them, and this is my country, not yours."

"That doesn't matter," Bolan replied. "Big fish eat little fish the whole world over."

"Meaning what?" she asked, puzzled.

Merging into traffic, Bolan explained, and soon Ziu gave a hard grin.

"Turn there," she said, pointing at an exit sign. "We will find what we need in that neighborhood."

Following her directions, Bolan soon found the poor section of Canton, something the tourists were generally not allowed to know even existed. There was a lot of trash, and graffiti was everywhere. Every building was in need of repair, and a few offices had their windows covered with tinfoil in place of shades. The street was in terrible condition with endless potholes, and ragged homeless individuals slept near steam vents from the underground tunnels.

Most of the people were walking or riding bicycles; the few cars in sight rattled along trailing blue smoke. Old men sat on wooden boxes on the cracked sidewalk playing dominoes, and a couple of young men smoking cigarettes lounged against cinder-block walls, apparently doing nothing as a full-time occupation. Several girls in short dresses and harsh makeup stood in alleyways watching every car that rolled past.

"I don't suppose you have such places as this in America," Ziu said sadly.

"Every major city has a slum," Bolan said.

"Slum? I do not know that word."

"Slum, ghetto, hood, inner city—they're all the same."

Bolan found a pawnbroker set between a bakery and a used-clothing store, and Ziu went inside to exchange his expensive military wristwatch for a medium-range camera.

The Glock would have gotten her much more money, and an infinitely better camera, but not all pawnbrokers had a shady side, and the deal might have generated a visit from the police, or worse, the military. Weapons of any sort were strictly forbidden in a Communist country. There really was no other way to keep a population enslaved. However, cameras were used by everybody.

Going to one of the larger shopping malls downtown, Bolan kept watch while Ziu strolled about with the camera, taking pictures of people and shops. Using the very last of the money, she bought a rice cake and ate it on a bench, then went to the washroom, leaving the camera behind.

Bolan almost smiled as a group of teenagers moved in fast to surround the bench, and then strolled away slowly, the camera no longer in sight.

A moment later, Ziu slipped into the car. "Did it work?" she asked breathlessly.

"We have the minnows," Bolan said, easing into gear. "Now we use them as bait to catch a shark."

Keeping as far back as possible, Bolan meandered through the traffic, trailing the gang. Unexpectedly, they turned into a farmer's market and disappeared among the stalls and pushcarts.

"Wait an hour," Bolan said, quickly getting out of the car. "If I'm not back by then, find your friends."

"I'll wait until dark," Ziu countered, slipping behind the wheel.

"Just do as I say," he growled impatiently.

"Stop wasting time," she snapped, passing him the folded newspaper. "Hurry, or you'll lose them!"

Realizing it would be pointless to argue, Bolan took the newspaper and walked away. Once he was among the bustling crowd, he stepped into a dark alley to slip out the Glock and tuck it into his belt under the windbreaker.

Returning to the crowd, Bolan soon found the gang again, pilfering small items as they strolled along. Following after them on foot proved to be a lot more difficult than in a car, as Bolan's height made him tower above everybody. Hunching his shoulders, the soldier tried to keep behind tent poles and flapping awnings as much as possible. He drew some puzzled stares from men, along with a few smiles from some of the women working the stalls. Zipping the windbreaker closed to prevent anybody from catching a glimpse of the guns, Bolan did what he could to avoid attracting any additional attention.

The smells of the market were a knife in his belly. There was no money for breakfast at the hotel that morning, but he would eat soon enough.

That was, if the kids didn't get away, Bolan added, as the gang went into a public toilet, only to slip out the side window. Okay, they knew he was following them. No need to be covert anymore.

Breaking into a sprint, he chased the gang around a corner and down a dark alley. As he came out the other side, he saw one of them vanish behind a rattling trolley car. He kept running, and when the car was gone, the gang was nowhere in sight.

They were good, Bolan noted, but not professionals. There was a Mexican restaurant on the opposite corner, and the front door was still swinging back and forth.

A gas station stood on the near corner, but even if he had the time to call Zia, there was no telephone, only a blank steel plate in the wall. Bolan had been seeing this happen more often these days. Cell phones were so cheap that pay phones were fast becoming a relic of the past.

Slowing to an easy stroll, he took his time crossing the street, and walked around the restaurant. The rear was closed off with a tall wooden fence, the only gate locked. Bolan used the keywire gun to open it, and hurried through.

There was the usual assortment of garbage cans and

empty wooden crates he would expect to find behind any restaurant. Thirty or so teenagers were clustered around the back door as if waiting for somebody to rush through. Each was armed with a weapon. A few of the younger members had only knives or baling hooks, while the older ones were carrying IMBEL shotgun pistols. The guns held only four cartridges, but Bolan had faced the weapons before and knew how extremely deadly they would be in the right hands.

"Nobody move!" he commanded in a low voice, drawing both his guns.

Instantly, everybody turned, their faces registering shock. Several of the boys growled, and a couple girls hissed like cats. Bolan had to reassess his opinion of one of them. The girl was so small he had naturally thought she was only twelve or thirteen. But now that she was facing his way, he could see she had a full womanly figure. She was at least eighteen, with the eyes of a thirty-five-year-old. Plus a hatchet. The young woman was going to be trouble.

"Drop the guns," Bolan ordered, clicking back the hammers of both pistols.

Nobody moved, then a few of the IMBEL pistols started to rise.

"Your leader will be the first one I shoot," Bolan stated coldly.

Snarling something in Chinese, the oldest youth pushed the other gang members aside and stepped forward.

He couldn't have been more than sixteen, but had the air of command. He was wearing a black leather jacket decorated with the symbol for Harley-Davidson, and heavy motorcycle boots. More important, there was a 9 mm Heckler & Koch pistol sticking out from behind a large belt buckle also bearing the logo for the American motorcycle company.

In ragged stages, the other gang members lowered the muzzles of their guns, but they didn't drop the weapons.

"Last chance," Bolan stated, putting two pounds of pressure on the six-pound triggers.

The youth studied Bolan closely, then spoke again. Hesitantly, the gang dropped the guns.

"Got a name?" Bolan asked.

With a sneer, the youth spoke rapidly in Chinese.

"Cut the shit," Bolan drawled. "You speak English, I've heard you. *Dong ma?*" That last was just about all the Chinese that Bolan knew, the word for "understand." The rest was a bluff. He simply assumed that since any gang this big probably did work with the Hong Kong underworld, they would out of necessity know a little English.

"*Dahng rahm.* I'm the leader," the youth said in perfect English. "The name's Talon, and these are the Wolves."

The Wolf Pack. Bolan had heard something similar with street gangs around the world. Funny how they all identified with the same wild animal.

"The name is Cooper," Bolan said, "and I've got a business proposition for you."

"What do you want to buy, eh?" Talon asked without any real interest. He tucked the thumbs of both hands into his wide leather belt, his fingers only inches from the HK pistol.

"Not buying, or selling."

"Then you're a fool to come here." The young woman chuckled, running her thumb along the edge of a knife. "There are thirty of us and just one of you!"

At those words, the gang smiled like beasts preparing for a feast.

Choosing a target, Bolan clicked the selector on the Glock and stroked the trigger.

The fenced-in yard became filled with the prolonged discharge of the German machine pistol, the muzzle-flame extending for a over a yard, as the spent brass shells arced away high. A wooden crate disintegrated into splinters and the ground underneath seemed to boil from the barrage of the eighteen rounds firing in two seconds.

Stunned, the gang stared at the gaping crater in the dirt, then looked up just in time to see Bolan slapping in a spare clip.

Nobody spoke for a few moments.

"Okay, not a complete fool," Talon said, shifting his stance. "What's the deal?"

"I want to make you rich," Bolan said.

"You want to make us rich," Talon repeated, saying each word separately as if trying to seize its true meaning.

"Sure you do!" a bald teenager snarled, reaching for something under his denim jacket.

Moving fast, Bolan drew the Glock again and fired once. The silenced weapon gave a hard cough that merged into the cry of pain as blood erupted from the thigh of the teenager.

Dropping the revolver, he grabbed the wound and staggered away to sit with his back against the wall. It was a classic street fighting technique. If hurt, guard your back.

"Dai!" the young woman cried, starting forward to wrap a scarf around his leg and make a tourniquet.

He kept his face neutral, but Bolan was impressed. She had pulled the cloth out of a leather bag hanging at her side. There were several more in there, along with what looked like rolls of bandages. He had never met a street gang sophisticated enough to have one member designated as the medic. This plan just might work.

Suddenly, the young woman grabbed the bottom of her T-shirt and pulled it over her head, exposing her naked breasts. A silver ring glittered from the left nipple.

Expecting something like that, Bolan drew both guns, aiming the Glock at Talon as he swung the AutoMag to point behind.

"Go for it," he growled in a voice from beyond the grave. The sound of rushing steps behind him instantly stopped.

"Ti-Wou, Feng, come over here where he can see you," Talon commanded. "May-Lee, put them way. This man is not interested."

May-lee sneered, lowering the T-shirt and tucking it into her pants.

"You're very fast," Talon stated as a fact. "You could have killed everybody here if you wanted."

"But then we couldn't have done any business," Bolan countered.

Nodding in thought, Talon walked over to a pile of trash and pulled out a couple of crates. He flipped them over and sat on one.

Holstering his weapons, Bolan took the other.

"Talk," Talon said with a gesture.

"You distribute drugs in this territory," he said. "Sell on the street corners and back alleys, but you keep very little of the money because you aren't the supplier. You're not in charge."

Talon said nothing.

"But that would all change if the current supplier was no longer in any condition to conduct business," Bolan continued.

"That would be very good thing for the Wolves," Talon

said carefully. "But the house of Mr. Dee is too well protected, too many guards with very good guns. AK-47, M-16, MP-5, and such. Much better than what we have." He paused. "Body armor, too. Not bulletproof vests, body armor. Understand?"

Bolan nodded. "Do you know his address?"

"Yes, of course."

"I do not."

Slowly, Talon smiled. "And if you knew his address, what then?"

"You could visit him in, say, an hour," Bolan said. "There would be many things of great interest for you to find, and all of them would be belong to you…and the Wolves, of course."

"Everything?"

"Everything I don't take."

Now the light of understanding came into the teenager's eyes. "Then perhaps we can help each other," Talon said with a wide grin, a gold tooth glinting in the sunlight. "Here, let me draw you a map…."

CHAPTER FOURTEEN

Rosewood Estates, Canton

Lying flat on top of a grassy hill, Bolan used binoculars to carefully watch the huge mansion below.

The place was a fortress, he noted. A military hard site.

The manicured lawn stretched for acres, and the main house was a mansion five stories tall, with two guest wings and four chimneys. There was also a greenhouse, an enclosed swimming pool, a private golf course, rose garden, stable with riding pasture, a tennis court and a helipad. The civilian version of a Black Hawk stood on a circular patch of pavement, a couple of guys in overalls tinkering with the engine. A wind sock on a pole showed which way the breeze was blowing, letting the pilot visually gauge the speed. A dozen cars stood in the garage, all of them of foreign manufacture—Ferrari, BMW, Rolls-Royce and a massive Hummer.

It was all very pretty, and a lie. According to the phone book, the mansion was owned by a Mr. Dee Jinn-wa, and according to Ziu he was the drug lord of southern China. Mr. Dee owned most of Rosewood Estates, along with a sizable chunk of downtown Canton.

The smooth green lawns gently curved upward, forcing an invader to cross a lot of open ground. A low stone wall around the patios offered perfect firing positions for the defenders. The outer perimeter was a tall brick fence, topped with an iron spike railing that rose ten feet into the air. Past that was an enclosed dog run, ten feet of bare dirt and then an inner wire fence. From their lack of barking, Bolan recognized the animals as military guard dogs, trained to rip out throats and groins, but never bark. Silent death on four paws. Chilling stuff.

There were several men on lawn tractors trimming the grass, each wearing a shoulder holster, as well as a couple guys walking on the flat roof. They were equipped with pistols, body armor and sniper rifles with telescopic sights.

On the rear lawn there seemed to be a party going on, unless this was how the local drug lord lived every day. A score of people were lounging around an Olympic-size swimming pool that had a waterfall cascading down an artificial mountain of artistically arranged granite boulders. Most of the women were Asian, but there were also a few of other nationalities. Variety was the spice of life, apparently. Many of the women were topless, lying on chaise longues to tan.

Smoke rose from a barbecue grill where liveried servants basted rows of browning spareribs, and there were more guards than Bolan could easily count.

The armed men stood well away from the swimmers and the pool, watching the outer walls. They seemed relaxed, not expecting any trouble, but ready for it. The big athletic-looking men stood balanced on both feet. These were more than bodyguards, they were private soldiers.

If Bolan wanted to blitz the place, he would have needed some major artillery. But that was not the plan for today. He was here to simply watch, and wait to be betrayed.

Just then a Harley-Davidson motorcycle rolled up to the front gates, and the driver removed his helmet to reveal that he was Talon. Briefly, the teenager talked excitedly to the guards. At first they seemed scornful, but he insisted, and finally they nodded in belief. Moving fast, one of the guards went directly to a wall phone, while the other paid the youth off with a fistful of cash.

As Talon drove away, a soft alarm began to sound, and everybody scurried into the mansion. More guards poured out of hiding and additional dogs were unleashed in the run. In moments, the girls were safely inside, the party over and the mansion sealed tight, surrounded by a cadre of armed men ready for business.

Crawling backward, Bolan got below the swell of the hill and ran down the slope to jump into the waiting car.

"Well, how did it go?" Ziu asked, lowering her gun.

"Tell you in a few minutes," Bolan growled, revving the engine to charge across a field of lush grass.

The car was still accelerating when Bolan reached the paved road, and Talon came into view. Slamming on the brakes, he brought the car to a rocking halt sideways across the road.

With screeching tires, Talon fought the bike to a ragged stop, then flipped up his visor and screamed in Chinese at the unseen people behind the tinted windows of the car.

Ziu stepped out from the passenger side and scowled. "Do you know who you are talking to?" she demanded hotly.

Sneering in disdain, Talon answered back loudly.

"I'm speaking English," Ziu retorted, "so that he can understand what I'm saying!"

"He? Who is this he?" Talon spit back furiously.

Lowering the electric window, Bolan showed the teen the business end of the AutoMag.

With a gasp, Talon recoiled and started to go for the

pistol in his belt, then stopped his fingers only inches from the checkered grip.

"Smart move," Bolan said, clicking back the hammer on the .44 AutoMag. "Get his gun."

Rounding the car, Ziu walked over to the teen and took the weapon from his belt. Dropping the clip, she thumbed out all of the cartridges, then raised the gun and fired the bullet in the chamber. As the spent brass was kicked out the side port, she made the catch, then thumbed it into the magazine, and slipped that back into the weapon, working the slide.

Bolan approved. Most modern automatic pistols would leave the slide kicked back to show the clip was empty. Putting a spent round into the magazine would make the slide go back into place, and the gun would appear to be fully loaded, even though it was empty.

Talon said nothing as she tucked the useless pistol back into his belt.

"The letter," Bolan said succinctly.

Searching his pocket, Ziu found the envelope and took out the paper inside. "It's in code," she muttered.

Bolan grunted in response. "I can guess what it says. He's to go to a special place and receive a substantial reward, after Mr. Dee sends word that somebody actually has attacked the mansion."

Astonished, Talon dropped his jaw. "But how..." he started, then snapped his mouth shut. "You going to kill me now?"

"Not if you follow instructions this time," Bolan said in an ominous tone. "I rarely give a second chance, so don't waste it."

"No, sir, I won't!" Talon said eagerly, his face shiny with sweat.

"Get moving," Bolan said with a neutral expression.

As the teen kicked the big Harley alive, Ziu walked back to the car and climbed inside.

"Why didn't you make him tell you the location of a dealer before?" she asked with a scowl, "and avoid all of this unpleasantness?"

"Because he only knew the lower-level dealers, and I needed somebody at the top of the organization," Bolan replied, watching the teen slowly drive away. "Besides, this way everybody is rushing to protect Dee at the mansion, leaving all the other locations relatively unguarded."

"Relatively," Ziu repeated, emphasizing the word.

"Nothing's perfect," Bolan replied.

Staying a block behind the teenager, Bolan followed him back into Canton, then past the downtown business district and out into the eastern suburbs. Shiny office buildings and busy shopping malls gave way to individual houses and strip malls, then melded into squat factories and ugly row homes crammed together like dirty slices of bread. Big trucks rumbled constantly along the roads and often there was no sidewalk, only gutters.

The occasional store had every window boarded shut, the sheets of plywood covered with graffiti and starting to splinter along the edges. Parking lots were closed off with tall wire fences, the top frothy with coils of concertina wire. The air was thick with the taste of exhaust and chemical fumes. The neighborhood was somber and gray, with all the warmth of a mortuary slab.

Bolan twisted the wheel to avoid a pothole. "Where is everyone?"

"They're at work. Everybody here works."

"Even the children?"

"There are no schools, only factories. The government denies that this part of Canton exists," Ziu said woodenly. "No tourists are allowed to come here under any circumstances."

"Good thing we're not tourists," Bolan grunted, loosening the Glock in his shoulder holster. It held the last magazine he had for the weapon, and there were only eight rounds in the AutoMag. Until he got more ammunition, he would have to make every bullet count.

Soon, the tightly packed row homes gave way to individual homes again, but the condition of the buildings continued to deteriorate. Most of the ramshackle houses were in poor repair, with tiles missing from the roofs. Windows were held together with duct tape.

The sole exception was a large three-story house. The roof was intact, there were bars on the windows and the walls were clean and bare of graffiti. The lawn was choked with weeds and the fence was in pieces, but these details almost seemed incongruous compared to the excellent condition of the rest of the house.

As Talon braked the motorcycle directly in front of the building, Bolan continued on to the corner and parked near a rusty fire hydrant.

"Better move fast," he said, throwing the car into Park and turning off the engine.

Nodding, Ziu scrambled into the rear seat and ducked low.

Joining her, Bolan watched the teenager stroll casually up the sidewalk and knock on the front door. A moment later, a slot opened in the door. Talon said something in Chinese and the slot closed again.

"Message from Mr. Dee," Ziu translated softly, squinting to see their mouths.

Suddenly, the door swung out, revealing that it was layered with armor. Filling the doorway was a huge man with an Uzi machine pistol in his grip. A British Webley

.445 revolver was tucked in a nylon shoulder holster. The two men started talking.

"'What the fuck do you want,' the guard is asking," Ziu said in a low voice. "'I'm here with a message for Miss Torqueville.' 'I'll take it to her.' 'No, I have to do this in person… Please, the car on the corner has a gun pointed at my head….' Matt, he knows!"

Instantly, the guard swept the teenager aside and swung up the Uzi to fire. The hail of 9 mm bullets shattered the driver's window, showing there was nobody behind the wheel.

Half a heartbeat later, Bolan threw open the car door and triggered the Glock. The silenced weapon coughed twice. The range was impossible, over a hundred feet, but a black dot appeared on guard's temple and his head rocked back hard.

As the corpse collapsed to the floor, Talon grabbed the Uzi and swung around, wildly spraying the weapon about.

Already in motion, Bolan dived to the side and came up firing. Talon recoiled as he was hit in the chest, his life spraying out the back of the leather jacket in hot jets of blood.

Springing across the threshold, Bolan holstered the Glock, grabbed the Webley from the dead guard's shoulder holster and kept on moving. As he expected, this was no crack house, but a major distribution center. The front living room was full of ordinary furniture, but it was only stage dressing to fool the idle curious.

A curtain closed off a doorway, and underneath Bolan found a brick wall filling the bottom half, a thick Plexiglas window closing off the top. Behind the bulletproof window was a middle-aged man wearing a revolver in a leather shoulder holster. He was frantically trying to stuff packets of white powder and pills into a metal drawer. In the background were four more men sitting at wooden desks. As they looked up with shocked expressions, their hands paused while dividing more white powder and piles of blue crystals into small plastic bags.

Stopping before the window, Bolan fired the AutoMag a fast five times, the big bore hand cannon booming like thunder. The massive .44 Magnum rounds slammed into the vulnerable metal frame that held the Plexiglas, and the window came free, to crash into the front man. Gushing blood from his nose, the fellow dropped out of sight, and Bolan emptied the Webley into the other drug dealers. As they fell backward into eternity, Bolan dived through the window to land in a crouch, and pulled the Glock.

Seconds later, there came the sound of booted feet pounding on floorboards, then a thick wooden door slammed open and six men carrying assault rifles burst into the counting room.

Stroking the trigger, Bolan unlashed the machine pistol. The remaining sixteen rounds discharged in two seconds, and the armed men were brutally hammered back into the hallway, their rifles briefly chattering into the floors and walls.

Tossing away the Glock, Bolan grabbed an M-16 assault rifle, along with a couple spare magazines from a twitching corpse. He spent a tense few seconds checking over the weapon, then rushed forward once more, sending short bursts into anybody he saw carrying drugs or holding a weapon.

Turning a corner, the soldier paused as a big man waddled into view. The fellow was carrying a QBZ assault rifle and wearing level five body armor.

Crouching low, Bolan fired the grenade launcher fixed under the barrel of the M-16. The 40 mm shell hit the armored guard like an express train but didn't explode, sending him smashing into the opposite wall. The double-barrel assault rifle went flying away, and Bolan shot the guard in the foot with the M-16. Yowling in pain, the man doubled over, and the Executioner shot the guy's exposed neck, the 5.56 mm hardball rounds coming out his groin. Shuddering all over, the dying man went limp, red blood splattering the floor.

Reloading the M-16, Bolan paused for a split second to fire a mercy round to end his opponent's misery, then moved to the stairs. What he wanted would be on the upper levels.

The second floor proved to be the storage room and interrogation chamber, with iron manacles on the wall set directly above a drain in the floor for easy cleaning. It also seemed to be the arsenal for the drug house; a wall rack held assault rifles, pistols, grenades, and even a few Armbrust rocket launchers. Bolan glanced over the array of weapons, then kept going. There was no time to stop. He had only minutes before the alarm was sounded and more guards flooded in from other houses. He needed to be long gone before then.

On the stairs, he easily avoided a trip wire attached to an antipersonnel mine hidden inside the wall. There were more, but that was the only one activated. He seemed to have caught the drug dealers by surprise.

On the third floor, he discovered a small kitchen, the number of mugs hanging on wall pegs giving him the total number of guards: fourteen. He had already dispatched over a dozen, which left one last man, plus whoever was in charge of this hellhole.

At the end of a hallway, Bolan saw a closed door and put a long burst from the M-16 into the panels. The wood was chewed away to expose sheet steel, the hardball rounds merely ricocheting off the thick metal.

Shouldering the assault rifle, he drew the AutoMag and fired on either side of the armored door. The big slugs smacked into the smooth plaster, kicking out clouds of dust. Somebody screamed in pain inside the office, and a heavy machine gun burst into life, the large caliber rounds punching a ragged line of holes in the armored door.

By the time the shooting stopped, Bolan had retreated to the far end of the hallway. Raising the M-16/M-203 combo, he aimed carefully, triggered the grenade launcher and ducked.

With just enough distance to arm itself, the 40 mm shell hit the door and detonated. The deafening blast shook the entire house, cracking the walls and blowing the door off its hinges.

Thick smoke was still swirling as Bolan rose and lurched forward. He felt sore all over from the powerful concussion, but he was absolutely sure the people inside were in much worse condition.

Pausing to peek through the bullet holes in the wall, Bolan saw only wreckage and smoke. Staying low, he swept into the office, both guns at the ready.

Lying on the floor near an open wall safe was the tattered remains of a man surrounded by loose piles of bloodstained cash. Bolan almost started to go for the safe when he saw there were two teacups shattered on the floor. Looking about, he saw a closet in the corner, the door slightly dented from the blast, but not breached. A safe room inside the office? Clever.

"Come out, or I use another grenade," Bolan ordered. There was a brief pause, then the door creaked open and out walked a disheveled woman clutching a briefcase.

"Of course! I surrender!" she cried, tears running down

her face. "Please don't shoot me!" The accent was French, but she spoke English perfectly.

"Drop the briefcase, and your gun."

"I…I'm not armed," she replied, placing the briefcase on the splintered remains of a desk.

"Spread the jacket," Bolan ordered.

She did, using only her fingertips, as if having been frisked many times before. Then, without being asked, she turned around to show that she did have a gun in a holster behind her back, and next lifted her skirt to reveal only ripped panty hose.

"You can search me," she offered.

He ignored that. The woman was a looker, sure enough, with curves in all of the right places. Even though her dress was torn in several spots it still looked expertly tailored, and she was wearing a lot of gold jewelry. Maybe she didn't sell the drugs, but she was an integral part of the machinery that did, and thus just as guilty as the dealers.

"Got a name?" Bolan demanded, snapping open the briefcase. It was packed full of cash, U.S. dollars, British pounds and Chinese yen. From the large denominations of the bills, he figured the briefcase held a small fortune.

"Gillain Torqueville."

"Okay, give me a reason to let you live," Bolan said.

She gestured at the briefcase. "That's full of money. Take it, all of it. It's yours!"

"That was mine the moment I entered the room," he growled, feeling the terrible pressure of time.

"I'll give you the name of my supplier!" she suggested, breathing deeply, her full breasts straining against the torn blouse.

"Mr. Dee? Already been there," he said honestly.

Her eyes went wide at that news. "But he…I… Okay, tell me what you want! Anything at all! It's yours!"

Solemnly, he raised the AutoMag and clicked back the hammer.

"For the love of God, tell me what you want!" she screamed, tears running down her cheeks.

A sound behind Bolan made him swing around fast to see a piece of the cracked ceiling crash to the littered floor. Quickly, he turned back, but the woman hadn't moved.

"I want you to retire," he said, walking closer to place the hot muzzle of the AutoMag against her throat. He could see the pulse of the carotid artery under her satiny skin. "Leave China forever, and you live."

"Nothing else?" the woman whispered, licking dry lips.

"Nothing more."

"Deal." She sighed. "Are...are you CIA, or MI-5?"

"It doesn't matter," Bolan said, removing the gun to close the briefcase. "The rest of the money in the safe is yours for doing nothing for an hour. No calls, no screams, no running. Understand?"

"Yes, of course," she said hesitantly. "But how do I know that I can trust you?"

"You're still breathing, and I'm not out of bullets," Bolan stated, letting her look into the huge barrel of the AutoMag.

She went pale, and nodded again. "Whatever you say."

Bolan heard the sound of running feet and turned with both the Glock and the AutoMag leveled.

Suddenly, the bloody man with the smashed nose from the lobby appeared, cradling a Neostad shotgun. As he raised the barrel, Bolan fired both guns. Mortally wounded, the man spun away from the double assault, his weapon discharging loudly into the floor and ripping up a chunk of carpet.

Bolan walked closer to the woman. "If we ever meet again, it will be your last moment on Earth," he said, taking the briefcase.

Dumbly, she nodded.

A few minutes later, he left the house carrying a heavy duffel bag and the briefcase. Stowing them both in the trunk of the car, Bolan slipped behind the wheel and drove away.

"Did you get what we need?" Ziu asked, looking him over for any wounds. He was covered with blood, but none of it seemed to be from him.

"How about some breakfast first, then we'll do inventory," Bolan countered, dropping a huge wad of bills in her lap.

Riffling through the stack, Ziu gave a low whistle. "Breakfast followed by…?"

"A new car, a shower, an hour of sleep and a long drive."

"To Fakkah?" she asked. "Then we're going to need a map. Plus some long poles, birdcages and canaries."

"Just in case the land is poison?" he asked, taking a corner.

"A fool is often judged by the depth of his grave."

In the distance, the sound of police sirens started to build in volume.

"Any chance of getting our hands on a chemical suit?" Bolan asked, shifting gears to lower his speed.

"None."

"Then it's a bad day to be a canary," he declared, heading for the northbound highway once more.

CHAPTER FIFTEEN

Justice Building, Washington, D.C.

Making notes on the screen with a light pen, Hal Brognola was carefully studying a computer monitor that detailed maps of every known drone attack. He felt positive that something other than an attempt at expanding China's borders was happening, but he just couldn't fathom the hidden agenda.

The intercom buzzed, and Brognola reached across the desk to tap a button. "Yes, Kelly?" He had asked his secretary to not disturb him, which meant this was a priority call from either the White House or Bolan.

"There's a call for you on line one," she replied crisply. "The President."

Brognola tapped a few buttons. There came a fast series of click and squeals as the NSA scrambler on the secure line activated.

The drone attack on the White House had come as a total surprise. The jets tasked with defending the structure against attack hadn't even had time to be scrambled. Luckily, there had been no deaths.

Brognola realized just how tough the building was when he saw that Chinese UAV utterly destroyed when it rammed headlong into a French door that looked about as resilient as a sand castle. The windows hadn't even cracked, and the only things harmed were a couple of potted ferns on the balcony.

Minutes later, the President and his family were safely on the way to Camp David, while the Vice President and his family flew to an undisclosed location. The members of the Senate and the House had scattered to the winds, and the only people left on the Hill were military troops, ready and eager for a chance to get even with the deadly UAVs.

The phone gave another series of clicks.

"Hello?" a garbled voice asked.

"Hold, please," Brognola said.

At last the phone began to hum, and the line cleared. "Okay, sir, we can talk now," Brognola said, leaning forward to activate a Humbug. The device was redundant, but he always preferred to be safe than sorry. Apologies were a lot cheaper than funerals.

"We found them, Hal!" the President said without preamble. "It's the damn Germans again. Lord knows which group, the Volksfyre perhaps. We had trouble with them before, just never on this scale."

"Germans?" Brognola repeated with a scowl. "That doesn't gibe with the intel I'm getting from my man on the scene."

"Trust me, Hal. The CIA went over the drone we recovered from the Airbus, and know everything but the name of the guy who dug the iron ore out of the ground. The electronics were German. The steel carried trace elements from an abandoned Stuttgart foundry.... It was made in Germany. That's a fact."

"Now we just have to find the base," Brognola said, loosening his necktie. "Or did the CIA pull another miracle out of their covert ass?" His stomach was tightening as if he was about to start a gunfight. There was something wrong here.

"That they did, my friend! The electronics were traced back to a shipment stolen five years ago from some little town in China. The black market dealer buckled under questioning from the Italian police, and Interpol found the warehouse where the drones were assembled."

"In Germany?"

"Right on the Rhine! There was a boat moored there, the *Glucksstern*, and we found it moored in Baffin Bay near the Arctic Circle."

"Where was that again?" Brognola asked with a scowl. "Sir, how hard is this intel?"

"Rock solid. NATO already has sent a full wing of heavy bombers to blow that ship out of existence." The President paused. "It's actually very clever to have a mobile base of operations at the top of the world. Using a trans-polar flight, you can strike anything in the Northern Hemisphere with relative ease."

"Germans at the North Pole..." Even as he said the words, Brognola knew it was nonsense. "Sir, cancel the attack. It's a diversion, or worse, a trap."

"What makes you think that?"

"Gut instinct," he stated, tapping the light pen against the monitor. "I've been studying the attacks, and this is Chinese. Absolutely."

"Even for you, I would need more than a feeling to change a major military operation, Hal. My people say it is the Germans."

"And Matt Cooper says it's the Red Star. My money is on him," Brognola stated forcibly. "Besides, there was no way for anybody to know the Vice President was on that plane. None whatsoever. That means the real target was the passengers. All of those millionaires, movie stars and congressmen."

"Now, how does that change anything.... Oh, publicity?"

"Yes, sir. That attack was designed to catch our attention and make the six-o'clock news."

"I can see your line of reasoning," the President said thoughtfully.

"And why was there only a single drone? Why didn't it explode when damaged and destroy the entire plane? Somebody wanted us to capture that drone intact, to send us on a wild-goose chase to waste time while..." He paused in consternation.

"While what?" the President demanded. "They prepared for the real attack, something major?"

"That's what I would do."

The President snorted. "Unfortunately, while I can advise and request, I do not command NATO."

"Then strongly advise the supreme high commander to recall his forces before—"

"Hal, it's already too late. The bombers are en route."

"Then we better start digging graves, sir," he growled. "Because after NATO gets the ever-loving shit kicked out them, the blood will really hit the fan!"

Canton

PAUSING BEFORE the back door of the apartment building, Sergeant Ming ran an EM scan for any magnetic trips, found nothing, then used a keywire gun on the lock. The door opened soundlessly.

Easing inside, he checked the mailboxes in the lobby and found the name of the person he was looking for on the nineteenth floor, the top level. Expensive and exclusive. Obviously, crime paid very well on the east coast.

His informants in the Tong said that somebody had just blown apart one of Mr. Dee's urban forts as if it were made of bamboo. A tall man, dark, not Asian, who took only money and weapons, but no drugs. The sole survivor of the attack, Gillian Torqueville, had been undamaged and was leaving China. Taken separately, these were matters of only minor interest, but combined they reeked of the CIA operative from Hong Kong, and thus needed to be promptly investigated in more detail. If the big American had escaped alive from the drone attack on the White Lotus, then he was a danger to the project.

Going to the basement, Ming killed the power to the alarm system and video cameras, then bypassed the dead elevator and took the stairs to the nineteenth floor.

The lock on the door was electronic, and with the power turned off, Ming simply pushed his way inside the apartment. A bodyguard snored softly on the sofa, a foreign-made Heckler & Koch MP-5 submachine lying across his lap. Ming slit the man's throat with a knife, then used a pillow to control the gush of blood and not get any on his clothes.

When the guard stopped thrashing, Ming did a quick check of the apartment—correction, of the penthouse suite, to make sure that he would be alone with the target. The place was amazingly clean, unnaturally so—rubbed, scrubbed and polished. He found that very interesting. So the target was a control freak, eh? Perhaps he could use that during the interrogation.

Just then, a door swung wide and bright light exploded across the living room.

Stepping into the shadows, Ming watched as the woman walked out of the bathroom. Her long black hair was held in place by an elastic scrunchy, she was wearing a silk nightgown that revealed every curve of her body, and she held a 9 mm Beretta tightly in her left fist.

However, Ming could see that the safety was still in place. She was concerned, but not frightened.

"Bohai?" she called out, advancing into the hallway.

That caught Ming totally by surprise, and it took him a moment to realize that the dead guard had to have the same name. "Bohai is dead," Ming said from the darkness.

That made her jump, and he charged.

As he appeared out of the darkness, she clicked off the safety of her pistol, but Ming got there before she could fire. He grabbed her arm to twist hard. The gun fired, the muzzle-flash stinging his cheek, but the slug missed, to smash a mirror on the wall. The pieces fell into a softly bubbling aquarium full of tiny fish.

Jerking the gun free, Ming tossed it away and crushed the woman close to check for more weapons. She would tell him all that she knew. Then she would die.

CHAPTER SIXTEEN

Fakkah, China

A few miles outside Canton, Ziu purchased some canaries at a small stall along the side of the road, while Bolan stayed with the new Geely SUV and kept watch for any hidden observers. The tinted windows cut down his visibility, so he cracked a window slightly.

If the town wasn't really dead, and the chemical spill was just a cover story, then the local canary dealers would be the best place to watch for unwanted guests. But the area was clear, and there were only a few workers in a nearby field weeding the rows of corn by hand. Bolan didn't think about corn, wheat, lettuce and such in conjunction with China. But logically, the nation had to have a massive agribusiness to feed a billion people.

"I also got lunch," Ziu announced, putting the twittering birds in the backseat of the car.

"Beef and broccoli?" he asked in jest.

"Southern fried chicken," she replied, patting the greasy paper bag.

"Any fries?"

"Fries?"

"Never mind." He chuckled, starting the engine.

Passing a shopping center full of tourists, Bolan stopped so that Ziu could make a few more purchases: fresh clothing, binoculars and some sports equipment, including a complete diving rig with pressurized air tanks. Bolan didn't know how well a scuba mask would work against poison gas, but it was all they could get on short notice. Hopefully, it wouldn't be necessary to test the apparatus.

IT WAS LATE in the afternoon when Bolan saw the exit for Fakkah. The turnoff had been permanently closed with a barricade of concrete dividers. There was no way around, so he kept driving and took every turn that went in the right direction. However, every road to Fakkah was closed, and at one point a railroad bridge was gone, the rushing river underneath filled with twisted steel beams.

"They blew the bridge," Ziu said, looking out the window and over the edge of the cliff.

"If there really was a toxic chemical spill," Bolan said, rubbing his jaw, "that would be a wise move. However…"

"Yes?"

He pointed. "Anything that deadly to humans would also kill most of the plants. At least for a little while. But I don't see any new growth, only old trees."

"You suspect the story about the spill was fabricated to chase people away?"

"Yes and no," he said, tuning off the engine and exiting the SUV.

Walking to a barricade, Bolan grabbed a fluttering piece of yellowed newspaper caught between two concrete dividers. Using a knife, he cut away much of the paper, but kept the banner along the top intact. Returning to the car, he passed the scrap of paper to Ziu through the window.

"Check the date," he said.

She did, and frowned. "I do not understand," she said. "This newspaper is from August five years ago. But the chemical spill happened in September…." She looked up with an anguished expression. "They sealed off the city, and then something happened to Fakkah?"

"Every weapon needs to be tested before combat," Bolan replied with a scowl. He had been expecting something like this.

"Oh Matt, he couldn't have! Not his own people!"

"Let's go see," Bolan replied, getting behind the wheel and starting the engine. "But I'm pretty sure that we're not going to need the scuba tanks, or the canaries."

Driving along the edge of the cliff, they encountered another destroyed bridge, and saw the river dotted with big chunks of broken concrete.

"The water is much more shallow here, and a lot slower," Bolan said, easing the SUV into some bushes. "We should be able to cross without too much trouble."

"I'll get the canaries," Ziu said, reaching into the backseat.

Stepping out of the vehicle, he snapped open a knife and started to cut off a branch. "Better not. The noise might give away our presence."

"To whom? You think there still might be guards?" Ziu demanded, leaning forward to look out the window.

He placed the leafy branch on top of the car and started on another bush. "Not human ones."

After a few moments, she grimly nodded and got out to help with the camouflage.

When the SUV was properly covered to avoid any aerial surveillance, they opened the trunk, got weapons and started for the river.

The grassy bank was slippery underfoot, but Bolan and Ziu made it down without taking a tumble. As they waded into the river, the rushing water rose only to their waists, but the current was strong and constantly tried to sweep them off their feet. Only the jumbled array of broken concrete offered any support, and both Bolan and Ziu were exhausted by the time they reached the other side. A field of tall grass gradually rose into a low hillock, the crest ragged with willow trees and wild rosebushes.

"Nothing in sight," Ziu reported, scanning the rolling landscape with the binoculars.

"Good. But stay alert for the sound of an electric fan," Bolan replied, checking over his weapons. The AutoMag was in a holster strapped to his waist, along with a Chinese-made combat knife. The silenced Glock rode in a shoulder holster, and the M-16 assault rifle was slung across his back. A lumpy war bag of spare ammunition hung off his shoulder, and binoculars were draped around his neck.

Ziu lowered her binoculars. "Is that what a UAV sounds like?"

"The American and British drones do."

"Good to know." The woman picked up a QBZ assault rifle and worked the arming bolt. Similar to the U.S. Army M-16, the Chinese weapon was a 5.56 mm machine gun, with a 35 mm grenade launcher attached underneath.

Dressed as if she was going camping, Ziu was wearing a brown fishing vest composed entirely of pockets, a dark flannel shirt, blue jeans and sneakers, her long hair tied in a ponytail. There was a pneumatic airgun holstered at her side, along with a combat knife, and a deadly 9 mm Norinco pistol in a shoulder holster. The massive Webley was tucked into another holster at the small of her back.

She had purchased the bulky airgun at a sports store that sold such things for paintball ranges, a current fad among the more affluent middle-class. Simply use a kitchen basting needle to add some epoxy glue to the fluorescent paint inside the balls, and they neutralized a security camera quickly and silently. The modified toy was an old and valued friend to the White Lotus Society.

"If we hear a drone, do we run or fight?" she asked, checking the ammunition magazine in the assault rifle.

"Both."

"Freeze!" she said harshly.

Instantly, Bolan stopped in his tracks and looked at where she was staring. There was a shallow hole in the ground, the earth freshly churned, and nearby were the splattered remains of what had most likely been a rabbit. Easing a hand into a pocket, he extracted the EM scanner and ran a fast check.

The readings were compatible with a standard Chinese land mine. Officially, the Communist government didn't make, have or use such devices, in accordance with a United Nations ban. Unofficially, the PLA had millions of the deadly antipersonnel devices stashed in armories around the country in case of an invasion.

"Are there any more of them?" Ziu asked, her hands white on the assault rifle.

"Plenty," Bolan answered, pressing a red button on the scanner. The device gave a low hum, and there came an answering click from under the soil. "However, I can deactivate them easily enough with a failsafe code."

"How could you possibly know... You expected these to be here," she said, tucking a loose strand of hair behind an ear.

"I would have been surprised if there weren't any land mines," he replied. "Shen-wa likes to fight from a distance, and China has millions of these in stock. They're a perfect match."

"Any chance that will work on a drone?"

"None whatsoever, unless Shen-wa is a fool."

"Unfortunately, that is one of the few things he is not," she replied with a grimace.

TAKING HIS TIME, Bolan found several more of the mines, and advanced slowly into the kill zone, carefully deactivating each one in turn. Ziu followed behind him, putting her boots into the impression of his footsteps. Just in case.

Reaching the rocky soil of the hillock, Bolan saw the scanner finally read clear. "Okay, we're safe from here on," he said, tucking away the device. "Just keep a sharp watch out for trip wires and deadfalls."

"Always do," she replied, studying the grass ahead of them as if it was crawling with deadly snakes.

Starting up the slope, Bolan tried to block out the sound of the river and listen for any sounds from the other side of the hill. But there was only an ominous silence.

Nearing the crest, he went flat on the ground and crawled the last few yards. Ziu stayed close to his side. Easing his way through the prickly bushes, Bolan carefully parted the fragrant leaves.

At first the little town of Fakkah seemed undamaged, then the terrible quiet hit him, and he knew the truth. This was a city of the dead. Wide swaths of farmland had clearly gone wild, with saplings battling one another for dominance in weedy fields. What looked like a soybean field was nearly choked with clumps of ivy, and grain silos were thickly covered with bird nests, something that would never be allowed to occur on a functioning farm.

The town of Fakkah itself was oddly still. The paved streets were full of potholes, and dotted with dirty cars stopped randomly in intersections, with more than a few crashed into the sides of buildings or wrapped around dented streetlamps.

Nothing moved, aside from a ragged Chinese flag

fluttering above the burned wreckage of what might have been a school, or possibly a courthouse. It was difficult to say for sure. Much of the town had been burned to the ground, whole sections of houses gone, as well as something large—a warehouse, or perhaps a market.

Oddly, there were no bodies on the sidewalks or on the pavement, but Bolan noted numerous piles of tattered rags. Bringing up the binoculars, he saw the rags were torn clothing, and lying scattered nearby were human bones, broken and gnawed clean of any trace of flesh. Just then, a pack of howling dogs raced into view around a movie theater, in hot pursuit of a small deer. They caught it on the front steps of a library and tore the screaming animal apart with their teeth. Red blood splashed across the granite steps, disturbing a pile of rags with a corroded rifle sticking out from amid the bones and boots.

Adjusting the focus of the binoculars, Bolan saw it was a bolt-action hunting rifle, but the boots looked military. That told a grim tale of civilians and soldiers fighting side by side. There were signs of combat everywhere: doors broken into homes, blast craters in the side of buildings where a missile had impacted, and the splintery stumps of trees surrounded by broken branches.

A nearby bush rustled.

"Two o'clock," Ziu said, reaching out from the leaves to point downward.

Looking in that direction, Bolan frowned. On the far side of the town was a large factory of some kind, the two tall brick chimneys rising above the destroyed community like the horns of a demon. There was no damage to the facility; the windows were intact and the outer fence still standing.

A metal door opened, and a man came out. He was wearing bright orange fatigues and had a pistol holstered at his hip. Looking about suspiciously, he pulled something out of a boot, then thumbed a match alive and lit a cigarette.

As the door closed, Bolan got a brief glimpse of working machinery, a conveyor belt and a lot more people in similar fatigues.

"No smoking allowed inside. That means delicate electronic equipment," Ziu whispered in a rush. "More land mines, or is this where they make the drones?"

"There's your answer at four o'clock," Bolan stated.

Moving her binoculars, Ziu inhaled sharply and a chill ran down her back. Off to the side of the building, where a parking lot should be located, was a wide stretch of pavement surrounded by a high barbed-wire fence. There were no cars in sight, only big cargo containers, row after row of them, spreading outward for acres.

"Those might be empty," she said.

"With no two containers stacked on top of each other?" Bolan retorted. "Take my word for it, those are live."

"Do you think Shen-wa is here?" the woman asked, looking hard at the factory, as if trying to pierce the brick walls with her eyes.

"There's no way to know for certain," Bolan answered, "but I'd say no. I don't read him as the type of man foolish enough to—"

"Keep all his eggs in one basket?"

"Exactly." He studied the acres of cargo containers. Some looked years old, rusty and streaked with dirt. Others seemed brand-new. "This must be his reserve army in case of trouble."

Suddenly, there was movement in the air above the parking lot—a small black object flying around the outer fence like a soldier on patrol.

"Damn!" Ziu muttered, then added a long curse in

Chinese, the words coming too fast for Bolan to keep track. "How many drones do you think the old bastard has built?"

"In five years?" Bolan grunted. "Too many."

"Hundreds?"

"Thousands, maybe more. The drones are only two yards across, while those containers are forty feet long by twenty feet wide. Do the math."

She did, and clearly didn't like the result. "With such an army, the major could take over China before attacking the rest of the world." Ziu sneered in open hatred. "Emperor Shen-wa! The godless Communists are bad enough, but with him in charge…" She gave a shudder. "What must be done?"

"We don't want to reveal our presence yet. We need to get inside that factory. If the drones are remote-controlled, then the communication chips must be preset before installation. If we could get one, we might be able to backtrack the command signals and find out where Shen-wa is located. Then we take the fight to him."

"An excellent plan, but how do we get inside?" Ziu asked, as another drone came into view, flying behind the first over the parking lot. "There are wild dogs in the streets, drones in the air, armed guards and steel doors. That factory is a fortress!"

"Yes, it is," Bolan said slowly. "Okay, we make the drones come to us, instead."

"And then what?"

"Come on, I'll show you," he answered, crawling backward out of the bushes.

A FEW MINUTES LATER, a thunderous explosion shook the trees and bushes on top of the hillock, twigs and leaves blowing high into the sky.

Immediately, one of the drones on patrol around the parking lot changed course and streaked over to investigate. Following a thin plume of smoke, the drone paused to hover alongside a copse of willow trees. Sprawled on the churned ground was the splayed body of an armed woman, her chest covered with blood and guts.

As the drone turned around to look for any companions, there was a motion in a tree, and Bolan dived out with a knife in each hand. Landing on the drone, he plunged the steel shafts directly into the louvered vents of the turbofans. Instantly, the spinning blades jammed, and the drone dropped heavily to the ground with a dull thud.

Rolling off the machine, Bolan got clear just as it started to slide down the grassy slope. He landed in a crouch, with the Glock in his hands. As the drone began to build speed, an antenna popped up from the armored hull, and the Executioner shot it off with a 9 mm round, the sound generated by the silenced weapon no louder than a hard cough. Struggling to take flight again, the damaged drone was just revving its engine to full power when the ground underneath violently erupted.

Broken pieces of the machine scattered, some bouncing along to set off other land mines, while a lone wing made it intact all the way down the hill to splash into the foamy river.

The noise of the explosion was still echoing when Bolan lurched into action. Using the EM scanner, he deactivated the other land mines as fast as possible, going from one piece of wreckage to another, grabbing anything electronic and stuffing it into an empty canvas bag.

Just then, there came the soft whir of an electric fan, and a second drone appeared over the crest.

With the gun ready in her hand, Ziu cut loose with a

stream of paintballs. The first few missed, but the rest splattered across the front of the armored craft.

Quickly retreating, the Sky Tiger blindly fired back with both 4.45 mm caseless machine guns, the barrage ripping a shallow trench in the dirt where Ziu had just been, and chewing bark off several willow trees.

On the move, Ziu fired another flurry of multicolored paintballs, and the drone backed away more, then started to spin very fast until it was a blur. Some of the fluorescent paint came loose, but the epoxy kept most of it in place, the spin only smearing the paint more evenly across the bulletproof eyes of the deadly war machine. Then Ziu dived to the side and tumbled down the slope of the grassy hillock.

Suddenly, an antenna popped up from the armored hull of the drone, and a split second later the machine violently exploded. The writhing fireball extended for several yards, and a halo of shrapnel shook the trees and bushes.

Reaching the bottom of the hill, Ziu paused to brush the guts of the dead rabbit off her shirt. Something hummed past her cheek just then, and she felt a warm liquid trickle downwards.

Galvanized back into motion, she dived into the rushing river and fought her way to the other side. A centimeter was as good as a klick, as her father always said.

Bolan was waiting on the opposite bank with the M-16 balanced in his hands. "Any damage?" he demanded, not looking at her. His eyes stayed on the sky above the hillock, a finger resting on the trigger of the 40 mm grenade launcher.

"Nothing serious," she muttered, slogging up the muddy bank. "Did you get the chip?"

He gave a curt nod. "Yes, let's go."

"Where?" she asked suspiciously, looking at the war bag hanging at his side.

Still keeping a close watch on the sky, Bolan started quickly for the hidden SUV. "To the nearest Red Star office to hijack a computer and hack their signal."

Ziu almost stumbled at that, but kept going, her face rigidly blank, her thoughts private.

As Bolan pulled away the cut pieces of bushes, the woman got into the vehicle and shifted into neutral. He started to push, and the car began to roll along the ground, gradually increasing in speed. Immediately, the soldier burst into a full sprint, and Ziu threw open the passenger-side door. With the car moving ever faster, the timing was tight, but he managed to get inside and pull the door shut just as a Sky Tiger appeared over the hillock.

Hovering in place, it stayed close to the wreckage of the destroyed drone, as two more appeared, then a dozen arrived to form a defensive line around the downed machine.

"They don't want somebody to steal any of the pieces," Ziu whispered, straining to steer the powerless car. It was moving at a fair clip by now, the trees flashing past and the soft ground crunching under the tires.

"Too late." Bolan patted the bag lying on the front seat. "I have most of the motherboard right here."

"Most?"

"We don't need anything more."

A curve in the dirt road took them out of sight of the hillock, but Ziu still kept the vehicle rolling along until the ground became level and their speed slowed. Reluctantly, she started the engine. With the paintball gun in his lap, Bolan kept a sharp watch on the sky for any movement, as she took a turn and drove back to the paved road.

"Are they going to attack?" she asked, effortlessly

merging into the flow of sparse traffic. There was only one other car in sight, and a ramshackle truck carrying stacks of wooden crates full of squawking chickens.

"Not without a clear target," Bolan said, shifting the paintball gun to his right hand and pulling the M-16 assault rifle closer.

"Then it's a good thing the windows are tinted," Ziu said with a smile. "Because you look about as Chinese as the American President!"

"Maybe even less." Bolan chuckled, loosening the AutoMag in his holster. "But my concern is that Shen-wa might have them attack every car in sight, purely as a precautionary measure."

Her smile vanished. "Hopefully he is not yet ready to start openly killing civilians."

"If he does," Bolan replied grimly, "just drive as fast as you can for a forest, and leave the rest to me."

The drones stayed on the horizon for quite a while, with more appearing, as if individually following everything on the country road. Trying to remain inconspicuous, Ziu did her best to match the speeds of the other vehicles.

"I've also been thinking about Shen-wa," she continued. "Since he does not know about us, the Red Star will be considered his greatest threat to success. So what are the chances that he has not already had the drones pound their headquarters, and every major field office, into the dirt?"

Bolan considered that. "You're probably right," he admitted. "Okay, where else can we get access to a supercomputer good enough to read the communications chip?"

"No problem. I can easily steal—ahem, obtain—a laptop for you. Or even a mainframe, if it is necessary."

"No good. When the motherboard goes hot, the ident chip will probably fry a split second later."

She frowned. "So we need a computer that can read the chip in a microsecond."

"A millisecond would be better."

"Then head north, toward Changsta," she replied proudly.

"If you're thinking about a university, I can't use it," he stated. "There would be too many civilians."

"Then how about the First Bank of China, owned and operated by the Tong," she said. "They're the Chinese Mafia, you know."

"Never heard of them," he lied with a straight face. "You sure the bank has a supercomputer?"

"Positive." Ziu smiled. "The bank is where the Tong... wash their money?"

"Launder."

She nodded. "Yes, launder. The White Lotus Society has been planning on hitting it someday to cripple their operations." She looked sideways. "And perhaps steal a billion or two."

"No harm in that. Do you know the layout?"

"Intimately."

"Then it sounds perfect."

Soon, the paved road merged with a busy concrete highway full of cars, vans, trucks and motorcycles. Ziu slipped between a couple of Great Wall trucks, the big eighteen-wheelers hauling pieces of a mobile house and concrete bridge abutments.

"They're not a forest," she muttered, flexing her hands, "but it'll do for now."

Never taking his sight off the black specks in the rearview mirror, Bolan grunted in agreement.

Slowly, the long miles passed, and eventually the drones fell behind to became lost from sight.

CHAPTER SEVENTEEN

Baffin Bay, Arctic Circle

Rising high and fast on deafening columns of flame and smoke, ICBMs launched from concealed underground silos in the United States, Canada, the United Kingdom, France, India and Russia.

Arching high above the Earth, the missiles breached the atmosphere and touched the hard vacuum of space, before angling back down and streaking in toward their assigned target.

Alarms sounded all over the world, and a score of nations began scrambling their jet fighters in preparation for war. Fleets of ships surged across the oceans, and submarines rose to start broadcasting on every possible wavelength. Within minutes, the internet slowed to a crawl, choked with the flood of frantic email messages, the servers for social media sites crashed, cell phone usage reached an all-time high and the commercial airwaves exploded with endless news reports denying everything.

Unnoticed amid the worldwide turmoil, a lone B2 stealth bomber taxied along the runway at a small NATO airbase outside of Brussels, and lifted off into a drizzly gray sky.

At Baffin Bay near the Arctic Circle, the quivering antenna jutting from the *Glucksstern* suddenly went still as it detected the disturbance high in the stratosphere. Instantly, the remaining cargo containers blew off their lids, and swarms of Sky Tiger drones poured forth to streak toward the heavens.

As the ICBMs began to converge on the rusty freighter, the Chinese drones cut loose with everything they carried: rockets, missiles, chaff and flares, the 4.45 mm caseless machine guns firing continuously, filling the air with a wall of high-velocity lead.

One ICBM veered away, then another. Two exploded. Then the drones ran out of ammunition, and triggered their emergency JATO rockets, accelerating so fast they almost tore themselves apart. Dozens of the drones rammed headlong into the descending international barrage, battering every missile aside and causing two of them to crash into each other.

Spewing fire and smoke, the wildly tumbling missiles crashed randomly into the vast polar ice fields, their assorted warheads thunderously detonating. Writhing fireballs dotted the frozen landscape, blowing gaping holes in the thick ice cap, and shattering mountains of compressed snow back into their primordial components.

However, no mushroom clouds formed above the furious explosions. The use of nuclear weapons in that area would have spread radioactive contamination across the oceans of the world, and eventually killed millions of people along the coastlines. The dreaded thermonuclear warheads had been wisely replaced by more conventional explosives: TNT, Bermex, C-4, thermite, and the ever-reliable fulminating guncotton.

Tons of ice and snow were thrown high, and there soon formed a monstrous blizzard that blanketed Baffin Bay until it was no longer possible to tell the land from the sky.

In perfect timing, the NATO stealth bomber crested the horizon and instantly launched a full salvo of Tomahawk missiles, then another and another until the bomb bay was empty. Banking away fast, the stealth bomber angled sharply upward as the cruise missiles separated to flash toward the shuddering landscape. Streaking around the cracking mountains and melting glaciers, the Tomahawks zoomed in toward the defenseless German freighter from a dozen different angles.

As they got within visible range, the last cargo container automatically triggered, and a blast of inert argon gas propelled a stolen Russian thermobaric bomb out of the hold. The NATO missiles were only meters away when the charge cleared the deck and detonated.

The initial blast partially melted the freighter, then the Tomahawks knifed into the lambent fireball, and their own warheads ignited, quadrupling the staggering force of the volcanic outpouring to effectively vaporize the German ship and everything in the hold.

Already weakened from the ICBMs, the arctic cap shattered into jagged shards, icebergs flying away like snowflakes. The volcanic shock wave rumbled across the top of the world, smashing aside mountains and splintering glaciers, supercompressed ice that hadn't moved in a hundred millennium. Orbiting mil sats and spy satellites registered the flash, and the crew of the International Space Station blinked at the unexpected diamond-point of blinding white light.

Slowly, the gargantuan forces began to dissipate, and soon there was nothing remaining of Baffin Bay but churning waves and a few lingering traces of ionized vapor.

Changsha, China

KEEPING HER EYES on the road, Ziu drove the SUV through the early morning traffic. She missed not having

Matt at her side, but this was something she had to do alone. It was funny how quickly she had become used to having him near. She still ached at the loss of Eugene, and would mourn for him when this was over. But at the moment there was work to be done.

There were no rickshaws, bicycles or even motorcycles in this part of the town, only expensive cars, many of them driven by a chauffeur. The Geely SUV looked horribly out of place among the streams of much more expensive BMWs, Jaguars, Cadilliacs, Porsche, and other imported vehicles. However, all vehicles had tinted windows, so that helped to some small degree.

Parking behind the People's Library, Ziu used the key-wire gun to open the service entrance. Slipping inside, she locked it again and descended to the basement. The stairs were a freckled terrazzo, and the cinder-block walls painted a soothing green. The air was cool down there, dry and clean, the stacks of books as neatly regimented as a chessboard. The metal bookcases were filled with extra copies of popular novels, new volumes not yet processed, and old textbooks waiting to be trashed. She found it amusing to think that information could became defunct over time. The Soviet Union had fallen, Pluto was no longer a planet, and anything dealing with making high explosives in your kitchen had been declared strictly forbidden. Oh sure, she knew that most of the information was available on the internet. But she also knew a lot of that was deliberately wrong, the chemical formulas scrambled by intelligence agencies around the world. Any attempt to homebrew TNT using that recipe would end with the amateur chemist lying on the floor in a pool of his or her own blood, coughing until merciful death finally ended an unimaginable agony.

There were no security cameras in the library basement,

as none of the material was particularly valuable. Stopping at the maintenance room, Ziu went inside to clip a black box onto a shielded cable, then did the same thing to the telephones lines. Closing the door behind her, she then squirted epoxy glue into the lock so that nobody could get inside again without considerable effort. Then she went directly to the security office and eased open the door, stun gun at the ready.

An elaborate control board filled half the room, a double row of monitors showing different aspects of the library above, including the roof and parking lot. Reclining in an office chair, a uniformed guard was puffing contentedly on a hand-rolled cigarette, the sweet Colombian smoke rising high into an exhaust vent. Nearby was an open box of fried rice and a thermos. The guard didn't hear Ziu enter, as he was intently watching a woman in the lavatory adjust her panty hose.

"Pervert," Ziu said in disgust, thrusting the stun gun hard against his neck.

The guard started to turn at the contact, then jerked wildly for a few seconds as 50,000 volts coursed though his body, and promptly collapsed to the floor, the joint falling from his slack mouth.

Grinding out the joint with the heel of her boot, Ziu checked to make sure the unconscious guard was still breathing, then bound his wrists and ankles with duct tape, sealed his mouth and rolled him into a corner.

Slipping into the warm chair, she started to flip switches, and the scenes on the video monitors abruptly changed from pictures inside the library to different views around the city. She had no guide, so was working purely on guesswork and luck, but she soon found Bolan lounging against the brick wall of a closed amusement park. There was nobody else in the vicinity except for a girl sweeping the street and an old man just opening the door to a small café.

"White online," she crisply reported into a throat mike, turning on the transponder clipped to her belt. "I can see you, Black. Everything is clear. You are good to go."

There was no response.

"White to Black, do you copy?" There was only the soft hiss of static.

Frowning, she adjusted the controls and tried again.

SIPPING A PAPER CUP of surprisingly good coffee, Bolan leaned against the brick exterior of the Grand Ballroom, a thumb tucked into his belt to keep a hand close to the Glock under his brown uniform windbreaker.

The morning air carried hints of fish, beer, diesel fumes and cotton candy. But mostly it just smelled of fried food. It didn't really matter where he was, every amusement park smelled the same. Whether serving corn dogs, French fries, egg rolls or falafel, there was always the heavy aroma of hot peanut oil. The air tasted fried. Now, there was a slogan for the Travel Channel.

A long row of flagpoles edged the brick pier, the flag of China snapping loudly in the cool breeze. The ornate safety railing was made of wrought iron, in a classic design of cherry blossoms. Past the stone breakers, a hundred sailboats dotted the choppy water of the river, a sleek People's Liberation Army patrol boat clearing the way for a Dutch cruise ship large enough to alter the local weather patterns. There was a helicopter parked on the top deck, alongside a carousel, right next to the putting green.

Briefly, Bolan wondered if Shen-wa was staying mobile, then decided against it. His read was that the old man liked to operate from the shadows, so he'd be deep inside something big—an abandoned missile base, deserted coal mine, something like that. Maybe even a deserted prison. Those also made the best bolt-holes.

Masked by the rising dawn, Bolan felt relatively safe standing out in the open with his back against one of the brick walls flanking the side entrance to the Changsha amusement park. Freshly washed, the shiny streets were deserted at this hour, aside from a few wandering pedestrians.

"—an you hear me?" Ziu asked suddenly through his earbud.

"Confirm, White, loud and clear," Bolan softly subvocalized into a throat mike. "I was starting to get worried. What took so long?"

"I must have bumped the transponder and changed frequencies. Sorry."

He glanced at an armored surveillance camera set on a pole thirty feet high. "Are you in the city system?" he asked.

The camera swung his way, then moved up and down, as if nodding yes. "No problem." She laughed. "I told you we do this all the time back in Canton. There are no police or military in the area. Everything is green."

"Good to know, thanks," he said, walking over to a fancy brick trash can and disposing of the coffee cup. "From here onward, don't say anything unless there's trouble."

"Confirm, Black. I wouldn't jiggle your elbow," she said seriously. "I've got your six. Good luck."

Just then, a bell rang, sounding remarkably similar to the famous Wall Street gong. Doors opened everywhere, and suddenly the sidewalks were flooded with hurrying people in business suits, all of them carrying briefcases. Tucking a clipboard under his arm, Bolan thought it resembled the running of the bulls in Pamplona, only this crowd was being chased by a time clock.

Waiting for the traffic light to change, Bolan dutifully crossed the street at the corner with everybody else. Adjusting his new sunglasses, the soldier warily studied the downtown skyscrapers. He was trying to remain covert by wearing the brown cap and jacket of a delivery service company, and carrying a clipboard. There was nothing he could do about his height, but the sunglasses hid his eyes, which helped to some small degree.

The main street was divided in two by a long median that was decorated with a small waterfall and rows of flowers. Pretending to check the clipboard, Bolan paused for a moment to look over the downtown buildings. Most were made of brick, five or ten stories tall, and each looked brand-new, as if the city had been built yesterday. But rising majestically amid them was a massive glass-and-steel skyscraper, eighty stories high. The morning sun gleamed off the mirrored windows, casting a reddish light across the city, as if it were painted in blood.

"Is that it?" Bolan asked softly, adjusting his collar.

"Confirm. The First Bank of China. Watch your ass."

"Always do," he replied, and started that way.

The lobby of the building was cool and crisp, the atmosphere tingling with the unseen aura of raw financial power. In controlled chaos, business executives were rushing about in orderly streams, sipping tea from paper cups while talking on cell phones.

Red carpet runners stretched across the blue marble floor, connecting the front revolving door to the elevator bank, the newsstand to the reception desk, like electronic circuits. Rivers of motion, they channeled a steady flow of humanity that never seemed to slow, much less stop.

A uniformed police officer was chatting with a pretty

woman in pink leg-warmers at the news stand. She was opening a fresh stack of newspapers and lying them out for the customers. People tossed coins into a plastic bowl and grabbed one without even slowing.

"The headline reads Glorious news!" Ziu said over the radio. "Xiban Prison Demolished Because There Is Such Low Crime in Central China."

Yeah, right, he thought, spotting the reception desk.

Starting that way, Bolan stayed on the red carpeting to not draw any attention. According to Ziu, her sources said that the Tong operated here under the business name Global Financial, and occupied the top five floors of the skyscraper, including a heliport on the roof.

The location of the Tong supercomputer had never been in doubt once Ziu mentioned there was a helicopter that a ground crew worked on every day, but it never went anywhere. That cinched it for him. Supercomputers were kept cold with a steady stream of liquid nitrogen. The exhaust fumes were harmless, but considerable, and government spy satellites could easily spot a hidden supercomputer by the thick plume of nitrogen gas escaping—unless there was a really big fan to disperse the cloud, such as a broken-down helicopter that was always being repaired. Back in Washington, D.C., the exhaust fumes of the machines used by the IRS, DOD and numerous other departments and agencies were vented to Georgetown University and mixed with the rising vapors from their much touted IBM Blue/Gene supercomputer. Hidden in plain sight. However, there was no way knowing if the Tong's machine was on the top floor, or a lower level, and the exhaust was simply vented up to the helicopter for dispersal.

"Okay, you're out of sight," Ziu said. "It's audio only now."

Sauntering to the reception desk, Bolan grunted in

reply. The listing of companies was in Chinese, English and Arabic. Global Financial did indeed fill all the top floors, with International Exports just under them, but the seventy-eighth floor was occupied by several small companies in private suites. Civilians would work there.

The reception desk looked like something out of the *Star Trek* movies, while the woman behind the counter looked like something out of Chinese *Vogue*.

She was tightly bound in a formfitting dress. Flat shoes encased her feet and ankles, and her red hair was pulled painfully back in a tight bun. She looked ready to have an Egyptian priest administer the tana leaves to finish the mummification process. Her nails were long and a deep red. Her bracelets matched her necklace, which matched her earrings.

As he stopped in front, the woman politely asked something in Mandarin.

"English, please, dear lady," Bolan replied in as thick a British accent as he could muster. Hong Kong and mainland China did a lot of business together, and everybody knew a few key phrases.

"My apologies," she answered smoothly in perfect diction. "How may I assist you today?"

"Hassan Properties?" he asked, glancing up at the listing and pretending to be confused.

"Suite four, on the seventy-eighth floor," she replied crisply, and turned to assist somebody else.

"What was that about?" Ziu asked as he walked away. "You could read the board."

Pausing for a moment, Bolan checked his clipboard. "No, that's no good," he muttered in annoyance, and continued onward.

"Understood," she replied in his earbud.

Going to a private elevator, Bolan pressed the call

button, and the door opened to reveal a beefy security guard. Clearly Asian, he was taller and wider than Bolan. His uniform had trouble containing his body, and his huge arms almost too muscular to fit in the sleeves. His black hair was oiled flat to his head, his shoes were polished to a mirror shine and a flesh-colored wire snaked out of his shirt to an earbud. There was a collapsible French police baton clipped to his belt, along with a military-style stun gun and a holstered Glock pistol.

He growled something in Mandarin.

"Can I help you, sir?" Ziu translated.

"Huh? Oh, sorry," Bolan said, and walked quickly over to the public elevator.

As he rode it to the top floor, people got on and off constantly, but he was finally alone for a moment.

"What was that about?" Ziu asked curiously.

"Wanted to see if guards wore body armor," Bolan said into the throat mike, turning his back to the security camera mounted in the corner of the cage. Turning again, he pretended to check the documents attached to his clipboard.

"Do they?"

"Yes."

"Is that trouble?"

"Only for them."

Continuing in silence, Bolan rode to the seventy-first floor and got off. The corridor was lined with offices, the frosted glass walls bearing small placards with the name of each company in three languages. Going to the end of the hallway, the soldier waited until nobody was in sight, then used the keywire gun to trick the lock on the exit and slip through.

The stairs were cold and slightly dusty from lack of use, which was as they should be, but Bolan used the EM scanner anyway, to check for proximity sensors or hidden video cameras. At the seventy-fourth floor, he found the stairs blocked by a locked gate, but once more the keywire gun removed the minor obstacle. However, there was another locked gate at the seventy-fifth floor, this time with a video camera on the other side.

Staying low, Bolan studied the motion of the device as it swept back and forth, covering the entire landing. As it moved past the gate, he stepped forward and unlocked it with the keywire gun, then sank back out of sight. On the next pass, he went through the gate and gently closed it, then hid under the stairs once more. On the following pass, he went back to lock the gate and then proceeded up the stairs.

At the next floor, he touched the fire door. It felt cool, nothing more. So did those on the next three floors, but the door to the eightieth level was very cold. Not icy, but a lot colder than the others. Checking for proximity sensors, this time he found nothing. However, the keypad proved to be a fake, merely attached to the wall near the door, but not wired to anything. On a hunch, he checked the latch and discovered that it was just welded in place. Another fake. There was no way to open the door from his side.

Studying the situation for a few moments, Bolan finally drew a knife and began running it carefully along the seam between the door and the steel jamb, cutting away the insulation. Soon he had a small pile of the stuff on the floor, and a steady cold breeze blew around the door.

Now he waited.

It was almost half an hour before he heard angry muttering from the other side of the door, and it opened wide. A young woman in a fur parka stood there, holding a thermograph scanner in her gloved hands. She gasped at the sight of Bolan, and he took her out with the stungun.

With the Glock at the ready, he eased inside and glanced around fast. He was in a small room full of liquid nitrogen tanks, white vapors rising from the hoses that connected to the complex-looking valves on top. A rack of fur parkas and gloves stood alongside a clear wall of polycarbonate, and on the other side were multiple rows of blade servers surrounded by swirling clouds of white fog. Bingo.

More important, there was nobody in sight.

Hauling the unconscious woman inside, he closed the fire door. Taking the key card from her, Bolan donned a parka, then passed the card over a blank metal pad on the transparent door. It hummed, then unlocked and slid into the wall.

Stepping through quickly, he heard the door slide shut behind as he proceeded directly to a line of workstations. All were empty, but one had a steaming cup of tea near the keyboard, and a black leather purse hung off the back of the chair.

Sitting in the chair, Bolan almost jumped out again as it began to mold itself to his frame, and then vibrate softly, massaging his shoulders.

"How are things outside?" he whispered, deactivating a couple of firewalls. The words were visible in the air, the room was so cold.

"All clear, no unusual activity," Ziu reported crisply.

Grunting in reply, he accessed the internet and went to a website maintained by the cyberteam at Stony Man Farm. He downloaded a tracer program, set it running, then pulled the broken piece of circuit board from his pocket and connected it to a USB port.

"Here we go," he whispered, tapping a button on the keyboard.

"Good luck!" Ziu replied.

Just for a moment, nothing happened. Then the circuit

board gave a puff of smoke, and the chips cracked. Checking the monitor, Bolan saw the program had worked, and he pulled up the coordinates to the source of the self-destruct signal. Central China…Yangtze River…

"He's at the Three Gorges Dam," Bolan whispered.

Ziu gave a low whistle. "That's the biggest dam in the world. You could hide an army inside the place!"

"I think that's the idea," he noted, emailing the data with a personal note to Brognola.

Deleting everything, Bolan tucked the useless circuit board back into his pocket, and was starting to leave when a door opened and a guard stepped into the cloudy room. He blinked in surprise, and the Executioner fired the Glock, putting two rounds into the man's rib cage. He heard the dull thwack of the soft lead smacking into body armor, and the guard doubled over, gasping for breath.

Pulling out the stun gun, Bolan started to approach the guard when the man straightened with a Norinco pistol in his hand.

Diving forward, Bolan jammed the stungun against the man's bare ankle and pressed the button. The guard convulsed from the brutal surge of electricity, and the pistol dropped to the floor. Then the guard collapsed on top of it, almost as if he did so deliberately.

With a growing sense of unease, Bolan rolled the guard over and scowled. The gun was made of thin plastic, the interior jammed full of electronic circuits and a mercury pressure switch. He recognized it instantly as a Dead Man, a fake weapon designed to be thrown away in surrender, which would then send out a radio signal to trigger a silent alarm.

"They know I'm here," Bolan snarled, heading for the exit. "We're going to plan B!"

"Confirm! Meet you at the rendezvous point."

Even though the numbers were falling, Bolan took the time to yank random blade units from the servers and smash them on the floor. He had a grenade, but this close to the liquid nitrogen tanks the blast would almost definitely rupture them and kill everybody on the entire floor, including the unconscious technician. She might know who her real employer was, but then again, she might not. Bolan had sworn a long time ago never to kill an innocent person.

Once past the plastic door, he used the AutoMag to smash the card swipe, then placed the grenade carefully on top of a pressurized canister of liquid nitrogen. The guards would have to go slow, and check everywhere for traps before continuing after him. Depending on how good they were at the job, that could buy him two, maybe three minutes. Not much time, but just enough if his luck held.

Heading directly to the roof, Bolan used the AutoMag on the electric motor inside the phony helicopter. It shorted out, then burst into flames. Something else to occupy the attention of the guards.

Going to the southwest corner, the soldier allowed himself a brief smile at the sight of the window washer rig still in place. Climbing onto the platform, he worked the controls and sent the rig hurtling down the outside of the skyscraper as fast as possible. The coils of rope hissed as they unfurled, and he tried not think about what would happen if the guards discovered his method of escape and simply used a pocketknife to cut the anchor rope.

A few harrowing minutes later, Bolan saw the sidewalk approach and waited until the very last moment before applying the brakes. He bounced to a halt just above the concrete, and hopped out to walk away quickly. At the first alley, he turned out of sight and started to run.

A second later, the window washer platform suddenly dropped the last couple of inches to loudly crash on the sidewalk. Then an endless length of braided rope began to tumble down from above and pile around the rig.

CHAPTER EIGHTEEN

The Badlands, North Dakota

Coming to a complete stop above the fluffy clouds, two Dragonfire drones dropped straight down through the clouds to land on a flat-topped mesa in the middle of the Badlands.

The barren landscape stretched for miles in every direction, and there were no outposts, settlements, roads or camps. Only endless acres of hard sand, rocks and cacti. Desolation extended to the horizon and beyond. The closest town was Fargo, hundreds of miles away.

Turning off their rumbling engines, the drones switched to battery power, and robotic cables snaked out of the hulls to start vacuuming up piles of windblown sand. The material came out vents positioned on the back of the machines, and soon their angular black armor was covered with sand, completely hiding them from any possible aerial observation.

According to the battle plan, the other three Dragonfire drones were similarly hidden at remote locations in Scotland, Siberia and Afghanistan, close enough to their assigned targets to be able to strike within minutes, but far removed from any possible chance of accidental discovery.

With the infinite patience of a machine, the drones waited to receive further orders, their deadly cargo of

Chinese nuclear bombs in the holds primed and ready to go at a moment's notice.

Three Gorges Dam, China

DURING THE LONG plane flight away from the city, Bolan and Ziu caught up on some lost sleep, and then had breakfast at a pancake house at the airport terminal.

"Lots of chain restaurants in China?" he asked, liberally pouring syrup over his buckwheat waffles. This was going to be a long day, and he would need fuel for the inner man.

"Such as waffle houses?" she asked with a laugh. "Why yes, of course. More and more."

"Not very traditional."

She dismissed that with a wave. "That is the old China. Today, if something is good, or useful, then we incorporate it into our society."

"All the while ignoring copyrights and patents."

"True. But has America ever thanked Greece for inventing democracy?" she asked, daintily wiping her mouth clean.

"The check is in the mail," Bolan replied with a straight face, then ruined the effect by smiling.

She laughed in return, then the two of them got busy discussing the details for the work ahead. First and foremost, they were going to need some modeling clay, and a small fire extinguisher.

After making some vital purchases, Bolan and Ziu rented a Hoover-TT van with four-wheel traction and drove the final hundred miles to the colossal dam. Several times the size of Hoover Dam in Colorado, even at this distance the Three Gorges Dam rose before them like a truncated mountain. There were plenty of signs, but nobody had to tell them this was the largest man-made structure in the world, aside from the Great Wall.

A sprawling parkland surrounded the hydroelectric facility, with a casino and several hotels. There was boating, swimming and water skiing in the placid lake, but the wild Yangtze River below was reserved for commercial shipping traffic and fishing.

Keeping a careful watch on the crowds of people, Bolan couldn't spot anybody who seemed to be watching the flow of new arrivals. That didn't mean they weren't under observation, it just meant that the Red Star operatives were very good, or more likely, keeping an eye on the civilians through a long-distance telescope.

Trying to blend in with the rest of the tourists, Bolan was wearing a Hawaiian shirt, white pants and deck shoes, along with the mandatory wraparound sunglasses. Ziu was in a white summer dress that showed off her figure and legs to full advantage. Both of them were also wearing shiny gold wedding bands, a decadent Western tradition that affluent Chinese couples had been emulating in recent years.

In the rear of the Hoover-TT was a picnic basket, bulky camera bags and some camping gear, most of it manufactured by Colt, Smith & Wesson and Glock.

"Remember that as honeymooners we need to appear in love," he said, patting her bare thigh.

"Just don't get carried away, dear." She smiled, twisting his hand away in a martial arts move, then sweetly kissing him on the cheek.

"Tough love, eh?" Bolan chuckled.

"Something wrong?" she asked, touching the scarf around her neck.

"No, just admiring the view," he said, looking out the window.

As the van was passing the public lavatories just at that moment, she frowned, clearly puzzled. Then her face brightened in understanding, and she demurely shifted the hem of the dress a little higher.

Just then, a helicopter flew into view overhead to land on top of the dam, and almost immediately departed again, receding into the distance.

"Somebody just arrived," Ziu said, sealing the plastic bag around her pistols.

Grimly, Bolan nodded and drove a little faster. Suddenly, he had a very bad feeling about the mission and decided to take out some insurance. "Any chance you could call the Central Military Committee and ask them to raid the dam?"

"Unlikely, at best," Ziu replied with a snort, then she slowly smiled. "However, I can ask one of my people call the Ministry of State Security to report that they have found a hidden weapons cache for the White Lotus Society. That will warrant a military recon, and when the drones arrive to kill them, the CMC will send in a battalion to invade!"

"Or simply bomb the dam out of existence," he added. "But either way, we should have enough time to finish the job."

She waited expectantly.

"Make the call," he said.

Pulling out a cell phone, she started tapping buttons.

Taking the right fork in the main road, Bolan drove the van down a serpentine route to the riverside camping spots, the loose gravel softly crunching under the tires. Bypassing the more popular areas, Bolan choose an isolated lot in a well-secluded area with many surrounding trees and bushes.

This was a couples-only section of the campgrounds, as

any type of normal conversation was flatly impossible. Ten of the center vents in the dam were open at the moment, the rushing streams of lake water creating a nonstop roar as they arched away to cascade down into the turbulent river. The spray filled the air with a fine mist, and several rainbows were visible in the early morning sunlight.

"This will do fine," Bolan said, turning off the engine. The noise from the dam was a palpable presence even inside the vehicle.

"I wonder why so many people visit a waterfall for their honeymoon," Ziu said casually, adjusting the throat mike hidden under a flowery scarf.

"It's probably the adrenaline rush of being so close to something so overwhelmingly powerful," he said, increasing the volume on his earbud.

"I know the feeling," she said, not looking anywhere in particular. But if he heard the remark, there was no indication.

Gathering their bags and backpacks, Bolan and Ziu strolled away from the campsite and meandered into the trees. Once they were out of sight, they took off toward the river, hopping a low fence and climbing down a steep embankment to reach an access road blocked with a barbed wire fence. Bolan kept guard while Ziu picked the lock on the gate. Then they slipped through and locked it behind them.

The gentle patter of rain had been added to the rumble of the multiple waterfalls, and they were soon drenched to the skin from the cold spray. From this location, they had an excellent view of the dam and river. On the far bank, a hulking elevator was slowly hauling an oil tanker up to the lake on top of the dam, while on the opposite side, another elevator was steadily lowering a barge heavily loaded with freshly cut trees.

After sprinting along a concrete road for a while, the pair clambered over a safety railing made of iron, and slipped on their backsides the last few yards to reach the edge of the water.

Unpacking their bags, Bolan and Ziu strapped on their scuba tanks and made sure that their weapons and equipment were secure and watertight. They would get only one chance at this.

"What if they open the valve while we're inside?" Ziu asked, checking the mouthpiece and hose of the pressurized tanks.

"Then it's been nice knowing you," Bolan answered, spitting into his mask to prevent fogging. "Shen-wa knew in advance that sooner or later somebody was going to try to get inside, so every possible entrance will be heavily guarded. But he wouldn't be expecting this."

"Who the hell would?" she said with a grimace, tucking a combat knife into a sheath.

Slipping into the shallows, Bolan and Ziu turned on the flashlights strapped to their wrists, then ducked underwater and started swimming upriver. Within moments, they were in a vicious downstream current, and it took everything they had to keep going. But eventually, they found a large circular opening and managed to swim inside.

The tug of the currents eased immediately, and they had a much easier job swimming. In the bobbing lights, they could see the metal walls of the tube, and followed the gentle upward curve of it until they broke the surface again.

Keeping a grip on the Glock machine pistol inside a sealed plastic bag, Bolan warily looked around the black interior of the tube, while Ziu checked out her Norinco. They had been unable to obtain a proper sound suppressor for her pistol, but she had cobbled together a homemade version with a piece of PVC pipe, duct tape and a lot of steel wool. It would work for only one or two shots, but that was better than nothing.

Taking out her mouthpiece, she grinned. "You were right," she said through the throat mike. "Look, right over there—climbing rings!"

"Standard safety precaution for any sloping metal surface," Bolan said, tucking the Glock into his belt before swimming closer to the wall. "Oil rigs, battleships, there's always something for the workers to hang on to in case of trouble."

"Very considerate of the major to provide them," Ziu said, clipping on her own rig.

"More likely it was the Beijing architects who designed the installation," he said, snapping a clip onto the ring, then hauling himself out of the water. The incline wasn't very steep this close to the river, but he knew it would get a lot worse farther on.

Half wiggling and half flopping, Ziu got out of the cold water to sit on a corrugated shelf set into the wall, which seemed designed for just such a purpose.

"How far do we have to go?" she asked, turning off the air tank.

"Until we find it," Bolan said, slipping out of his shoulder straps and placing the air tanks aside for the moment.

"Fair enough," she replied, opening a plastic bag to take out a dry towel and start wiping her face and hair.

Stripping naked, Bolan opened more sealed bags to towel himself dry, then get dressed in a pair of utilitarian green coveralls and sturdy work boots.

"Now, I have no idea what the guards will be wearing, but that isn't important," Ziu said, slipping into a sport bra. "Just watch for the sidearm. Some of the Red

Star operatives may toss away their assault rifles to try to pretend they're just workers here, but there will not be enough time for them to remove their gun belt, so…" She stopped.

Strapping on a shoulder holster, Bolan said nothing, his expression neutral.

"Sorry," Ziu said with a nervous chuckle. "I keep forgetting you've done this sort of thing before."

"Never hurts to be reminded of the basics," he said diplomatically, working the slides of the Glock and AutoMag.

When Bolan and Ziu were ready, they started to walk up the sloping black tube, switching their climbing ropes from one ring to another. The darkness ahead seemed nearly impenetrable. Their flashlights helped some, but the stygian gloom was unrelenting. They felt like ants walking into the barrel of a cannon, and tried not to think about what would happen if the civilian operators of the dam decided to open the valve for this particular spillway. Umpteen thousand gallons of water would come rushing at them from a half mile above. At least the end would be quick.

The nonslip rubber soles of the work boots helped both Bolan and Ziu to keep from falling, but once or twice they slipped, and had to crawl back onto their feet using the ropes.

After a few hours, they took a brief rest.

"I wonder why Shen-wa didn't put a couple of video cameras in here?" Ziu asked, trying to catch her breath. Sitting in another of the small alcoves, she let her boots dangle over empty blackness, the bottom of the spillway lost in the distance.

"Can't send a signal through steel this thick," Bolan said, chewing a protein bar. He reached out with a knuckle to rap on the metal wall. "Besides, if a civilian inspection team came through, that would blow his cover."

"True enough," she said, taking a sip of water from a canteen. "Besides… Damn, what is that awful smell?"

"This is the culprit," Bolan said, lifting a dead carp into view. "It must have gotten trapped here the last time the spillway was used." He sniffed. "Not long dead. A day, maybe two."

"Is that good?" she asked.

"Neither good nor bad," he said, tossing it away. The carp hit the tube wall and slid away into the darkness.

Screwing the cap onto her canteen, Ziu said nothing. A single slip, and that was what would happen to them. The only consolation was that by the time they reached the water they could be going so fast that death would be instantaneous.

After that, they kept conversation to a minimum and concentrated on the task at hand. The process seemed endless—shuffle forward a yard, switch the clips and repeat. Soon a dull pounding could be heard, almost like approaching footsteps. It continued to grow in force and power until it shook the steel walls.

"We're close to the turbines," Ziu said, touching her throat mike.

Frowning, Bolan held up three fingers, two fingers, one, and then five.

Switching frequencies, Ziu tried again. "Better?"

"Loud and clear," he replied.

"Must have bumped it in that fall," she said in annoyance.

He started to answer, but then noticed something looming in the shadows ahead. For one heartbeat, he thought it was a wall of water coming their way, but then relaxed when he realized it was the sluice gate of the spillway.

Bisecting the tube, the huge, thick plate was swiveled into the open position.

"If…if the gate is open why are we still alive?" Ziu asked in a small voice.

"The spillway has a dozen of these to control the flow," he said, starting forward. "This is just the bottom gate."

Proceeding closer, Bolan and Ziu gratefully found that the tube was almost level at that point. Clearly, it was to aid the staff when they needed to work on the gate.

Shuffling along the expanse of rusty metal, Ziu went through the gate to attach both their ropes to rings on the other side. Then she removed the air tanks and let them slip away.

Meanwhile, Bolan got rid of his tanks, then began fingering the walls until finding the puckered scar where the section containing the gate had been welded to the spillway. Pulling out a wad of modeling clay, he slapped it against the wall, then pressed in a thermite grenade. A few feet away, he did so again.

"Ready?" he asked, slipping a finger into the ring of each military canister.

"…set, go," Ziu replied.

After jerking both rings free, Bolan turned and ran.

He barely got through the gate when a gentle red glow banished the darkness, and a wave of soothing warmth flowed through the tube. But that quickly changed into an uncomfortably bright orange light, then a searing yellow and finally a blinding white light. Waves of hellish heat washed over Bolan and Ziu, along with the terrible stink of melting steel. They tried to inch a little farther behind the gate for protection.

After several minutes, the light slowly died away, and the soldier shuffled closer for an inspection. There was now a large hole in the wall, the bright red metal still dripping off, to plummet away and hit the tube below.

Spraying the edge of the hole with a mini fire extinguisher from his pack, Bolan watched the foam explode into vapors at first, then sizzle, and finally just bubble from the intense heat.

Advancing carefully, he shone his flashlight into the hole to see a section of granite, some burned concrete and the interior of a dark hallway, a painted arrow on the wall pointing in both directions.

Pouring the contents of his canteen on the granite yielded little result aside from making steam, so Bolan also used Ziu's and finally got the heat down to a more tolerable level.

Going first, he quickly scrambled through the hole, his gloved hands starting to burn even from this brief contact with the slowly congealing rock. He hit the scorched tiles and rolled clear just in time for Ziu to arrive in a belly flop.

Stiffly, they rose and drew weapons. This section of the hallway was dark, but there were bright fluorescent lights at either end.

"No sound of a fire alarm," Ziu whispered in obvious relief.

"There's nothing here that could burn," Bolan replied, straining to hear anything over the turbines. But there was nothing aside from the invasive vibrations of the massive hydroelectric generators. "Okay, let's move. If they open the spillway now, we'll drown without the air tanks."

"Complain, complain," she muttered, clicking off the safety on the 35 mm grenade launcher.

Suddenly, they heard the sound of running footsteps. With nowhere to hide but the painfully hot hole in the wall, both of them dropped to the floor to offer as small a target as possible.

"Sidearms," Ziu reminded him curtly, leveling the QBZ assault rifle.

But the advice proved to be unnecessary. Three men came charging around a corner. Dressed in gray uniforms, they were all wearing body armor, and two were carrying QBZ assault rifles, while the third was holding a toolbox. They gasped at the unexpected sight of the armed man and woman, and instantly leveled their weapons.

Aiming high, Bolan and Ziu put a spray of 5.56 mm rounds into their unprotected faces, yielding grisly and very permanent results.

"Take the armor," Bolan advised, as she scavenged through their pockets for spare ammunition clips.

"What about you?" Ziu asked, stuffing a grenade into the camera bag hanging at her side.

"Only slows me down," he said. Hearing a sound from behind, he spun around in a crouch, the assault rifle at the ready, to see a tall woman in civilian clothing carrying an Atchisson autoshotgun.

Bolan cursed, Ziu dived for the hole and the stranger opened fire, the sputtering roar seeming to fill the universe.

CHAPTER NINETEEN

Beijing, China

Located deep beneath the massive August 1st Building, the tactical command center of the Central Military Commission was illuminated only by the light coming off the ring of high-definition plasma monitors lining the six walls.

On display was a real-time view of the world from several orbiting military satellites. A vector graphic showed the status of every branch of the Chinese military and police, and spy satellite data revealed the position of enemy troops and fortifications of every nation along their vast borders. An overlapping chain of radar rings edged the country, and a similar sonar version showed all underwater activity along the coastlines.

Usually reserved for a computerized graphic of weather patterns over Beijing, the center monitor now showed a real-time view of the Arctic. There was a new lake that had been recently formed at the exact location formerly known as Baffin Bay.

Aside from the high-definition monitors, the conference room was decorated with ceremonial swords, infamous war axes, bejeweled shields and silk tapestries, priceless antiques from the many thousand years of turbulent Chinese history. There was even a brick from the Great Wall to remind everybody in attendance that anything was possible, if a person was willing to pay the price.

There were no technicians in the room to operate the monitors, nor were there any guards, serving staff, aides, secretaries or personal assistants. This was the heart of the national defense grid, and only high-ranking Communist Party officials, generals, admirals, the executive director of the Red Star, the chairman of the CMC, the appointed premier and the elected president were in attendance.

Like many of his predecessors, President Xu Qishan was an old man by the time he came to power. His skin was leathery and unnaturally dark, and his shoulders were hunched, as if the years were heavy weights he had to carry. He moved slowly and wore thick glasses, but his eyes were bright with intelligence, and his voice was loud and strong, still carrying traces of the raw physical strength that had helped him survive the bloody revolution and decades of political intrigue.

"Are you sure about that?" Admiral Bo Yintao demanded.

"See for yourself. There is no radioactivity," Premier Hua Bangua stated bluntly, leaning back in his chair. "Whatever NATO destroyed, they did without nuclear weapons."

"It might have been a test," Brigadier Deng Huang suggested. "Or perhaps just a public display of their strength."

"As if we do not already know how well-defended the Western nations are," Colonel Lixue Jin-ping muttered, rubbing a puckered scar that ran along her face. Where it touched her scalp, the black hair had turned stark white.

"Sir, this must somehow be connected to that idiot Shen-wa!" General Zhao Ke roared, slamming a fist onto the conference table. "If we allow him to continue with this insane plan, soon China will become engaged in a nuclear war with the entire rest of the world!"

"If America declares war on China," stated Wen Ang, chairman of the CMC, "then the very first thing they will do is—"

"Launch nuclear weapons," Colonel Lixue stated firmly.

"Worse."

"Worse?"

"Their President will have Congress cancel their debt to us," said Zhaogu Yangdong from the Ministry of Defense. "We will lose a hundred billion euros like that!" He snapped his fingers in demonstration.

"Then they'll arm the nukes," General Zhao added.

"Perhaps, perhaps not," Premier Hua said slowly, speaking as if every word was a precious jewel not to be wasted.

Raising his hand for a moment of silence, President Xu carefully poured himself a small cup of fragrant black tea from a Ming Dynasty teapot. Nuclear war with the West. Nobody wanted that anymore. Not even the hated Russians. The foolish days of politicians thinking that such a conflict could be won by anybody were thankfully long gone.

"What nonsense," snorted a major from the new Ministry for Space Defense. "The Americas are too weak, too soft and out of control." He spoke as if it was a self-evident fact and couldn't be contested.

"It is not nonsense!" a senior general bellowed, throwing a sheath of papers across the polished table. The sheets went flying, but nobody moved. "The Americans are our staunchest friends, and the single biggest threat to communism, combined!"

"The Soviet Union collapsed purely because of their seductive way of life," Chairman Wen added scornfully. "Conquest by rock music and blue jeans."

"The West are both decadent and strong," Brigadier Deng added fiercely, brandishing a clenched fist. "They're living contradictions in everything they say and do! The very antithesis of noble communism!"

"Which makes them more dangerous than the Russians, or Japan," said the director of Bureau Six, Counterintelligence. He was a thin man with a thin mustache. "I must agree with the earlier statement. While Major Shen-wa's initial goal of Chinese expansion was highly laudable, it has gone horribly wrong. We must now consider the distasteful option of exercising termination with extreme prejudice."

"You mean kill him."

He gave a small nod. "Exactly."

"With the greatest reluctance, I must agree. The major is out of control," President Xu stated, setting down the priceless antique cup. "We must stop him in any way possible."

Encrypted data started to scroll along the bottom of the screens, giving the technical analysis of the polar explosions.

"They used Tomahawks," Admiral Bo stated, using the English name for the cruise missile.

"And a lot of them," Colonel Lixue said in agreement. "Four…no, six. Plus something else…a thermobaric device?"

"Classic overkill." Admiral Bo sneered. "How American."

At the end of the table, a man politely coughed. "Returning to the more pressing matter," said the executive director of the Red Star. "Unfortunately, nobody knows where Major Shen-wa is hiding."

"Nobody?" demanded the head of the Ministry of State Security. "Perhaps you simply have not asked the right people strenuously enough." Adjusting the nylon patch covering a missing left eye, the man slowly smiled. It was an unpleasant sight.

"On the contrary," the director whispered in a tight voice. "I can assure you that my people are unmatched at forcibly retrieving information. Major Shen-wa has vanished from the face of the Earth."

A dull thud caught everyone's attention.

"What was that?" Colonel Lixue growled, pulling a fat fountain pen from a uniform pocket and depressing the clip. There was a hard click, and the bottom shattered to reveal a short gun barrel.

"Is that a weapon?" the chairman demanded, pointing a finger.

"As if everything the minister for State Security carries isn't," Colonel Lixue replied, sneering.

Holding a cell phone as if it was a grenade, the minister didn't bother to deny the declaration.

They heard another thud, much louder than the first, and the room shook slightly. A little dust rained down from the ceiling, and one of the wall monitors went dark.

Everybody turned to stare in surprise, and the dead monitor exploded into the conference room, spraying out electronic debris. A split second later, Sky Tiger drones began to pour out of the smoky hole, one after another, with their machine guns blazing.

The politicians and soldiers were torn to pieces before anybody could react, the bodies jerking wildly from the brutal assault of 4.45 mm rounds ripping through their bodies.

Only the president wasn't harmed, and he fought to control his pounding heart as the swarm of drones flew around the room again and again, as if searching for anything else to annihilate.

Staring at the gaping hole in the ferro-concrete wall, the president felt as if his head was going to burst from all of the unanswered questions he had. How had the machines gotten this far inside the building? Why hadn't any alarms sounded? And where were the guards!

Just then, a drone left the rest and came closer, to hover above the table directly before him. The warm wash of the turbofans blew everything loose off the surface, secret documents sailing about like playing cars caught in a summer storm.

Licking suddenly dry lips, could see into the barrels of the caseless machine guns jutting from the black ceramic hull, as well as what looked like High Mountain–class antipersonnel rockets and Viper missiles. Fear froze his muscles, making it difficult to breath.

Softly whirring, the drone moved closer, then gently landed on the table, crushing the priceless Ming teapot under its armored chassis. Hot jasmine tea gushed across the polished wood, washing away pools of warm human blood.

"Hello, old friend," a familiar voice whispered from somewhere inside the machine.

At those words, his fear instantly turned into vitriolic hatred, and Xu leaned forward as the armored hull of the drone cycled apart, and a small plasma screen lifted into view. There was a burst of colors and static, which cleared into a picture of Major Shen-wa Fen.

The traitorous Red Star agent was in full dress uniform as if this were a parade ground. In the background were dozens of people in white lab coats hunched over consoles, operating complex controls and whispering into throat mikes.

"I...am impressed," Qishan managed to say without his

voice cracking. "This is quite an achievement, even for a demented bastard such as yourself."

If the insult was even noticed, Shen-wa paid it no heed. "You should not be overly surprised," he said, the words slightly out of time with the moving of his mouth on the screen. "After all, I helped design and construct the building. I would have been a fool to not incorporate a few items that I considered of possible use in the future."

"Like a secret entrance?"

"Exactly. Now, here is the sum of the matter," he said. "You and the other members of the CMC have betrayed the Chinese people, and as of this moment I am taking over control of the nation."

"Killing me accomplishes nothing," Qishan stated stubbornly. "The Central Committee and the armed forces will never obey a usurper!"

"But getting control of our nuclear arsenal does," Shen-wa countered with a hard smile. "With the rest of the world busy licking their own wounds after my Dragons strike, all I must do is destroy a couple of small towns with our own missiles, then blame the West, and everybody will rush to fall into line." He grinned. "Here is my offer. Give me the access codes for the master computer complex in Xiang, and you may leave the building alive. If not..."

The circling ring of drones instantly rattled off long bursts from the machine guns, destroying countless historical artifacts. The bodies on the floor jerked about from the ricochets off the walls as if briefly alive once more, then the fusillade stopped and a heavy ringing silence filled the room.

"D-do I h-have your word on that?" Qishan asked in a quaking voice, the words sounding strange as if somebody else had spoken instead of him. "The c-codes for my life?"

"You do, old friend." Shen-wa laughed, tucking a pipe into his mouth. "And you know that my word is good. Correct?"

"Yes, it is," Xu acknowledged woodenly, massaging his temples. "I can see that there is no choice in the matter."

"None at all."

Feeling oddly calm, Xu sighed in resignation. "Then all I have to say is...Long live China!"

"Eh?" Shen-wa demanded, suddenly alert. "What was that again?"

In a blur of motion, President Xu reached into his uniform jacket, pulled out his wallet to press it against his forehead and squeezed. The disguised .44 derringer hidden inside the soft leather boomed, removing half his face and sending brains, blood and gore spraying across the room.

As the nearly headless corpse limply collapsed in the chair, the screen showed Major Shen-wa throwing away his pipe to insanely scream in frustration. Then it went dark, and every drone in the room streaked away, to crash through the exit doors and begin to kill everyone in sight.

Level Nineteen

BOLAN AWOKE slowly with a throbbing headache.

Breathing in deeply, he charged his body with oxygen to clear his mind, and soon realized that he had been stripped to his underwear and firmly tied to a wooden chair. There were large ugly bruises all over his body, and a nasty buzzing in his ears.

Testing the ropes, he found that they weren't done by an expert. There was a little give in the knots around his right ankle. He worked at tightening the muscles and then relaxing, to gain more play.

Meanwhile, he looked around for Ziu and found her also stripped down to her underwear and tied to a chair. She had just as many bruises, and her ponytail had been undone, probably so their captor could search for any hidden weapons. There was nobody else in sight.

The room itself was large and well lit, with a concrete floor and cinder-block walls. There was one door, metal, with no lock. Dirty chains hung in a corner over a drain, and there was an ugly assortment of handsaws and machetes lying around.

With a snort, Bolan dismissed that as purely a trick to soften them before questioning. If they were actually in the hands of a psychopath, they would have awakened with the hamstrings in their legs already cut, making it impossible for them to run, or even walk, ever again. A little snip, and you were wheelchair bound for the rest of your life. After that, escaping from anywhere was problematic.

Focusing his mind to banish the pain, Bolan redoubled his efforts to get his leg loose. It was blatantly obvious that the tall woman with the Atchisson had fired a split second before he and Ziu had been able to get off a round, and she'd cut them down, not with fléchettes, or Double-O buckshot, but stun bags. That would explain the fist-size bruises, and the simple fact that they were both still alive.

"Matt..." Ziu groaned, and opened her eyes to look about.

"Over here," he said, rocking his chair to attract her attention.

Groggily, she turned that way, smiling weakly. "We almost did it..."

"We're not dead yet," he growled, yanking upward with

all his strength. The ropes scraped the skin from his leg, hair coming off and blood welling, but his foot came free. Triumphantly, he wiggled the toes to help restore circulation. The next part was going to really hurt.

"Ziu, if that door opens, you scream 'above you' at the top of your lungs," he ordered brusquely. "Understand? Scream your guts out."

"Why…?" she asked, shaking her head.

"Just do it!" he barked.

Quickly, she nodded. "Yeah…okay."

Seeing no reason to delay any further, Bolan threw himself forward and managed to stand awkwardly balanced on one leg. Flexing his knee a few times, he then leaped as high as possible and turned over, to come crashing down on the chair.

The wood loudly shattered under his two hundred-plus pounds of hard muscle, and the ropes came off. Rolling over, he got his hands in front of him, and went over to release Ziu. In a few minutes she was free, and she groggily helped undo the last of his bonds. But her fingers kept slipping, and it took a lot longer than he would have liked.

"Now what?" she asked.

"Sorry about this," he said, and slapped her with an open palm across the face.

Her head rocked from the blow, and she kept turning around, to stab out with a flat hand toward his stomach. He bent out of the way, then ducked low as she then went for his eyes in a martial arts move, her fingers bent like tiger claws. Then she stopped moving, her face flushed.

"Why did you do that?" she demanded in a clear voice. "I could have killed you!"

"It got you awake and functional again," he said, rubbing his sore wrists. "Now stay angry, and keep focused!"

Going to the blades near the drain, he wasn't surprised to find they were just for show, the edges dull. It would take days to sharpen this junk into any kind of an efficient weapon.

"Guess it did, at that," she muttered, weaving her long hair back into a ponytail to get it out of her face. "Okay, now what?"

"We escape," he growled, picking up a splintery piece of the broken chair and rubbing it against the rough cinder-block wall.

CHAPTER TWENTY

Strolling along the sidewalk on top of the colossal dam, a guard paused at a brick kiosk to reach into a wastebasket and pull out a brown paper bag.

Checking to make sure nobody was looking, he unscrewed the cap of the bottle inside and took a quick swig, then sprayed out the illegal whiskey again as something flashed by close overhead. The hot wash riffled his hair and churned up the loose dirt on the bridge with hurricane force.

A jet fighter! he realized in growing horror.

He tossed the bottle away, and it landed with a crash as he clawed at the hand mike hanging over the shoulder of his gray coveralls.

"Base, we have incoming!" he bellowed, thumbing the switch. "This is post nineteen, and we have incoming! Repeat, we have an incoming jet fighter!"

A dark shadow quickly passed over the dam again, but much lower this time, the buffetting wash making him stagger.

"Confirm, nineteen!" a voice crackled over an earpiece. "Can you identify?"

"A...Chengdu J-10 or maybe an 11," he said, squinting upward through the window of the kiosk while adjusting the transponder clipped to his belt. "But definitely one of ours! I mean that it's Chinese, not American or Russian!"

"Did it see you?" the voice demanded brusquely. "How many of them are there? Just jets, or are there also helicopters?"

"Two jets, no troop carriers," he reported crisply, years of training taking over without conscious effort. "Wait, there's something in the distance...."

Grabbing a military monocular from a wall peg, he stepped to the open doorway and looked skyward, pressing a button for maximum computer enhancement. The view zoomed out, as he swept the skies to find another plane heading for the dam. A big plane... He blinked. No, it was six planes flying in a straight line to hide their numbers. This was an invasion!

"Red alert!" he cried quickly.

But that was as far as he got before the kiosk shuddered from a hail of rounds punching through the window and brick walls. Glass exploded into his face, and red pain filled the universe.

Staggering blindly away from the damaged kiosk, he tried to continue the report, but it was difficult to breathe. His lungs felt as if they were on fire. The hot wind came again, and he grabbed on to the iron pipe of the safety railing for support, hearing the stuttering sound of a machine gun. Torn into shreds, the gory corpse went over the railing, to plummet down the front of the gigantic dam. It took a very long time for the tumbling body to finally disappear into the foggy mists at the bottom.

Alarms began to sound as doors were slammed open, and dozens of armed guards rushed out onto the roadway running along the top of the dam. Assuming defensive positions, they began opening fire with their QBZ assault rifles as a full wing of PLA jet fighters flashed by, their nose cannons spitting death. Half the guards died in the pass, their tattered bodies blown to pieces.

Screaming in terror, one of the guards broke ranks and ran away. But the rest stayed in formation and pumped 35 mm shells into the sky, trying for a lucky hit and hoping the HN-5 Red Cherry portable missile launchers would arrive soon.

Unexpectedly, another jet appeared from the east, flying high along the roadway and dropping a line string of cylindrical objects. A few of them splashed harmlessly into the lake behind the dam, and a couple went down the front, but most impacted onto the paved roadway and burst into roiling clouds of a villainous green gas.

As the spreading fumes reached the guards, they began to jerk and foam at the mouth, then collapse, their hair, skin and clothing going oddly pale, and then a ghastly shiny white.

Automatically, every door slammed shut and loudly locked tight, the intake vents for the air system cycling closed as the entire half-mile-wide structure became hermetically sealed.

As the J-11 jet fighters bombed the roadway with another string of poison gas canisters, wide patches of grass on the nearby hillside ripped apart as squat rectangular boxes rose into view to the thumping sound of working hydraulics. The protective front panels dropped away to reveal a metallic honeycomb of antiaircraft rockets.

Each of the A-100 launchers was equipped with an individual radar dish that spun on top, and the computer-controlled weapons independently chose a target in the sky and fired. Smoke bellowed from the aft ports and flames erupted from the front, as dozens of 300 mm rockets were launched, row after row of them, until the sky seemed filled with nothing but spiraling contrails.

"Big Dog to wing," the chief pilot said calmly into a throat mike. "Everybody, open fire!"

Nimbly swerving out of the way of the lifting rockets, the pilots checked the HUD displays, released the defensive flares and chaff, then unleashed a Vympel and a PL-12 missile. Locking on to the radar dish of each launcher, the guided missiles streaked in almost too fast to watch. Violently, they slammed into the empty A-100 launcher, the detonations tearing gaping craters in the sylvan hillside.

Just then, each of the big 300 mm rockets exploded in midair, the blasts sending out large clouds of dark material. Spreading fast, the clouds soon formed a thick umbrella over the Three Gorges Dam that was much too dense to see through.

Banking hard, the pilots of the Chengdu J-11 checked their X-band radar to find it also oddly blocked. Instantly, they performed a barrelroll to gain some needed distance, then swung about to flash over the dam on a recon pass to see what the enemy was trying to hide. But the moment the jets passed through the dark clouds their turbofan engines sputtered, flared, briefly stalled, and then died completely.

Suddenly down to only battery power, the pilots bravely fought to level the flight path of their dead fighters, and banked hard to angle toward the distant countryside.

Just then, Type-63 surface-to-air missile launchers rose from the battered hillside, and now dozens of 102 mm heat-seeking missiles lanced upward.

Once more, every jet released flares and chaff, then one pilot banked to release everything on board. Thunderbolt, Vympel, Falcon and HOT missiles dropped off the wings, then ignited and streaked away. In pyrotechnic fury, four... five...six of the incoming SAMs were blown out of the sky, then the rest converged upon him like rabid wolves. The salvo of missiles punched completely through the jet fighter, exploding on the other side, then the massive stores of fuel and ammunition detonated into a massive fireball.

"Big Dog to wing, eject, eject, eject!" he yelled into the throat mike, then yanked the armed switch alongside his chair.

Instantly, the explosive bolts lining the cowling crackled like firecrackers. The cockpit flipped back to vanish in the wind, and Big Dog braced himself as the minirockets under his chair loudly surged into hissing life.

Riding fat columns of fire, he and his fellow pilots were unable to move, or even speak, during the brutal acceleration. Through tearing eyes, they watched their jets dwindle into the distance, and then violently explode as the enemy missiles found them with pinpoint accuracy.

As they rose into the clouds, the massive dam, lake and river disappeared, then the rockets cut off, and parachutes burst from the back of the chairs. Carried on by sheer inertia, the pilots experienced a brief sensation of free-fall, then the chairs started to descend, and the parachutes jerked open to billow wide. The jolt was hard, but nothing compared to what they'd endured before.

Taking a moment to catch their breath, the pilots then scowled as they floated through the dark cloud of swirling particles, the strange material going into their mouths.

"What is this shit?" Quicksilver demanded, making a spitting noise.

"Tastes like...ash," MoonDancer replied in growing surprise. "This is volcanic ash!"

"Clever," Big Dog muttered hatefully. A few years ago a volcano had erupted in Iceland, the windblown ash disrupting air travel for most of Europe. If any jet got near, the stuff would be sucked into the hot engines and instantly bond to the spinning blades of the turbofans, knocking them off balance, and making the engines stall.

Even as he drifted away on the polluted breeze, he had to grudgingly admire the brilliance of the enemy below. Major Shen-wa had armed ordinary signal rockets with volcanic ash and basically brought down an entire wing of the finest jet fighters with carefully thrown handfuls of dirt.

"What now, sir?" Thunder King asked in a tight voice.

"We land and get out of here," Big Dog replied tersely. "Handguns and good intentions aren't going to breech that monster!"

"I guess this is now a job for the groundpounders," MoonDancer added, obviously thinking along similar lines.

Carried along to the west by a gentle breeze, the six pilots watched an open field of wildflowers come steadily closer, and they prepared to hit the ground running, when dark specks rose from the trees along the field.

"Drones!" Big Dog snarled, clumsily hauling out his service pistol and starting to shoot.

The rest of the PLA pilots did the same, and the Sky Tigers responded with long bursts from their 4.45 mm machine guns, bright tracers showing the strings of hot lead sweeping among the men and women trapped in the dangling chairs. Quicksilver was stitched across the chest and slumped over, her service pistol falling away.

"I'm not going to die like this!" Thunder King snarled, slapping the emergency release of the web harness on his chest. "See you back in Beijing!" As the harness came free, he dived out of the chair, trying for a small pond near a beaver dam.

Still shooting at the drones, MoonDancer could only

grunt as he saw the man miss and hit a flat rock with horrible results.

Raging with frustration, Big Dog suddenly got a wild idea and clawed for the cell phone tucked into his shirt. Dragging it out, he hit speed dial.

"Hello, dear! I'm glad you got back safely," his wife laughed in relief. "Should I come get you at the base or—"

"I love you! There's ash in the smoke!" he bellowed over the rushing wind and his banging Norinco pistol. "Call the CMC! Don't send helicopters! Machine guns and SAM batteries are everywhere. Heavily defended! I love you! Tell them there's ash in the smoke! There's ash in the smoke!"

"Smoke? Ash?" she asked in confusion.

Just then, the glowing line of tracers swung his way. He shouted her name one last time, there was a searing burst of white-hot pain, then an eternity of nothing.

Swirling around the helpless pilots, the Sky Tigers riddled them with nonstop gunfire until the ejector seats landed amid the flowers. Nearly reduced to hamburger, the bloody corpses did nothing as their rescue parachutes filled with the breeze and dragged them into the nearby forest and out of sight.

Only seconds later, there came a fast series of hard explosions as the land mines hidden among the dense foliage were triggered. The bedraggled remains of the pilots and ejector seats were briefly blown back into the sky, only to ingloriously tumble back down again in tattered pieces too small to trigger any further explosions.

Level Nineteen

FLANKED BY FOUR armed soldiers. Lieutenant Zhang Meiron waited as the door to the cell was unlocked. In her hands was a wooden box containing a can of butane and a small sledgehammer. Although no expert at torture, she felt more than confident that with the proper inducement the two prisoners would tell her everything long before Ming arrived back from Changsta.

As the lock disengaged, the door was yanked out of the hand of the soldier. Without thinking, he reached for the latch, and it came right back to smash into his hands, the bones audibly breaking. He fell down with a cry and was dragged out of sight as the door slammed shut again.

"What in the… Fire!" Zhang yelled, dropping the box to draw a Norinco pistol.

The rest of the startled soldiers cut loose with their QBZ assault rifles, but the soft lead rounds merely dented the steel door, failing to penetrate. The door opened again, and there was the missing soldier, his hands tied in front, and a sharp wooden stick pressed to his throat.

"Don't shoot!" he screamed, as a bruised hand extended from under his arm, and the Norinco pistol started blasting.

Three of the soldiers died on the spot, blood gushing from ruined throats. The last man only got a graze on the shoulder, and he fired back, the first soldier jerking wildly at the barrage of 5.56 mm rounds slamming away his life. Then the Norinco fired again, ending the confrontation.

Turning away, Zhang sprinted for the elevator. She heard the sound of running bare feet and somebody tackled her around the knees. She went down and hit her jaw on the floor, the blow cracking a tooth. Blood filled her mouth.

Rolling over, she lashed out with two fingers twisted together, but the other woman blocked the strike with her wrist, the hand becoming a fist that punched her squarely in the left breast.

Sickening pain exploded in her chest, and Zhang blindly rammed out with the heel of her hand, catching the prisoner on the side of the nose.

Reeling back, Ziu used that momentum to spin and ram a fist in the other woman's stomach. But the blow didn't go in as deeply as expected, the muscles there firm and trained.

Instantly, Ziu jumped back to avoid the expected high-low strike of twisted fingers trying to remove an eye, and a fist in her own stomach.

Panting for air, the two women circled one another, then Zhang sneered and went for the pistol on her hip. Ziu dived forward to land in a roll and come up to ram the heel of her hand into her opponent's nose just as the gun cleared the holster. Blood gushed from the impact, and Zhang jerked her head back…only to keep on going and drop limply to the floor, her nose flat to her face, the shattered bones driven deep into her brain.

Snatching the pistol, Ziu pumped two rounds into the chest of the Red Star operative, just to make sure.

"Get dressed," Bolan said, passing over an assault rifle. "I'll watch the stairs."

She took the weapon, paused, then fiercely hugged him. "Eugene was right," she said, turning away from the larger woman to kneel and start stripping one of the much shorter men. "You are a very dangerous man."

"It's just indigestion," Bolan said with a thin smile. "Those waffles were awful."

Snorting a laugh, Ziu pulled the pants off the corpse and began to remove the body armor. "Maybe we should wear some of this next time," she suggested.

Just then, the elevator gave a soft ding and opened.

Instantly, Bolan and Ziu swung their weapons around and fired, the soft lead rounds drilling into the group of people wearing gray uniforms, punching their remains to the floor.

"That one looks okay," Ziu said, lowering the assault rifle to start getting dressed again.

There was a lot of spilled blood on the clothing, but taking the pants from one man, and the shirt from another, she managed to get dressed in relatively clean clothing. As expected, all the boots were much too big, so she put on two pairs of socks, and that did the trick. She felt filthy, but was armed once more, and that was what mattered.

Joining her, Bolan saw that she was dressed correctly, and took the undamaged body armor off the corpse. Unfortunately, nobody was carrying grenades or a radio. Then something caught his attention, and he reached among the bodies to extract an angular rifle with an amazingly large barrel. It was a QBZ 35 mm grenade rifle. Rummaging about, he located a bandolier of shells.

Suddenly, an alarm began to clang.

"Here they come again, my friend," Ziu growled, tucking a spare ammunition clip into a pocket.

But just then, they heard a distant explosion, and a tremor shook the area.

"Somehow, I don't believe the Red Star is going to worry about us anymore," Bolan said, pulling on a pair of pants and zipping them closed. "I think the CMC got your message."

"I am thankful for the enemies of my enemies," she muttered, kneeling to search for more clips.

"Amen to that," Bolan added, draping the bandolier across his new body armor, then shoving a spare Norinco pistol behind his back. "Now let's find Shen-wa."

"Agreed."

Heading down the stairs, they heard a lot of commotion, cursing and gunfire coming from high above, but it soon faded into the distance. Reaching the bottom level, they encountered a steel door without visible hinges, securely locked with a glowing biometric pad in the shape of a hand.

Retreating a safe distance, Bolan sent a couple of 35 mm rounds into the door, blowing it out of the jamb. Even before the smoke cleared, Ziu fired a long burst from her QBZ assault rifle through the jagged opening, as the Executioner sent off a couple more rounds. Men screamed as the shells exploded, then Bolan and Ziu charged into the next room, their stolen weapons spraying hellfire.

CHAPTER TWENTY-ONE

Lake Yangtze Resort

A dull throb came out of nowhere, the odd noise barely discernible above the rush of the choppy water. Steadily, the sound increased in volume and power until it was louder than thunder, the hammering pulse visibly shaking the trees of the forest. A split second later, a hundred Chinese military Jingsha and Zubr-class hovercrafts charged into view from over a rocky hill and raced down the slope, safely bypassing a score of hidden land mines.

Streaming past a construction site, they flowed onto the artificial lake, the armada maintaining a tight battle formation as it skimmed across the smooth expanse of blue water, the combined wash of the powerful turbofans under their armored skirts churning the surface into white foam.

Ruthlessly, the gunners of the Jingsha hovercrafts opened fire with almost a thousand 14.45 mm machine guns at anything seen: inflatable toys, diving boards, rowboats, canoes, log cabins, cargo freighters, sailboats, fishing shacks, trawlers, fuel stations, wooden docks, canvas tents, campgrounds, hotels, restaurants, even the cars in the parking lots. The steel-jacketed rounds of the heavy machine guns chewed a swath of destruction along the shore of the man-made lake.

Several times the gunners exposed a machine-gun nest

hidden inside a boathouse, or a disguised SAM battery underneath a canopy of leafy vines. Both were immediately taken out with a devastating 102 mm rocket from a multiple rocket launcher, the blast leaving behind only smoke and twisted debris.

Privately, the crews of the Jingsha hovercrafts were thankful that so far there had been no sign of any civilians in the area, which only made sense. Nobody sane would have stayed after the public destruction of the J-11 jet fighters. However, their orders from the acting president had been brutally clear: they were to neutralize everything on, or near, Lake Yangtze with ultimate prejudice.

Meanwhile, the deck crews of the Zubrs kept launching torpedoes to race ahead of the flotilla, and depth charges off to the sides. Every few seconds, a section of the lake would jump, and a geyser would erupt from the surface, the white plume of boiling water spewing out a score of dead fish in every direction. Then a large explosion occurred directly in front of the hovercrafts as a torpedo triggered an underwater mine.

Once they reached the deep water, the Jingsha gunners relaxed, but the Zubr deck crews redoubled their efforts to search for traps. The pinging of the radar units could actually be heard above the muttered roar of the turbofans, and anything under the water was a legitimate target. The onboard supply of torpedoes and depth charges was dwindling fast, but the armada had only fifteen miles to go before the real battle commenced.

Only minutes later, a huge crane rose into view in the distance with a sleek yacht dangling from an array of thick lifting straps. Then a line of clanging buoys spanning the lake marked the end of the safe water for swimming and fishing.

Through binoculars, the commander of the attack

group could see the rapidly approaching top of the Three Gorges Dam. Sandbag nests had been established sporadically along the wide expanse of concrete, along with multiple rocket launcher boxes and a couple pieces of field artillery.

"Where did they get those?" the executive officer of the hovercraft demanded of nobody in particular.

"I do not know and I do not care," the commander replied grimly. "Have the rocketeers shoot the buoys, then prepare the crew for ground combat! We're taking back the dam!"

"Shoot the… What was that again, sir?"

"The buoys! Shoot the buoys!"

"Yes, sir!"

When the first buoy was hit by a 102 mm rocket, the entire span of them simultaneously exploded, the thundering chain of detonations forming a fire wall of annihilation before the speeding military crafts. But as the first Jingsha hovercraft sailed past the churning section of the lake, all the sailors cheered in victory. Then they abruptly stopped as hundreds of Sky Tiger drones poured out of the dam like a tidal wave of death.

Instantly, the gunners in the front Jingsha hovercraft cut loose with their machine guns once more, while the crew in the aft Zubrs yanked aside heavy sheets of canvas to reveal neat rows of Black Shark drones.

Lifting off the deck in orderly rows, the military drones surged ahead of the speeding hovercrafts to spread out in a defensive formation. Then the Black Sharks opened fire with their machines guns, rockets and missiles. Charging straight for them, the Sky Tigers did the same, but also began issuing thick volumes of dark smoke.

"Ash!" the commander growled, tightening his grip on the binoculars.

"The new filters will take care of that nonsense," the executive officer boasted proudly.

"Hopefully," the commander grimly countered, releasing the binoculars to loosen the Norinco pistol holstered at his side.

In controlled chaos, the two groups of drones merged into a single massive dogfight, spiraling, turning, swirling in a robotic maze of aerial combat, the muzzle-blasts from the hundreds of machine guns looking like demented fireflies within the swirling cloud of volcanic ash.

Unable to determine one drone from another, the gunners in the hovercrafts couldn't assist their robotic partners, and raged in furious impotence, with their hands on the triggers of the hulking 12.7 mm tandem machine guns.

Then enemy missiles started coming toward the military hovercrafts, and the crews expertly released huge amounts of flares and chaff. The sizzling displays were nearly blinding, but the missiles took the bait and exploded all around the armada in futile pyrotechnics. Shrapnel peppered the sides of the armored ships to no effect whatever, and a few of the crew on the open decks got struck, but their heavy level five body armor did the job. The armada sailed through the roiling explosions without the loss of a single craft, or sailor.

Now everybody held their breath as the lead Jingsha entered the swirling cloud of ash. Then they started cursing as only Chinese sailors could when the big engines stuttered, stalled and promptly died.

Coasting along on sheer momentum, the hovercraft eased down to the choppy surface of the lake and started bobbing about in the rough waves. Then the next one died, closely followed by a score more. Before the black cloud could reach them, the crews of the Zubrs got busy. MRL pods cycled alive and swiveled about, choosing targets and launching row after row of deadly Flying Viper heat seekers.

Programmed to identify the silhouette of friends, the computer-guided missiles bypassed the hovercraft and the Black Sharks to slam into the Sky Tigers and blow them apart. The first salvo cleared the air before the armada, but the enemy drones kept coming, and unfortunately, there were a lot more Sky Tigers than there were Flying Vipers. Soon, the reserves were exhausted, and the Sky Tigers swarmed over the stalled hovercraft, raking the decks with machine-gun fire and hammering them with short-range rockets. Pulling on gas masks against the ash, the crew bravely fought back with assault rifles and grenades launchers. But for every drone they destroyed, fifty men died.

Then a Jingsha exploded, the stores of ammo and fuel triggered by the incoming rounds. As the hovercraft sank into the crystal-blue water, the Sky Tigers swooped low over the wreckage to shoot the floundering crewmen before they could get away.

Just then, the sky darkened.

Reloading his service automatic, the commander squinted through the swirling ash to dimly see hundreds of massive cargo planes flying high over the lake. Their rear hatches dropped, and out came gleaming white parachutes, row after row of them, on and on, until the air was solid with descending paratroopers, their assault rifles firing nonstop.

Confused for only a microsecond, half the Sky Tiger drones curved away to meet the new threat, while the rest continued to attack the enemy hovercraft.

The lake water near the dam danced from the incoming lead as if it was raining, and a thousand ricochets bounced off the paved roadway, killing dozens of guards in spite of their body armor and helmets. Then the first of the grenades arrived, and a maelstrom of 35 mm rounds from the airborne assault rifles blew the sandbag nests apart, slaughtering the rest of the guards, toppling the artillery pieces and blowing up the MRL pods. Only a single pod got off a charge, the lone 102 mm rocket streaking away to skip across the lake like a thrown stone, and plow into a Zubr and blow it out of the water.

Suddenly, multiple salvos of 300 mm rockets rose from hidden bunkers in the forest, closely followed by a fiery barrage of Red Cherry missiles.

"High Mountain, repeat, High Mountain!" the commander subvocalized into a throat mike.

Immediately, a low whine cut the air and two Gazelle gunships rose from the last Zubr hovercraft. Quickly modified to use only canned air, the gunships moved slowly, but their gunners made up for that deficiency by rallying with every weapon on board—the 20 mm nose cannon, side-mounted 12.7 mm machines guns and the 53 mm rocket pods. The gunships almost looked like they were exploding themselves from the fiery wash and smoke of so much discharging ordnance.

The gunships were also carrying HOT antitank missiles, but those were reserved only for emergencies. If it all possible the PLA navy wasn't to damage the trillion-dollar Three Gorges Dam, even at the cost of their own lives. Of course, everybody knew that was why Shen-wa had established a firebase here, but there was nothing to be done about that.

Caught at point-blank range, the Sky Tigers fell in droves, and soon the cloud of ash started to clear. Then the drones clustered around the two Gazelles and bodily rammed the spinning turbo-blades on top. The armored blades sliced apart several drones, then they shattered, and the intact gunships plummeted into the lake, the faces of the startled pilot and gunner visible for only a moment before being swallowed by the murky depths.

Meanwhile, several miles downstream from the raging battle, a wing of Z-8 transport helicopters came around a bend in the mountain valley, and charged straight upriver, the gargantuan dam rising before them like the edge of the world.

Many of the pilots and crews had never seen anything that massive before, and briefly the airwaves were filled with a flood of profanity. Then hidden gun emplacements in the forest lurched into operation, and the armored helicopters rocked from the brutal assault of the heavy machine guns. But the crews did nothing in return, grimly concerned with only a single goal—getting closer to the dam.

Throwing out massive stores of flares and chaff, and launching salvo after salvo of antimissiles, the big Z-8 transports reached the base intact and threw open their hatches. Dozens of soldiers wearing bulky backpacks jumped out to run closer to the towering wall of concrete, then they twisted the controls on their jetpacks and flew upward on twin columns of blue-white exhaust.

A split second later, a flight of HOT antiarmor missiles arched over the forest to obliterate the helicopters in a stentorian hell storm of screaming men and exploding metal.

In spite of the heavy body armor worn by the soldiers, they moved faster than arrows, the hard acceleration distorting their faces into a demonic rictus. However, speed was of the essence. The experimental jetpacks had an extremely short flight time, and every second counted.

As they flew over the safety railing on top of the dam,

the first wave of soldiers turned off their jetpacks to land in a staggered row, and swung up their assault rifles to mow down a group of guards trying to right an MRL pod.

The next moment, the second wave arrived, and they cut loose with grenade launchers, violently blowing open the reinforced steel doors that gave access to the facility.

A few seconds later, the third wave crested the safety railing just as their jetpacks died. Half the soldiers managed to grab the iron pipe and cling with both hands, but the rest tumbled back down the half mile to the foggy bottom of the dam, screaming in rage and frustration. Some of them impacted near the smoking wreckage of the helicopters with wet crunches, and the rest plunged into the raging river, the heavy jetpacks dragging them down to vanish forever.

As the remaining PLA soldiers poured into the gaping doorway, Sky Tigers appeared to attack from behind, while the guards inside the dam began firing an electric minigun from behind a sandbag nest. Behind them was a large iron gate, the lock shiny where it had been hastily welded shut.

Moving fast, the rear soldiers blocked the doorway with a searing curtain of fire by throwing canisters of thermite, while the front soldiers cut loose with hissing flamethrowers even as the minigun killed the front ranks. The lances of chemical flame rushed over the falling soldiers to engulf the guards. Shrieking in pain, they stopped shooting and staggered about blindly, beating at their burning faces with fiery hands.

Suddenly, flame-retardant foam gushed from vents in the ceiling, but that only served to hide the twitching corpses of the fallen guards. Unstoppable, the thermite continued to rage.

Hovering outside, the drones poured death into the

wall of flames, but the company of soldiers had already taken refuge behind the sandbag nest. Since there was no lock on the gate anymore, they simply blew it open with shaped charges of high-explosive plastique, then charged deeper into the bowels of the colossal facility, using the flamethrowers to destroy every security camera they encountered.

A nearly invisible trip wire attached to an antipersonnel mine killed a handful of soldiers, but the rest managed to reach the end of the corridor alive, and close a second gate, to lock it tight against the arrival of more drones.

Bypassing the obvious trap of the elevators, the soldiers kicked open the door to the stairwell, and threw down concussion grenades to trigger a series of explosive devices built into the walls. Attaching nylon ropes to the iron-pipe banister, they quickly rappelled down the center of the stairwell, firing their assault rifles in short bursts into the busy darkness below….

Central Command, Project Keyhome

SCENES OF DESTRUCTION filled every wall monitor and the dead and dying lay everywhere as the fighting spread inside the dam. Using the victims as makeshift shields, Red Star guards were falling back to established defensive positions of sandbag nests, where they rallied and fired assault rifles and heavy machine guns into the advancing troops.

However, the PLA soldiers were not only wearing body armor, but also carrying heavy plastic shields. One could hold the heavy sheet of plastic, while another fired around the edge. Working in teams, the men and women came on and on, a flood as unstoppable as the tide. The assorted rounds from the Red Star guards merely slapped into the plastic shields and stayed there, trapped like flies in amber. Then a monitor flickered into blankness, closely followed by another.

A swam of drones poured down a corridor, firing their minirockets. The plastic shields were blown away, often carrying off hands and arms. As the mutilated soldiers fell, the ranks behind cut loose with grenade launchers, the sheer volume of 35 mm shells hammering the drones back, tearing off chunks of their ceramic armor, and then blowing them apart like clockwork toys.

Slamming open a door, a Red Star guard began to activate a Red Cherry missile launcher, but before he could shoot, a PLA soldier appeared with a flamethrower and engulfed man and machine in a lance of fire. A human torch screamed, then the missiles exploded harmlessly, and the PLA advanced again.

Never having experienced this sort of fighting before, the technicians in the room were silent. The only noise came from the humming control boards, and a samovar softly bubbling in the corner kitchenette. Then the refrigerator rattled as it started a cooling cycle, and everybody burst into excited conversation.

"How did they—"

"Does this mean that—"

"Have we lost?"

"Silence!" Shen-wa roared uncharacteristically, the single word filling the room. "Control yourselves! This sort of response from the August 1st Building, from whoever is in charge of the country at the moment, was inevitable. We have not lost yet!"

"Sir?" a young corporal asked, hugging a clipboard as if drawing strength from it.

"Have faith," Shen-wa said kindly. "How soon until the reserve drones arrive from Fakkah?"

"Ninety...eighty-nine minutes, sir," a technician reported, checking a scrolling monitor on her console. "They're just passing through the Changsha district."

"Any problems?" Shen-wa asked.

"Unexpected heavy resistance from gunboats in the river," another technician stated, "but otherwise...no, sir. No significant problems. The jets cannot find them, and tanks are too slow to catch them."

"Excellent. Well done," Major Shen-wa said, taking a chair and crossing his legs. "Close and seal all primary doors. Release the VX nerve gas, and shunt all available electricity from the generators to the tesla coils on level six." He chuckled. "A couple million volts of man-made lightning will take care of these big-city fools, eh?"

Some of the tension left the faces of the people, and they willingly returned to work.

Disgusted beyond words, the major tried his best to show the disdain he felt for these cattle. In truth, the base was compromised, and the battle already lost. But these paper-pushers weren't soldiers, merely civilians in uniform. He needed to keep up their flagging courage with ridiculous lies until they were no longer needed.

The refusal of the president to surrender had seriously derailed his plans for seizing control of China before starting the World War. Now, China would have to take care of itself against the rest of the world without his wise guidance, and Project Keyhome would simply assume control of the nation afterward.

Reaching into his shirt pocket, he removed a small black box about the size of a cell phone. Thoughtfully, he ran a thumb across the satin-smooth plastic. The power of an exploding sun rested in the palm of his hand. It was quite exhilarating, almost intoxicating, and it took an enormous amount of willpower to not open the box and use it immediately.

"Should I open a relay to the main transmitter for you, sir?" asked a technician, looking up from her console.

"No, not quite yet," Shen-wa said, obviously debating the matter. "On the other hand, yes, do so at once. Just in case."

"Yes, sir. Establishing the link…now."

With a low vibration, like a cell phone set to not ring, the little black box went live. Slowly, Shen-wa smiled.

Just then, the armored door to the room cycled open and Sergeant Ming Bohai squeezed through the widening crack. Going directly to the major, he saluted, then bent to whisper, "Sir, the base is compromised. We need to evacuate immediately."

"Not yet, my friend," Shen-wa growled, glancing toward the battles filling the few remaining monitors.

Most of the screens were dark by now, the cameras destroyed or the wires cut by the PLA soldiers. The rest were distorted by static, or rolling out of control, except for one. Using a direct link to an orbiting telecommunications satellite, that monitor showed a map of the world with four blinking red triangles in America, the United Kingdom, Russia and northern China. His secret army of sleeping Dragons.

"How did the CMC find us, sir?" Ming asked with a scowl.

Major Shen-wa frowned. "That is unknown. Lieutenant Zhang has a couple of prisoners on level nineteen who might have been able to supply that information, but she has not responded in the past hour, so I think she is no longer with us." He tried to generate some feelings for the missing woman, but there was nothing, not even disappointment over the loss of an excellent sex partner.

"One of them might be the CIA agent from Hong Kong," Ming said with a frown. "I have been tracking him across the country, and he is very good. The best I have every encountered."

"Is he too good?" Shen-wa asked pointedly.

Confidently, Ming smiled. "No, sir. The CIA agent will die at my hands."

"The CIA..." Shen-wa muttered as if expelling a rotten piece of fruit from his mouth. "Make his death memorable, Sergeant. Make him pay for all of this." He waved at the dark monitors.

"It will be my pleasure, sir," Ming stated, working the slide on a .50-caliber Norinco pistol.

"No, you stay with me for the present," Shen-wa ordered, pulling out the black box again. This time he flipped open the lid and tapped a few buttons.

On the wall monitor, the pulsating red triangles abruptly changed to solid black and began to move. At their control boards, the technicians noticed the change and started to speak, then silently went back to work.

"Time to target?" Ming asked, his eyes bright with excitement.

"Fifteen minutes," Shen-Wa said with a slow smile. "After which the entire world will be too busy trying to stay alive to bother us anymore."

"Then there is no need to prepare your shuttle?" Ming asked, looking over the busy technicians, a hand resting on his holstered weapon. There were twelve people in the room. The escape craft held only two, and there were ten rounds in the pistol. It was a simple matter of subtraction.

"None whatever, old friend," Shen-wa said with a chuckle. "Soon, the world will be on fire. Then my army of drones will carve out a new China, a golden age will be forged and there will be peace at last."

"Except for Japan," Ming added knowingly.

On a monitor, the PLA troops rushed down a corridor and lighting bolts crackled out of tesla coils hidden inside the floor, walls and ceiling. Every soldier died instantly, their lifeless bodies jerking wildly as the ammunition in their weapons exploded, blown off random parts of the galvanized corpses.

"Japan and America. Washington must pay for their crimes against me," Shen-wa growled, hunching lower in the chair, his face a twisted mask of barely controlled insanity.

Then his features brightened. "By the way, Bohai, I have a little gift here that you might like."

CHAPTER TWENTY-TWO

The grenade bounced down the terrazzo stairs and rattled across the concrete floor.

Snarling curses, the group of Red Star guards hastily scattered, then saw that the arming pin and safety lever were still in place. Furious over the pointless trick, the men surged back into position just as three more unprimed grenades bounced down the stairs, closely followed by three more. Thoroughly confused, the guards entered the stairwell and looked up, trying to see what was going on.

Hanging over the safety railing two levels higher, Bolan instantly fired the QLB/QLZ grenade launcher, the 35 mm grenade streaking down and exploding on the concrete floor amid the guards and grenades. The overlapping detonations filled the stairwell with a maelstrom of thunder and flame, blowing the guards into ragged pieces.

Carefully running down the blood-spattered stairs, Bolan and Ziu reloaded their weapons. Then they checked the dead for any usable ammunition, and Ziu used her knife to hack the hand off a lieutenant.

"This isn't going to work," she muttered, tucking the grisly appendage inside her bra to keep it pressed against her warm skin.

"Only one way to find out," Bolan growled, taking a broken radio from a sergeant and shoving it into a pocket.

A soft whirring noise from above drew their attention.

Swiftly angling their weapons upward, Bolan and Ziu fired their launchers in unison, the two 35 mm shells slamming into the Sky Tiger just coming out of the stairwell. The double explosion cracked the ceramic armor and knocked the drone aside, the stream of 4.45 mm caseless bullets from the chattering machine guns making the bedraggled corpses jerk about wildly.

While Ziu hastily shoved another shell into the breech of the grenade launcher, Bolan fired the launcher twice more, shattering the rest of the armor and blowing off pieces of the wobbling drone. Electrical short-circuits crawled all over the damaged Sky Tiger, and a split second later it detonated into a fireball. As the searing charge of thermite vaporized the remains of the drone, the weakened stairs gave a low groan.

"Move!" Bolan shouted, but Ziu was already dashing for the doorway.

They dived through the opening just as a chunk of the stairs came crashing down onto the dead guards, closely followed by a rain of partially melted debris. In only a few moments, the doorway was blocked solid.

Staggering down the long hallway, they shot out a video camera in the corner of the ceiling, then blasted a wall clock and a water fountain. The fountain merely erupted into a spray of gushing water, while the clock exploded, spewing out a deadly spray of fléchettes, the razor-sharp shards of steel chewing a circular patch inches deep into the opposite cinder-block wall.

At the end of the hall was a seamless slab of burnished steel equipped with a glowing biometric panel.

Biting a lip, Ziu placed the disembodied hand on the glowing plate, while Bolan removed the battery from the radio and pressed it against the raw, tattered flesh at the end. Both of them felt a tingle of electricity as contact was made.

For a long moment, nothing happened. Then there was a soft beep from the plate, and the massive door started to ponderously move aside with the sound of working hydraulics.

As soon as there was a large enough crack, Ziu tossed the hand away and swung up her assault rifle to trigger a long burst at the door. The hail of 5.56 mm bullets ricocheted off the armored exterior to scatter into the next room. Somebody unseen behind the wall screamed, and a guard fell into view, an Atchisson autoshotgun tumbling from her hands.

Suddenly, an old man shouted something in Mandarin, and a dozen weapons began to shoot, the opening door hammered with a barrage of bullets from chattering assault rifles and banging pistols.

Retreating for some needed yardage, Bolan fired a 35 mm shell into the splayed corpse on the floor. The distance was short, just barely enough, but the body violently exploded, spraying organs and intestines across the room. The gunfire stopped as a chorus of startled cursing erupted, along with the sound of running boots.

Charging around the door, Bolan and Ziu cut loose with their weapons, ruthlessly gunning down anybody wearing a gray uniform. A few of the guards fired back, but they missed Ziu completely, and hit Bolan only once in the chest, his body armor absorbing the impact of the 9 mm pistol round as if it were no more than a thrown snowball.

"Where's Shen-wa?" Ziu demanded, working the arming bolt on the QBZ assault rifle to eject a bent round caught in the ejector port. The brass case sprang free to sail away and land with a musical tinkle on the littered floor.

"We just heard him a second ago," Bolan snarled, dropping the clip to check the load.

"There's nobody here over thirty, much less as old as the major," Ziu said slowly, looking over the scattered bodies.

However, the big room was empty aside from the still forms of the dead guards, a small kitchenette with a bubbling samovar and a curved row of elaborate consoles facing some wall monitors. Most of the monitors were blank, or filled with crackling static, but three were still functioning normally. Two of the monitors showed PLA soldiers fighting drones somewhere in the facility, while the last one displayed a map of the world with four black triangles moving steadily toward New York, London, Moscow and Beijing. Each of the triangles was marked with the international symbol for nuclear radiation.

"He's going to nuke our own capital?" Ziu gasped in growing horror. "B-but that's insane!"

"So maybe we better get out of here," Bolan said in an odd tone.

Astonished, Ziu turned to stare at him, then saw that he was looking at a trail of bloody shoe prints that led directly to a blank section of the wall—and just stopped.

"Yeah, screw it, let's go," she replied, nodding in understanding.

Aiming their grenade launchers, Bolan and Ziu mouthed a slow count to three, then fired. The pair of 35 mm rounds hit the wall and violently exploded, spraying out jagged chunks of broken plastic to reveal a brick-lined tunnel. In the distance they saw two running figures heading toward the airtight hatch of a submarine.

Instantly, Bolan and Lee charged forward, their weapons

blazing away in assault rifle mode. Bouncing off the brick walls, the 5.56 mm rounds were funneled toward the major and the sergeant, and both men staggered, bleeding from numerous wounds. The last of the grenade shells slammed directly on the hatch, denting a hinge and warping the wheel lock.

Brutally rattled by the combination of concussion and shrapnel, Shen-wa and Ming staggered, then turned to shoot back with their handguns, the sound of the 9 mm Norinco pistols completely swamped by the discharge of the massive .50-caliber rounds.

Hit in the leg, Ziu cried out and dropped to a knee, blood gushing from the wound. Tossing away the empty rifle, Bolan drew his spare 9 mm Norinco pistol and hit the floor, triggering round after round.

Stepping in front of the major, Ming acted as a living shield while Shen-wa struggled to open the damaged hatch. His huge pistol boomed .50-caliber death, the heavy slugs zinging off the concrete floor, barely missing Bolan.

Unexpectedly, Ziu cut loose again with the assault rifle, the stream of 5.56 mm rounds peppering the steel hatch to ricochet off and wound both Shen-wa and Ming.

With blood trickling down the side of his face, Ming swung around with the reloaded Norinco, and Shen-wa turned around holding a Glock, his thumb flicking the selector on the side.

"Down!" Bolan shouted, recognizing it as his lost weapon.

Grinning, Shen-wa stroked the trigger, and the Glock 18 machine pistol roared, a stuttering flame extending from the muzzle as the entire clip discharged in two seconds flat. From far down the tunnel there came a guttural cry of pain and Ziu stopped firing.

As Shen-wa returned his attention to the wheel lock,

Ming reached up with a clenched fist to smash the overhead light, then began blasting away again with the bigbore Norinco.

Rolling from one side of the tunnel to the other, Bolan continued to return fire, but now he was literally shooting in the dark, and had to gauge his hits purely by the sound they made. Which gave him an idea. Going onto his back, he shot out more of the lights until most of the tunnel was in complete darkness.

"Very clever." Ming chuckled. "But I have a gift for you, Yankee!"

Knowing what to expect, Bolan rolled flat against the brick wall and braced his weapon with both hands. He would only get one chance at this….

There was a brief pause, then Ming began to walk forward while firing two powerful handguns, the different size muzzle-blasts briefly illuminating him in stark relief.

Aiming between the two flashes, Bolan walked the Norinco up the sergeant, listening to the dull thump of bullets hitting body armor, then the wet smack of the rounds finding flesh.

With a low groan, Ming sank to the floor. Bolan put a round through the top of his head, ending the matter forever.

Just then, light exploded along the tunnel as Shen-wa pulled aside the hatch and clambered through.

Sprinting forward, Bolan shoved his Norinco pistol between the closing hatch and the curved steel jamb. The heavy hatch slammed shut on the gun with a loud clang, the impact pinching the barrel, and Bolan released the useless weapon.

Muttering curses, Shen-wa tried to free the hatch, then began blindly shooting short bursts with the Glock.

In the thin slice of light coming through the partially open hatch, Bolan could see the corpse of the sergeant, and his weapons, the .50-caliber Norinco pistol, and his own .44 AutoMag. Grabbing both guns, he shoved one over the top of the hatch, the other under the bottom, and fired.

A high-pitched scream told him of a hit, and Bolan risked taking a look through the crack. Gushing life from a hole in his neck, Shen-wa was lying on the perforated deck of the minisub, a small black box in his hand. Weakly, the dying man attempted to aim the Glock at the box, and missed, blowing off one of his own fingers. Then he tried once more.

Triggering both weapons, Bolan put a volley of hot lead in the old man's head, the double Magnum Express rounds punching out his eyes and exploding out the back of his head in a ghastly spray of bones, brains and blood.

Shoving the guns into his belt, Bolan grabbed the hatch in both hands and slowly forced it open. There was nobody else in the tiny submersible.

Grabbing the black box, Bolan snapped it open to find four buttons marked with Chinese pictographs. Lurching out of the hatch, he raced back up the tunnel and into the light. He found Ziu sprawled in a pool of her own blood, breathing rapidly, and attempting to bandage her wounds with strips of cloth torn from her shirt.

"What do these mean?" he demanded.

"B-begin…pause, die, kill," Ziu whispered hoarsely.

Glancing at the wall monitor showing the progress of the four black triangles, Bolan paused for what seemed a very long time, then made the gamble of his life and pressed the third button. If "die" didn't mean self-destruct…

In perfect unison, the four black triangles briefly flared into blazing white circles, then faded away completely.

"Did...the n-nukes...go off?" Ziu croaked, forcing herself into a sitting position.

Gently, Bolan picked her up in his arms and started for the escape sub. "We'll find out soon enough," he said, entering the darkness once more.

EPILOGUE

Arlington Cemetery, Virginia

Rigidly formal in their full-dress uniforms, the seven U.S. Marines fired their M-4 rifles three times into the sky, as the empty coffin for Eugene M. Snyder was lowered into the cold ground.

"He was a good man," Hal Brognola said, as a military bugler began to play the final song.

"That he was, Hal," the President agreed, his head bowed in respect.

As always, the last note of the song seemed to cling to the air, but finally silence returned to the grave site, and the two men turned to stroll away as several members of the Snyder family began tossing handfuls of loose dirt into the grave.

An entourage of thirty Secret Service agents stayed at a discreet distance from the President, allowing him some private time with Brognola. In the distance, a dozen Apache gunships hovered just outside the boundaries of the cemetery, while a contingent of Navy SEAL snipers kept careful watch on their commander in chief from the portico of Montecello on Jefferson Hill.

"So what was the final outcome, sir?" Brognola asked, walking along the neat rows of identical headstones.

"Total victory. The drones dropped out of the sky like flaming meteors," said the President. "Homeland Security had emergency teams at the locations within an hour, long before the self-destruct charges burned through the casings of the nuclear bombs."

"I'll assume that Shen-wa needed them armored so that enemy gunfire wouldn't set them off early."

"Or worse, distort the primary sphere, and make it impossible for the nukes to detonate," the Man agreed. "However, it was still a hell of a gamble."

"Not so much gamble as an educated guess," Brognola countered, their footsteps softly crunching as they moved onto a gravel path. "Shen-wa was a trained combat soldier, just like Cooper. They need weapons to be easy to operate. Things get pretty wild in a battle, and if you have to fiddle with stuff to make it work, then you die. It is as simple as that."

"So it would seem," the President said, looking across the vast green fields of fallen heroes. "It is a pity that Cooper couldn't retrieve the blueprints for building the stealth drones. However, our scientists have seen enough to try to retroengineer the machines. The Pentagon thinks we can have a prototype up and running within a year."

Dourly, Brognola gave a grunt. "As will the United Kingdom, Russia and India."

"True. Once more, the balance of power is maintained. Peace at the edge of a sword."

"Better than no peace, at all, sir."

"Absolutely, my friend."

"So what happened to the rest of the drones?"

"The ones still deactivated at Fakkah got bombed out of existence by the Chinese Air Force. As for the rest of them..." The President smiled. "When the army finally invaded the control room, they smashed everything. Without any commands to guide them, the Sky Tigers went to default mode and flew to the Three Gorges Dam. They just stayed there, hovering in the air."

"Waiting for more instructions?"

"Exactly."

"Good Lord, it must have been a massacre!" Brognola chuckled.

"A slaughter would be a more accurate description." The President grinned back. "By the way, did the young lady who officially has no name survive her surgery?"

Brognola nodded. "She's fine, sir. Taking some R & R with Cooper at a safe location."

"Good. They deserve it." The President said nothing more for a few minutes as they walked along, then stopped to place a hand on the other man's arm.

"Hal, is there anything we can do to thank the White Lotus Society? Privately that is, without seriously annoying the new Chinese government?"

"Well, now that you mention it," Brognola said, pulling a sheath of documents from his jacket pocket. He passed them over, and the President started reading. "The Farm will be upgrading a lot of their older weapons, helicopters, computers and such, next year. It shouldn't cost us too much to pack the stuff up and send it to them." He grinned. "I happen to know where we can get a lot of big cargo containers on the cheap."

"Damn straight you do." The President laughed, giving back the documents. "Very well, send them whatever you wish. Carte blanche."

"Thank you, sir."

Just then, a wing of F-18 jetfighters streaked overhead in the classic "missing man" formation, a solemn tribute to all the men and women, soldiers and civilians, who had given their all to protect the innocent, and strive for the ultimate goal of peace.

"May the good Lord grant that we never have to see that formation again," the president declared, giving a brisk salute.

"Amen to that, sir," Brognola agreed, doing the same. "Amen to that."

* * * * *